Highland Silver

Highland Outcasts
Book 4

By
Elizabeth Rose

ARE YOU SIGNED UP FOR DRAGONBLADE'S BLOG?

You'll get the latest news and information on exclusive giveaways, exclusive excerpts, coming releases, sales, free books, cover reveals and more.

Check out our complete list of authors, too!

No spam, no junk. That's a promise!

Sign Up Here

www.dragonbladepublishing.com

Dearest Reader;

Thank you for your support of a small press. At Dragonblade Publishing, we strive to bring you the highest quality Historical Romance from some of the best authors in the business. Without your support, there is no 'us', so we sincerely hope you adore these stories and find some new favorite authors along the way.

Happy Reading!

CEO, Dragonblade Publishing

Author's Note

*(The **Highland Outcasts Series** features secondary characters from my MacKeefe Clan. The stories about the characters who are making guest appearances can be found in some of my other series, such as **Legacy of the Blade, Madman MacKeefe, Daughters of the Dagger, Legendary Bastards of the Crown, and The Highland Chronicles**, amongst others.)*

Some of the MacKeefe Clan heroes, heroines, and secondary characters seen in this book are:

Old Callum MacKeefe (Oldest living man in Scotland)

Ian MacKeefe (Callum's son – MacKeefe Clan chieftain)

Storm MacKeefe (Ian's son – also a MacKeefe Clan chieftain since they have holdings in both the Highlands and the Lowlands)

Heroes of the Highland Outcasts Series:

Gavin MacKeefe – hero of *Highland Soul*

Cam MacKeefe – hero of *Highland Flame*

Nash MacKeefe – hero of *Highland Sky*

North MacKeefe – twin brother of Nash, and hero of *Highland Silver*

Prologue

Northumberland, England

"HIDE, MATILDA, AND do not make a sound. Stay with your mother, and keep out of sight. Do you hear me? Your life depends on it." Robert Montclair hunkered down, looking into Matilda's eyes with concern as the warning bell in the courtyard rang out loud and clear in the night.

Matilda was only six years of age, but understood this look on her father's face. It was one of extreme concern. She'd recognized it several times through the years when her father was highly disturbed. Usually, it was before he headed out to battle. There was trouble tonight, there was no doubt about it. Something was extremely wrong, but she didn't know what.

"Papa, what's happening?" asked Matilda, not understanding the sense of urgency that had taken over her family's manor house on the border so late at night. One minute she'd been sleeping soundly, and the next, her mother had pulled her from her bed and they ran to her father's solar. Matilda looked across the room to see her older brothers strapping on their swords right over their night clothes. They looked nervous, and she swore their hands shook.

"Robert, I'm frightened," said Matilda's mother, Ann, wringing her hands together. "Is it the Scots?" she asked, looking over toward the partially open window. "Have they entered our living quarters?"

"Aye, I believe so," answered Matilda's father. With their manor house being so close to the Scottish border, they were always in danger of an attack. Up until now, they had been lucky but, tonight, it seemed as if their luck had run out.

Matilda's father gave her a quick kiss on the cheek before standing up and hugging his wife in a manner that almost seemed as if he were saying goodbye forever.

A guard knocked at the partially open door and quickly stuck his head inside the room.

"My lord, they've entered the manor and are ransacking everything," he reported. "They have killed off the guards at the gate, and the servants are running in fear for their lives."

"We've got to stop them," commanded Matilda's father, strapping a few extra blades to his weapon belt. "Do whatever it takes to keep them from getting to the solar. I have to protect my family."

"Aye, my lord. I'll do my best," answered the guard, disappearing from sight.

"We'll kill them, Father," called out Matilda's eldest brother, John, who was ten and eight years of age. He had never participated in a real battle, but was almost as skilled with a sword as any of her father's men.

"I'm ready to kill those bloody Scots, and send them straight to hell," yelled Andrew, her second brother who had just turned sixteen. Andrew was a hothead, always looking for a fight. He pulled his sword from his scabbard, vengeance filling his eyes.

"Robert, don't let the boys fight. They're too young," cried out Ann. "Please," she begged him. "I don't want to lose my children."

"I'm sorry, my dear. I don't have a choice." Matilda's father shook his head sadly. "We need every blade to protect our manor until help arrives."

"You're all going to die," cried Ann in hysterics, making Matilda feel very frightened and uncomfortable now. Was this really true? Were they all going to die tonight at the hands of the Scots? The thought horrified her, making her legs shake.

Spying an eating knife on the table, Matilda ran over and picked it up, gripping it tightly in one hand. "I'll kill them, too," she shouted, mimicking her brothers.

"Matilda, nay," said her father. "Put down the knife. You will not fight anyone. You need to hide with your mother. Your lives depend on it."

Matilda looked up to see the fear in her father's eyes. This only confirmed her mother's accusations. What her mother claimed would happen, would surely transpire before this night was over. Matilda's heart ached. Even at her young age, she knew this would be the last time she ever saw her brothers or father. She felt it in her heart that this night would not end well. Aye, death surrounded them and there was no escaping. She and her mother would probably die, too.

"If anything happens to me . . . take the children to my brother, Gilbert's," her father instructed her mother. "Tell him what happened, and he will look after all of you." Robert untied a pouch of coins from his waist and shoved it into his wife's hand. "Use the money I have hidden in this manor to live on. You know where it is. It will be enough for you and the children to get by on, for quite a while."

"Nay," cried Ann. "You hid that money for our future. For all of us, including you. If anything happens to you, I won't be able to go on."

"You have to, darling." Robert grabbed his wife by the shoulders and stared into her eyes, trying to calm her down. "I'll do my best to protect the boys, but their help tonight is crucial. I have trained them personally, and they know how to fight. It is up to you now to watch over our daughter. Ann, I am sorry for my bad choices. I regret my mistakes."

Matilda didn't know what that meant, but she saw her mother break down in a way that she'd never seen before. Looking over to her brothers, she witnessed fear in their eyes now that hadn't been there earlier. The sounds of clashing swords and shouting men had become even louder. They were getting closer, and would approach the solar at any minute.

"Let the boys hide with us," pleaded Matilda's mother.

"Nay, there is only room for two," answered Matilda's father in a rushed voice, glancing back at the door. "They're almost here. Now, hurry, there is no time to waste. Get behind the hidden panel and don't come out until you no longer hear fighting."

"Robert," cried Ann. "I don't want you or the boys to die."

"Go!" he shouted. "I sent a messenger to my brother earlier when I suspected there might be trouble tonight. I can only hope Gilbert will arrive here in time to help us."

Robert pushed Matilda and her mother into the cramped hiding space in the wall. Matilda still gripped the knife tightly, not wanting to let it go. Once they were inside the small enclosure, her father replaced the wooden panel in front of them to close them in. It was small and stuffy in there, and so dark that it frightened Matilda. She could feel her mother's arms shaking as she pulled her closer, but Matilda couldn't see her face. She also heard the soft sobs her mother was trying to conceal, as well as the loud beating of her own heart in her ears.

A bang was heard as the door to the solar burst open. The sound of running feet and clashing swords filled the air. There was a crack on the side of the panel where it didn't close snugly. Matilda peeked out, wanting to see what was happening. She froze as she watched in horror, seeing the battle unfold before her very eyes.

Several warriors entered and fought her father and brothers. They were big, burly men with lots of muscles and big swords. Matilda's brothers were no match for them. John and Andrew were young, and still wearing their nightclothes instead of chain mail. They also hadn't the strength, nor the skills with a blade that these barbaric Scots possessed.

It didn't take long for the Scots to get the upper hand. Right before her eyes, her brothers were struck down one after the other. It caused such fear to sweep through Matilda that she could not move, and neither could she look away. She barely found the will to breathe. Her mother peeked out as well, and gasped and held a hand over her mouth, pulling Matilda closer. Tears streamed down her cheeks and her body trembled. Both Matilda and her mother whimpered softly.

"Naaay," her father screamed, seeing his boys go down. He fought like a madman, taking on a man now who looked different from the others. His attacker didn't wear a plaid like the Scots. Instead, he was dressed in a tunic and braies, like an Englishman would wear. His back was to Matilda so she couldn't see the man's face. All she could see from her position, being so low to the floor, was two silver bands attached to the back of the man's boot heels.

"I can't believe this. You bastard!" shouted her father. "I should have known you'd betray me and team up with the bloody Scots. How could you do such a thing? What is the matter with you?"

"I'm sorry, Robert, but I have to look out for myself," came the man's answer. "The Scots have offered me protection as well as all the wealth I'll ever need if I give them your share of the bounty. It is too good of an offer to turn down."

"No offer is worth selling out your own kind. How can you do this? You have no wife or children, and you just killed my boys!"

The man's head turned quickly toward Matilda's brothers and then back to Robert. "Nay, you fools," he spoke to the Scots. "I said not to kill any of the children. What did you do?"

"We canna leave any witnesses," said one of the Scots, picking up a pair of silver candlestick holders and shoving them into an oversized bag he carried over his shoulder.

"You'll die for this!" screamed Robert. "You will all die by my hand for taking the lives of my boys."

"Now, now, Robert," said the Englishman, still parrying with

Matilda's father. "You have been a thorn in my side ever since we teamed up. I never trusted you. I am sorry about your children, but the Scots are right. I can't leave any witnesses alive to tell anyone what happened here tonight."

"You are nothing but a murderer and a thief!" Robert's sword clashed with the man's once again. Matilda's father was trained with a sword and he was one of the best knights ever. But this man was just as good. It was obvious he had some sort of training, too, or most likely, lots of experience in battles.

"I'm a thief? Hah!" spat the Englishman. "I heard from one of my spies that you managed to secure some treasure on your own without including me when you secretly met with some wealthy nobles lately."

"Nay. I didn't steal from the nobles, I swear. It was just one stolen piece I procured that I took off a bandit I met on the road when he tried to attack me. The opportunity fell into my lap. What was I to do? I was going to tell you about it."

"I don't believe that for one moment. Then again, it no longer matters. You have more than your share of stolen goods. Much more than me."

"That's to be expected. I have a family to support. You don't."

"You have more than you can possibly ever use. I'm also sure you've been hiding some of the goods as well. I believe it's time to share them with me now."

Stolen wealth? Matilda wondered what that meant. This man was calling her father a thief, and she didn't like it. Nay, this man was naught but a liar! Her father had never stolen a thing in his life. He was a good man, and honorable. He paid allegiance to their English king. He was a knight who had taken vows. What she was hearing couldn't possibly be true. She opened her mouth to speak to her mother, but her mother held her finger to her lips and shook her head, warning Matilda to stay quiet.

Their swords clashed as the Scots continued pilfering everything in sight, sticking things into bags to take with them.

Stepping over the dead bodies of Matilda's brothers, they acted like it meant nothing to them that they'd taken the boys' lives for a few baubles.

"I trusted you," spat Matilda's father. "We were friends. Why are you doing this to me? Because of you, my boys are dead."

"I didn't know they were going to kill the boys, but I suppose it is for the best," the man answered. "I told you. I need to look out for myself. The Scots are right. We can't have loose ends. And speaking of family, where is that lovely wife and daughter of yours, Robert? I know they must be hiding here somewhere."

"Nay! They're not here," shouted her father. Matilda heard fear in his voice. "They're at my brother's," lied Robert, still fighting the man while the Scots ransacked the room, collecting things they wanted.

"My cup," whispered Matilda, spying the ornate silver chalice on the edge of a small end table. Her father had given it to her for a present just yesterday for her sixth birthday. It meant the world to her. She'd never owned such a beautiful or valuable piece. It had green, malachite gemstones embedded in the ornate etchings and white stones on the base. A pink gemstone heart graced the middle. Raised designs of swirls and different shapes made it the most beautiful piece she'd ever seen.

She started to reach for the panel, meaning to go out and grab it, but her mother's hand clamped around her wrist. Matilda looked back, able to see a streak of light coming from the crack, lighting up her mother's face. Tears streamed down the woman's cheeks as she shook her head, holding her finger up to her lips once more, warning Matilda to remain still and quiet.

"Good thing for them they aren't here, or they'd be buried along with you and your sons today," snarled the attacker, still fighting with her father.

"You'd really kill a woman and a child?" asked Robert. "You are naught but a demon."

"I'm sorry, Robert, but I can't leave any witnesses. It's too risky. You see, the plan is failproof, but only with no one able to identify me. Your sons had to die, and now, so will you. Good-bye, old friend." The man thrust his sword through Matilda's father's heart, causing Matilda's eyes to widen, and her heart to almost stop.

Her father stumbled backwards, knocking into the small table before he fell to the ground in a puddle of blood. Matilda watched in horror, unable to believe this was real. When her father hit the table, the silver goblet fell to the ground with a clank and rolled in a half-circle on the floor in the rushes.

Matilda heard her mother gasp loudly and then clamp a hand over her mouth as she peeked out a crack on the opposite side of the panel, having seen her husband fall.

"What was that noise?" asked the attacker, looking around.

"What noise?" asked a Scot, rummaging through a drawer.

"I think those wretched females are hiding in here some-where. I should have known that Robert was lying." Footsteps were heard, and when Matilda peeked out the crack again, she saw the feet of the man stop right in front of the hidden panel.

"Get back, Matilda," whispered her mother softly, pushing her deeper into the hiding place. "Whatever happens, don't make a sound."

"I won't, Mother," she whispered back, crawling and hiding in a small area that could only fit a child.

Matilda heard the sound of the panel being pulled off, and her mother screaming as the man yanked her out into the open.

"Leave me alone," cried Ann, but the man just chuckled.

"I knew you were here somewhere. Too bad you couldn't keep quiet, or I might not have found you."

"I won't say anything, I swear. Just please, don't hurt me," begged Ann.

"Where is your daughter?" he demanded to know. "Is she in there, too?"

"Nay! She's at her uncle's," lied Matilda's mother, but Matilda could tell the man didn't believe her.

"I'll find that brat but, first, you've got to go. You've seen my face and know too much. I can't let you live."

"Nay, please," cried her mother, but it was too late.

Matilda heard the sound of the man's blade sinking into her mother's flesh and then her body hitting the ground. There was no denying that her mother had just lost her life as well. Matilda's little body shook in fright. She kept her eyes squeezed closed, trying to be silent just like her parents had instructed her to do.

A Scot ran into the room, shouting. "We've got to retreat," he called out. "There is a troop of Sassenachs headed right toward the manor house. They outnumber us three to one."

"I can't leave until I find that wretched girl. I'm sure she's here somewhere. Start a fire. We need to burn this place to the ground. Leave no trace as to who we are."

"Aye," answered the Scot rushing out the door.

Matilda's eyes shot open, and she saw the shadow of the man hunkering down, looking into the hiding place. His hand reached inside, grabbing around, searching for her. It came so close to her that she thought he would touch her. She closed her eyes and didn't even dare to breathe.

"If we dinna leave now, we'll be discovered," yelled another Scot coming into the room. "The fire's already started and it is spreadin' quickly."

Hearing this caused the man to back out of the hiding area and stand.

"Damn it, this is going to come back to haunt me someday, I just know it," he ground out.

Matilda opened her eyes again, seeing the back of the man as he reached down over the dead bodies of her parents and snatched up her silver goblet. "We almost missed this. Your king will like it," he said with a chuckle, tossing it to the Scot. "After all, it was probably his to begin with. I should be protected for life now, with the worth of this fine piece."

"They're comin' fast. We need to leave now." The Scot ran out the door, but the Englishman came back to the hiding place, once again, reaching inside. This time, his hand brushed against

Matilda's night dress.

"Come out, you wretched whelp," warned the man, gripping her nightdress tightly and pulling. The cloth started to rip.

Matilda looked at the eating knife she'd been clutching, knowing she had to do something to stop him and to save her own life. She was all alone now, and had to be brave. She would fight, just like her father and brothers. Raising the knife up, she brought it down with force, stabbing it hard into the back of the man's hand, pulling, causing a long bloody opening to appear. Blood squirted out, soiling her bed clothes.

"Aaaah," he cried out in pain, pulling his hand away. "You shouldn't have done that, you little witch."

"The English have entered the manor. We have to leave, now," came the cry of a Scot from the corridor.

Matilda's attacker remained hunkered down by the opening of her hidden compartment. "You say a word about any of this, and I swear I will hunt you down like a dog and kill you," he warned. "Stay there, if you want. And die in the fire." He closed up the secret hiding place, wedging a chair against the panel and ran from the room, leaving Matilda behind.

Through her tears, peeking out the crack, Matilda saw the back of the man leaving the room. She had never even seen the man's face. Something about his voice seemed familiar, but she couldn't place it, and didn't know who he was.

Shouting was heard in the distance, the sound of running feet, and clashing swords. But in the solar, all became quiet. After all, the dead could not speak. Her family had perished tonight, she realized, and only she was left alive. Matilda peeked through the crack again and could see the bodies of her family lying on the floor. She pushed against the panel but it would not open. Smoke from the fire started to enter the room. Tired and feeling faint, Matilda closed her eyes and sobbed. She'd never felt as alone as she did at this very moment.

Then she heard men entering the solar, and she bit her lip, holding back any sound so she wouldn't be discovered. She didn't move. She couldn't. Her body, frozen in fear, stayed still, since she was too scared now to even cry.

"Damn it, nay! They've killed my brother," shouted someone who sounded a lot like her Uncle Gilbert.

"Bid the devil, they even attacked Robert's wife and young boys," said one of his soldiers. "What kind of monsters are they?"

"Nay! God's eyes, this can't be true," yelled Uncle Gilbert.

"We're too late, my lord," said another, hunkering down to check Matilda's brothers for signs of life. "The boys are dead."

"Robert, you fool," Gilbert ground out, reaching down to close his brother's eyes. "Why didn't you leave this place and come live with me years ago like I begged you to do? Damn it, I told you this place was not safe, but you didn't listen."

"His wife is dead, too," said one of his men.

"Such a waste of lives," said another.

"We'd better go." The guard checking for signs of life got to his feet. "The fire is spreading quickly and smoke is already filling the room. Soon, we'll be trapped."

"Go, find the ones responsible for this," commanded Gilbert. "I want them to pay for what they did."

"Aye, my lord," answered a guard as he headed to the door.

Matilda let out a whimper, still too frightened to even call out for help. Gilbert's head snapped up, looking around the room. "Wait. Where's Matilda? Where is my niece? God's bones, I hope they didn't abduct her."

It was then that Matilda could no longer hold back her sobs, and she started crying from within the hidden area. She pounded on the secret panel, wanting to be let out.

"Matilda?" Gilbert got down on his knees and pulled away the panel, looking into the small, darkened space. "Is that you, my dear? It's all right. You can come out now. I will keep you safe."

Matilda dropped the knife and slowly crawled toward him. Her hand came across the velvet bag of coins that her father had given her mother before they hid away. She picked it up, clutching it to her chest. And as she exited the hiding place, she spotted the small rose quartz heart on the floor that had once been embedded in the silver goblet. It must have dislodged when the cup hit the floor. She snatched it up, slipping it into the bag with the coins. She stood up, and fell into her uncle's strong arms, crying uncontrollably. The room was filling with smoke now, and it was getting hard to breathe.

Her Uncle Gilbert hugged her and picked her up, holding her tightly. Matilda turned her head and her eyes roamed over the floor and the bodies of her dead family as the smoke started to fill her eyes. She whimpered. It was a horrendous sight to see her loved ones gone, and the vision would be embedded in her mind for as long as she lived.

"Don't look, dear." Her uncle pulled her head over to his shoulder and she hid her eyes, not wanting to see more.

"My papa told me and Mother to go to live with you if anything happened to him," she told Gilbert.

"Aye, and you will. From now on, you'll live with me and will never have to return to this godawful place again."

"What should we do with the bodies?" asked one of Gilbert's men who was still there.

"There's no time to collect them with the fire spreading. We'll have to leave them and come back later for their remains," said Gilbert. "Let's go!"

As Gilbert left the room carrying her, Matilda's curiosity made her look over his shoulder once more. She said her silent goodbyes to her parents and her brothers, hoping their souls would go to heaven. Anger filled her heart for what had transpired here tonight. It was at that moment that she decided she would someday hunt down the man who had done this to her family, and kill him. Even if it took a lifetime to do it, she would never give up her search.

Matilda would learn to fight with a sword, just like her father and brothers. She would be able to protect herself and those she loved so nothing like this would ever happen again. From this day forward, she swore she would never be helpless and vulnerable, even though she was a female. Once she mastered the sword, she would find the man she had stabbed with the eating knife. She might not have seen his face, but the scar she'd put on his sword hand would identify him, as well as the silver bands on the back of his boot heels. Matilda's life had changed tonight, and so had she. After what she'd experienced, she was no longer a child. Life's hardships made one grow up quickly.

Before, she had always thought she'd be raised as a lady, and marry for alliances. But now, she knew she would not depend on someone else to protect her, ever again. Nay, she would not hesitate to kill if she had to – the first being the bloody bastard who took the lives of those she loved!

◆◦◇◦◆

CHAPTER ONE

Hermitage Castle, Scotland, 19 years later

"WELL, NORTH, TODAY is the day that ye're finally gettin' yer sentence." Gavin MacKeefe leaned back on the wooden chair with a tankard of Mountain Magic cradled in his hands, staring down into the cup.

"Aye, I bet ye're glad." Cam took a swig of the potent whisky, brewed by the oldest man in Scotland – their chieftain, Storm MacKeefe's grandfather, Callum MacKeefe.

"I, for one, am happy I'm no longer an outcast," said North's twin brother, Nash, who was the most recent one to secure his place back in the clan again. "However, it wasna easy to convince my new bride that I had to leave her to help ye, North. Ye'd better appreciate this." Nash scowled and took a swig of Mountain Magic.

North, on the other hand, wasn't drinking. Instead, he paced back and forth in the great hall of the MacKeefe Clan's border castle, nervous to find out what Old Callum had planned for him. At Nash's wedding, Callum had hinted that North was going far away, and wasn't going to like it. If North wasn't at Hermitage Castle, or in the MacKeefe Clan's Highland camp, he wasn't going to be happy, he was sure.

"I just want this over with as quickly as possible," complained North. "I helped all of ye with yer punishments, and now ye're welcomed back into the clan. I'm the only one left. I dinna want to be an outcast anymore." North ran a weary hand through his long, brown hair and looked up at the dais once again, waiting for the announcement of his sentence. "What is takin' them so long?"

"Here they come now," said Nash, nodding toward the door.

An entourage entered the great hall, being led by Storm MacKeefe. His grandfather, Callum, hobbled along right behind him. Storm's mother, Clarista, and his wife, Wren, who were both English, followed him up to the dais. Storm's two sons walked over and stood next to him. Renard was a redhead and twenty-five years of age. The younger of his sons, Hawke, had long, dark hair and was only ten. Neither of them looked like Storm who had long, blond hair, that was now streaked with gray.

Something was amiss here. North could tell.

Storm raised his hand in the air to get the attention of the crowded great hall. "I have an announcement to make," he said. "Please, quiet down." Once the room had stilled, he continued. "My faither, Ian, will no longer be chieftain of the MacKeefe Clan . . . for now."

The crowd became restless. Comments were heard as people wondered what was going on. The clan had two chieftains, since the MacKeefes had holdings in the Lowlands as well as the Highlands.

"What's wrong?" called out Gavin.

"Is Ian still feelin' ill?" asked Cam.

"Aye," said Storm with a sigh. "Ian is still ailin', and I'm no' sure he's goin' to get better."

"Why?" asked someone from the crowd.

"What's wrong with him?" shouted out someone else.

"We're doing all we can to heal him," Wren told the crowd, glancing back over at her husband.

"Get out of my way, Boy," came a deep voice from behind North as a man pushed into him from behind. North moved quickly, and the man fell to the floor.

"Chieftain," said North in surprise, reaching out to help Ian MacKeefe, who slapped his hand away.

"I hear ye talkin' about me as if I'm no' even here," spat Ian. "I'm no' old, I tell ye. The fae folk take care of me with their remedies. I'm goin' to live forever."

The room became suddenly silent at their chieftain's nonsensical outburst.

"Da," said Storm, motioning to his guards. "Ye need to rest. My men will take ye to yer chamber."

Two guards rushed over to help him, pulling Ian to a standing position. When he stood up, a small pouch fell from his pocket, landing at North's feet.

"I think ye dropped this, Chieftain." When North picked it up, the scent of a strong herb spilling out of the pouch assaulted his senses.

"Give me that." Ian snatched it away from North, quickly shoving it into his pocket. Then he leaned over and whispered to North. "It's a secret. It is what's keepin' me young."

"What is it?" asked North.

"It's fairy dust. Dinna tell a soul. Especially no' my wife."

"My lips are sealed," North whispered back, thinking Ian had truly lost his mind. The scent from the pouch smelled familiar, but North couldn't place it.

Once the guards took Ian away, Storm continued.

"As ye have all seen, it is mainly my faither's mind, as well as a few other symptoms that are troublin' him. We still havena identified his ailment."

"Is it fatal?" asked a woman.

"Will he die?" called out a little boy.

"He's no' goin' to die," spat Callum, being just as ornery as ever. "My Mountain Magic will heal him. Just give it some time. There is nothin' to fret about, I assure ye."

"Callum, excuse me for sayin' so," North interrupted. "But yer Mountain Magic has been kent to make a man go mindless, no' heal his way of thinkin'."

Everyone laughed, since what North said was true. Old Callum's potent whisky was so strong that it sometimes knocked a man unconscious for days at a time.

"Haud yer wheesht, North, or I'll make sure yer punishment is twice as nasty as any of the others." Callum shook a bony fist in the air, probably trying to look threatening. Instead, it almost made him seem as if he'd gone mad as well.

North closed his mouth, thinking of the undesirable punishments of his friends, Gavin and Cam, and of his brother, Nash. He knew how bad they were since he had been sent along on each of their journeys, and had helped them. Therefore, he had endured their punishments as well. His friends and brother were once again accepted back into the clan. Sadly, North was still an outcast. The whole thing was silly in his opinion. They were only branded as outcasts in the first place for breaking some of Callum's stupid rules of his Horn and Hoof Tavern in Glasgow. Did any of this really matter?

"Sorry," said North, clearing his throat, sitting down on the bench next to his brother.

"Dinna make this worse for us," Nash said in a hoarse whisper. He had promised to go along with North and help him in exchange for North helping him, even though his new bride, Kellina, was waiting for him back in the Highlands.

"Until my faither is healed, my sons, Renard and Hawke, will be in trainin' to become the next chieftain to take his place," Storm continued.

The crowd was very upset at hearing about Ian.

"I'll do all I can to help out," promised Renard, trying to win over the crowd. "Of course, I ken that I'll never be able to fill my grandda's shoes."

"I promise to do all I can as well," said Hawke, even though he was just a child. Even at ten years of age, the boy was twice as big as most lads his age, and already seemed threatening. North was sure that either of Storm's sons would someday make a good leader for the clan.

"We have not yet given up hope on my husband, I assure you," said Clarista. "It might just be a temporary thing, and we are praying he'll get better."

"That's right," agreed Wren. "I have sent word to England for the old gypsy woman, Zara, who raised me to take another look at him. She couldn't find the cause earlier, but she is skilled in healing and I'm sure she'll help find a remedy to cure Ian."

"Hmph," mumbled Gavin under his breath to his friends. "Zara will probably use her witchy magic or those Tarot cards of hers to do somethin' to him."

"Like expel a demon?" Cam asked, taking another swig of whisky.

"We will hope for the best. That is all we can do," Storm continued. "In the meantime, there is business to attend to. North, please approach the dais."

"That's me." North sprang up from the bench so quickly that he almost knocked his brother to the floor.

"Careful, Brathair," griped Nash. "Ye almost spilled my Mountain Magic, and that will only be another punishment from Callum if ye do."

"Come up there with me, Nash," North all but begged his brother.

"Me?" Nash took a drink. "Whatever for?"

"Ye're comin' with me wherever I am sent. Ye promised. Be at my side when I receive my punishment as well."

"Ye did promise him," mumbled Cam.

"Ye'd better go," agreed Gavin.

"Fine." Nash let out a sigh and followed his brother up to the dais where North's sentence would be determined. Nash and North were twenty-four-year-old twins, but they were not identical. North was taller with more chiseled features and had silver eyes. Nash was shorter but quicker, and had eyes of hazel. They both had long, brown hair.

"North MacKeefe, are ye ready to be punished for losin' Storm's silver chalice, given to him by the king?" asked Callum.

"Well, to be accurate, I didna actually lose the goblet. It was stolen by thieves," North pointed out.

"After ye saw to take it and use it without askin'," snapped the old man.

Nash leaned over and whispered, "Dinna anger him, North. Ye do, and we'll never get back to the Highlands."

Callum overheard him and scowled. "Ye broke more than one of my rules, North MacKeefe. However, since losin' the cup is the biggest offense, yer punishment is to track down the chalice and bring it back to my grandson where it belongs."

"What?" both Nash and North said together.

"How can I do that?" complained North. "I dinna ken where it is."

"We dinna even have any idea who stole it," added Nash.

"I'll never be able to accomplish this task. I'm doomed to fail. I'll be an outcast forever." North was feeling so upset, realizing it would be next to impossible to be accepted back into the clan now. Thoughts filled his head of moving to Ireland or France, or possibly even joining a new clan. He would do whatever was necessary, but leaving the MacKeefes was the last thing he ever wanted to do. The MacKeefes were his family. All he had were his clan and his brother. This was not going to be easy at all.

"We are lucky enough to have a lead," said Storm. "If no', I would have talked Callum out of this punishment anon."

"A lead?" asked North. "So ye ken who stole it?"

"Go ahead, Renard. Tell them, since ye are the one who discovered the clue." Storm nodded to his red-haired son.

Renard cleared his throat before speaking.

"Hawke and I overheard somethin' on our latest journey. It had to do with a couple of pirates who recently visited Glasgow and are now tryin' to sell an ornate silver goblet."

"That's right," said Hawke. "The pirates' names are Goldtooth and Coop. They are part of the crew of the *Falcon*."

"The *Falcon*?" asked Nash. "I've heard of that pirate ship."

"Isna it run by three brathairs who used to be English fishermen?" asked North.

"Aye," Renard answered. "Tristan is the captain of the *Falcon*. His brathairs are Mardon and Aaron."

"None of them are any guid," added Hawke.

"That's why those thieves in the tavern seemed familiar." Gavin slapped the table and stood up. "The day the goblet was stolen, I saw two shady men hangin' around inside the Horn and Hoof. I couldna put my finger on it, but now I remember seein' them in port a few years ago. They were with the whole crew. They tried to steal from me, but I was too swift for them to catch."

"Aye, I remember." Cam stood up as well. "Gavin and I were tastin' the whisky as well as some of the lovely tarts that day on the docks."

"Sit down, Gavin and Cam," North told them. "No one cares to hear about yer drinkin' and whorin' escapades."

"Well, this will be easy then," said Nash. "We'll just find these pirates and take back the goblet. Then my brathair will be welcomed back into the clan."

"As long as they're no' back on their ship already," said North. He turned and looked at Callum and the others. "Where can we find them?"

"Well, that's a little tricky," said Callum.

"What do ye mean?" North didn't like the sound of this.

"Renard, would ye care to explain?" asked Storm.

"Sure, Da." Renard continued. "Hawke and I were over the border in Northumberland a few days ago when we heard this gossip. We were visitin' Montclair Castle, where our clansmember, Onyx, has a sister. It seems the pirates are inland right now and tryin' to sell off some of their stolen guids."

"Northumberland? Bid the devil, please dinna tell me that is where ye are sendin' me," complained North, not wanting to leave Scotland.

"There's no guarantee they're even still there," protested Nash. "Why dinna ye just have my brathair make ye a new goblet, the way Gavin made shoes for Callum after he ruined his."

"Nay," said Storm. "Learnin' to be a silversmith takes a lifetime. It isna anythin' like makin' a simple pair of shoes. I'm afraid we dinna have the time for that."

"Then I'll buy ye a new one," North offered.

"With what?" mumbled his brother. "Do ye ken what a silver chalice like that is worth? Brathair, ye dinna have that kind of money."

"He's right," agreed Callum. "Besides, if ye did that, ye wouldna learn yer lesson. Yer best bet is to be off now to try to find the cup. And if the pirates have already sold it, then ye'll have to hunt down the new owner."

"And do what?" asked North. "Steal it back? After all, I canna afford to buy it. Therefore, how do ye think I am goin' to be able to bring it back?"

"That is no' my problem," said Callum with a tsking noise from his mouth. "Do it however ye have to, but bring that goblet back to my grandson, or ye'll never be accepted back into the clan."

"Well, guid luck with that one," said Cam with a chuckle, pouring himself more Mountain Magic.

"Nash, we'll tell Kellina to start lookin' for another husband since ye'll return in five or ten years from now," added Gavin. It seemed like he and Cam were thoroughly enjoying Nash and North's discomfort.

"I dinna like yer attitude, boys," spat Callum. "Ye two have sharp tongues, and they need to be controlled."

"We're just jestin'." Gavin chuckled again and cradled his tankard in his large hands.

"Aye," agreed Cam. "The twins ken that." He greedily drank from his mug.

"Well, I dinna ken it," continued Callum. "And now, because of it, I've just decided to send ye both along with North and his brathair on this mission."

"What?" gasped Gavin, almost dropping his tankard.

A stream of whisky came shooting out of Cam's mouth. He wiped his face with the back of his hand. "But we're finished with our sentences," he protested. "We shouldna have to go with him."

"Plus, we've got wives waitin' for us back in the Highlands," Gavin reminded him.

"So do I, yet I am helpin' my brathair," said Nash.

"I helped both of ye with yer punishments, and they werena half as hard as this one is goin' to be," North ground out. "I canna believe ye'd desert me just because ye are no longer outcasts. I thought ye were my friends."

"Aye," agreed Nash. "We didna let either of ye down, and I think ye should help us find the cup."

"Storm?" Gavin looked up with begging eyes, hoping for help.

"Ye're no' really goin' to send us to England, are ye?" Cam spoke to Storm as well.

Storm looked over at Callum who had his arms crossed over his chest and was slowly shaking his head back and forth.

Then Storm shrugged his shoulders and answered. "I'm sorry, but it's my grandda's decision, so he has the final word in this. I ken yer situation, bein' just married, and I feel yer pain. Although, I have to agree with Callum that more eyes lookin' will help North find the goblet sooner."

"Then it's decided!" Callum raised his finger in the air. "Now, off with all four of ye, and dinna return unless ye have Storm's goblet in yer possession."

"Davita's goin' to kill me," mumbled Gavin.

"I promised Yvaine I wouldna be long," said Cam.

"I havena even had but a few days alone with my new wife," Nash told them.

"I'll send a missive to let yer wives ken what is goin' on," offered Storm.

"Well, I suppose we ought to get started." North sighed,

feeling as if this were naught but a fool's journey. There was no way in hell they were going to hunt down an expensive silver goblet stolen by pirates. Even if they did find it, they didn't have the funds to buy it back. If they had to steal it to get it, they could all end up in an English prison, and might even lose their heads before this was over. Nay, they were not going to fare well in the long run, he could see that right now.

"Godspeed and have a guid journey," called out Callum, cackling like an old hen.

"Guid luck," Hawke said, waving as North, his brother, and their friends slowly headed to the door.

"Guid luck?" North blew air from his mouth. "We'll need more than luck to pull off this fool's errand."

"Ye might want to start buildin' our caskets right now," Nash called over his shoulder. "Because if the English dinna kill us, our wives will. That is, if we even happen to return at all."

❖

CHAPTER TWO

Northumberland, England

MATILDA MONTCLAIR STAYED hidden under her cloak, sure to hide the sword strapped to her side as she wandered down Grope Lane in the bad part of town. Having come to town with her cousin, Marcus, and his wife, Amethyst, and two guards, she was lucky to have slipped away on her own at all.

This was nothing new to Matilda. She'd been searching the questionable parts of town for the last nineteen years, looking for the man with the scar on his hand who had killed her family. Every time they had journeyed to another castle or another town, she'd looked there as well.

She made sure to walk down the center of the street instead of next to the buildings. It was safer. Oftentimes, people threw garbage or emptied chamber pots right out the second-floor windows. The wooden buildings were built close together, and the upper stories jutted out further than the lower floors.

The sun was starting to set now, and it wouldn't be long before Marcus figured out she wasn't in the clothier's shop looking for a new dress like she'd pretended to be. She'd sneaked out the back door and through the streets until she got to Grope Lane.

If she was going to find the man she sought vengeance on, he was probably conversing with the beggars, the thieves, and the whores. Then again, her father had seemed to know him, so mayhap he was a noble instead. She had no idea where to look anymore. Her Uncle Gilbert had searched as well, many years ago. He'd always come up empty-handed. It was as if the attackers had just disappeared from the face of the earth.

Still, Matilda didn't give up. Through the years, she'd learned to wield a sword, and she was ready now if she did find him.

Her hand wavered at her waist, and her eyes darted back and forth as she sauntered down the street, listening and looking for clues. Nineteen years was a long time to wait, but Matilda had learned patience, if nothing else. For all she knew, the man might be dead by now. Mayhap she should have given up this quest like her Uncle Gilbert had urged her to do years ago. Still, part of her was so unsettled that she just had to keep looking. She needed to find justice for her family. For the people she'd loved and lost.

Wandering past the tavern, two whores eyed her up, and a drunk called out to her. She ignored them all.

"Over here, Missy. I'll give ye a copper for a roll in the hay." A dirty man in ragged clothes tugged at his belt, looking down to the tent under his braies.

"Nay, you won't! This is our territory," snapped the whore, shoving the drunk and knocking him down.

"If you want a roll in the hay, it'll be with us, not her," said her friend. They both looked like they wanted to kill Matilda, when she had done nothing but walk past them.

A shiver ran up Matilda's spine as she wandered further and further down Grope Lane, hoping today would be her lucky day and that she'd find some kind of clue. Garbage crunched under her feet. Her long cloak dragged in the muddy ruts of the road. The place smelled foul, and all she wanted to do was to go back to the castle, but her bad memories made her stay. There was an odd feeling in her stomach tonight. It was one of excitement and horror, all mixed in one for some reason. She was sure she would find something today.

Matilda stepped around a pig in the road, and dodged two

barefooted, dirty children who were trying to catch it. She stopped at the table of a woman who had broken and blackened teeth. She had goods on her table that Matilda was sure were all stolen from nobles. Silver spoons, hair combs, and even a bracelet made from copper with a green stone in the center, looked like items of a lady. She picked up the bracelet, pretending to be interested in buying it.

"Have you seen a man with a long scar down the top of his right hand?" she asked. "He'd be older by now, and probably wears boots with silver bands on his heels."

"There are plenty of men with scars in this part of town," answered the woman. "But if he's wearing heels with silver bands, he's not a peasant. What's his name?"

"I – I don't know."

"Well, what does he look like, then?"

"Well, I'm not really sure. I've never seen his face. I only know he wears silver strips on the heels of his boots, and has a scar down the top of his right hand."

"What do you want with him?" The woman squinted her eyes and looked Matilda up and down.

"I'm sorry. I can't tell you that."

"Why come to me, then?" asked the woman suspiciously. "This sounds like trouble."

"Nay, you won't be in any trouble if you tell me information, I promise."

The woman scrunched up her face and shook her head. "I don't know who you're talking about. Now, are you going to buy the bracelet or not, my lady?"

"What?" Matilda looked up in surprise. She had thought her identity had remained hidden, but this woman obviously saw right through it. "What makes you think I'm a lady?" she asked, putting the bracelet back down on the table.

"A noble on Grope Lane sticks out more than a lustful cur wanting to bed a willing tart. You're not safe here, and should go back to where you came from right away if you know what's good for you." The woman started scooping her goods into a bag, looking one way and then the other. "I'd be in big trouble just talking to you if anyone found out."

"But what about the man I asked about? The one with the scar? Have you ever seen him?"

"You have come here before asking that question, and I urge you to give up your search. No one is going to give you any information. Why should we even care?"

"Just look at this silver chalice fit for a king," she heard someone say. Matilda quickly turned her head to see a short, stout man holding up . . . her silver goblet, if she wasn't mistaken. Her heart sped up. This might be her lucky day after all.

This could very well be the goblet that was given to her by her father on her sixth birthday. Still, she had to get a closer look at it to be sure. She rubbed the rose quartz heart in her pocket, the way she always did when she worried. For some reason, caressing it helped to calm her. Taking it out of her pocket, she studied it in her open palm. This was the only thing she had left to remember her loving family by. Everything else had been burned, ransacked, or stolen so many years ago. This heart stone should fit on the side of the goblet, where it once made its home. If it did, then she'd know for sure this was the goblet that had been stolen from her on that awful day.

She slipped the stone back into her pocket, pulled her hood lower over her face, and slowly walked over to the table where the man was trying to pawn the cup. She had to see it close up. She had to know if it was hers.

"This has gemstones on it, and looks like you stole it from a noble," said the man behind the table, surveying the goblet. "If I buy it and get caught, I'll lose my head." He put it back down on the table. "I don't want it." He held up his palms and shook his head. "It's too expensive and will only bring me trouble."

"Nay, I didn't steal it from a noble," swore the man. "I got it in a tavern in Scotland. So, ye see, it's safe for ye to buy it. No one around here, noble or not, will be lookin' for it."

"That's right," said the man who was with him. This one was a big, burly pirate. Both of them wore colorful clothes and had head scarfs holding back their hair. "Besides, ye can always pluck off the gems and sell them separately and then melt down the silver. So, how much will ye give us for it, Matey?"

"I don't know," said the man, picking it up once more and inspecting it, turning it over in his hands. "It looks like it once belonged to a king or something. This is only going to raise suspicion." He glanced back up at the men. "You look like pirates, and I don't do business with pirates. Nay, I don't want it." He put it back down on the table once again.

Matilda silently walked up behind the pirates while the men were engaged in a heated conversation with the man behind the table.

"Goldtooth, I told ye, we shouldn't try to sell it," growled the shorter man with the barrel chest. "We should have just given it to Tristan as part of the crew's booty like I wanted to do in the first place."

"Did you say, Tristan?" asked the man behind the table. "I know who he is, since he used to sell me fish. He's the captain of the *Falcon* now. You are pirates! I was right."

"So, what if we are?" asked the shorter pirate. "Who really cares?"

"I don't want any trouble. Please leave." The man held up his hands once again and backed away.

"Coop, ye are a fool for sayin' my name aloud," spat Goldtooth. "We'd better get back to the others. Tristan will have our head if we don't return to the ship in time."

"Well, if ye don't want it, then I'll just be takin' it somewhere else." Coop reached out for the goblet, but Matilda was faster. She snatched it up from the table, quickly inspecting it to assure her that this was her long-lost chalice after all. In her hand was her last remembrance of her father.

"I'll take it," she said. "How much?"

"Wait a second," said Coop, looking at her oddly. "Ye're a

woman."

"And a noble," said Goldtooth, reaching out and pushing her hood from her head. "She's goin' to turn us in."

"He's right. It's not for sale anymore," said Coop, sounding very anxious.

"Hand over the goblet, Wench." The big man held out his open palm and smiled, showing off his front, gold tooth. Now, Matilda knew how he got his name.

"Nay, I don't think so." Matilda took a step backward, drawing her sword. She realized that all the vendors were quickly packing up their things and hurrying away now, leaving her alone with the two pirates. "This is my chalice. It was stolen from me when I was a child, and I'm taking it back." She dropped it into an open bag hanging over her shoulder.

"Don't think ye scare us with that blade," spat Coop. "Ye probably don't even know how to use it."

"Are you willing to find out?" she asked, raising her chin, trying to act brave although her insides were shaking.

"We've been wieldin' blades since before ye were born, Wench." Goldtooth drew his sword from his waist belt.

"She's a girl, ye fool." Coop pushed Goldtooth's hand away. "Look, my lady, that chalice is not yers. We stole it from Scots, not an Englishwoman."

"Those same Scots stole it from me years ago," she told them, still holding out her sword, stepping backwards. She knocked right into someone, spinning around and aiming the sword at them next. It was yet another pirate glaring down at her.

"What's goin' on here?" asked the older pirate she'd just bumped into. He had weathered skin and little wrinkles around his eyes.

"Stitch!" gasped Goldtooth, seeming alarmed. It made Matilda realize that this pirate named Stitch must be their superior. "This wench took somethin' of ours, and needs to give it back."

"What is it?" asked Stitch, looking at the other two from the corners of his eyes.

"It's a silver goblet," Coop blurted out, getting a swipe in the arm from Goldtooth in return.

"Don't tell him that," mumbled Goldtooth.

"Well, he asked," replied Coop in a hoarse whisper.

Stitch continued. "If ye two have booty on ye like that, ye need to hand it over to Tristan. Are ye tryin' to keep some of the goods for yerselves? That'll get ye both hanged from the yardarm if the captain hears about it."

"We didn't mean any harm, Stitch, honest we didn't," said Coop, sounding like he was pleading for his pathetic life.

"Tell that to Tristan."

"Nay!" The big guy held up a hand. "Please, don't say a word, Stitch. We'll split the booty with ye – we'll give ye half," said Goldtooth, trying to make a deal.

Stitch looked over to Matilda next. She still had her sword drawn, but he didn't at all seem alarmed. His confidence made her feel insecure, and the tip of her sword wavered.

"Ye know, this is no place for a lady," Stitch told her. "Ye're going to get yerself killed."

"I can protect myself," she boasted, raising her blade higher.

"Don't be a fool," he growled, seeming to be losing patience with her.

"I'm not a fool."

Before she knew it, Goldtooth was behind her, holding a blade to her throat. She gasped in surprise, not even having seen him move so fast and come up behind her. The tip of her sword lowered, but she didn't let go.

"Mmm, she smells good," said Goldtooth in her ear. "I haven't had a good lightskirt in a while now."

"Leave her," commanded Stitch. "Drop the blade, my lady, if ye know what's good for ye."

"Never." To let go of her sword now would be to surrender and lose her life. If she did as they said, she might as well give up because they'd probably rape her and take her back to their ship. Be strong, she told herself. Mayhap there was still a way to get out of this yet. She needed to think with a clear mind and couldn't let fear creep in.

"Hand over the goblet," demanded Coop, dragging her from her mindless plan.

"It's mine," she ground out. "You'll have to kill me to get it." As soon as the words left her mouth, she regretted them.

"That can be arranged," said Goldtooth, pressing the blade closer to her neck, and gripping her tighter around the waist. His stench assaulted her senses, and made her want to retch.

"Nay. Leave the girl be. Let's go." The order came from Stitch and, for this, she was thankful.

"But what about the cup?" asked Coop. "We can't leave without it."

"I'll get it," said Goldtooth, reaching for her bag.

Matilda quickly moved her sword to block him, cutting the man on the hand.

"Ow! Ye stupid wench!" Goldtooth removed his blade from her throat, holding his bleeding hand. Matilda stepped away from him, keeping him at the end of her sword.

"Matilda? Matilda, where are you?" yelled a man from atop his horse as a horse-drawn wagon came barreling down the street following him. Two guards atop their steeds were behind the cart.

"We need to go. Now!" said Stitch, taking off at a run with Coop right behind him.

"Damn ye, Wench, ye ruined everythin'," spat Goldtooth, still holding his hand and running after his friends. They quickly disappeared from sight. Matilda lowered her blade and let out a deep sigh of relief.

"Matilda! There she is," cried Amethyst from the wagon that was being driven by a servant. Marcus hopped off his horse, drawing his sword and running up to her.

"Cousin, are you all right? Who were those men and what is going on here?" he asked her.

"They're no one. Just . . . pirates," she answered, hesitant to tell Marcus at all since she knew how angry this was going to make him.

"After them!" Marcus ordered his men, but Matilda stopped them.

"Nay! Wait. They didn't harm me. Let's just go, please." These men weren't the ones who killed her family, and she had no qualms with them. She sheathed her sword and hurried over to the wagon.

"Matilda, what is going on?" Amethyst grabbed her and hugged her as she climbed up onto the bench seat next to her. "I was so worried about you. Why were you even down here on Grope Lane to begin with? What were you thinking?"

"She came here because she is still searching for the man who killed her family," said Marcus. "Cousin, this ridiculous notion has got to stop. You're going to get yourself killed."

"But I'm getting closer," she said. "And I'll never give up, you know that. Not until I get justice for my family."

"My father searched for your family's attackers for nearly a year and couldn't find them. What makes you think you can do so, especially after all this time?"

"I can and I will," she said stubbornly.

"You're never going to find them, because they don't want to be found," said Marcus. "Besides, you're a woman!"

"And what does that matter?" asked Amethyst, giving her husband the evil eye. Amethyst was an independent woman who had met her husband after she'd convinced the archbishop to assign her as assistant to her uncle, the Master Mason. Together with her uncle, she helped build Marcus' castle. If anyone would ever understand Matilda, it was Amethyst.

"Amy, please," mumbled Marcus, not wanting to get into an argument with his wife that had anything to do with women. He'd been down that road before, and Amethyst had always won.

"Please, don't argue," said Matilda. "It was worth coming to Grope Lane, because I found something today that was stolen from me when I was a child." She pulled the silver goblet out of her bag, and held it up, and smiled.

"What's that?" asked Amethyst in awe. "It's beautiful."

"This is my silver chalice, given to me by my father on my sixth birthday."

"Matilda, that could be any chalice," snapped Marcus. "You were too young to remember it, and you're probably wrong."

"Nay, I'm not. I'll prove it." She dug into her pocket, looking for the stone to put back into the empty indentation on the chalice to prove her point. To her horror, the stone was gone. She must have dropped it when the pirate grabbed her. She started feeling panicked as the wagon turned and headed back up the street. "I have to go back. I lost something. Stop the wagon, please."

"Nay, keep going," commanded Marcus, riding next to her, glaring at Matilda. "And if you step one foot out of the wagon before we get back to the castle, young lady, I swear I'll knock you over the head and lay you over my horse for the duration of the ride home."

"But Marcus, it's important," she insisted, turning around on the bench, looking down Grope Lane. It was dark now, and she'd never find it without a torch, which she didn't have. With all the garbage in the street, as well as all the thieves watching their every move, she was sure it was as good as gone by now. She'd found one treasure today, but at the same time, traded it for another.

"You have sneaked away from us too many times with this ridiculous notion of looking for vengeance on your family's attackers," grunted Marcus. "From now on, when we come to town, you will stay home in your chamber, watched over by one of my guards."

"Nay," cried Matilda. "Marcus, how can you be so mean?"

"Husband, that is a little extreme," Amethyst told him. She reached out and touched Matilda on the arm, letting out a deep sigh. "However, he is right, Matilda. It is a dangerous game you play. This is no place for a lady, and you're going to get hurt or possibly even killed if you keep wandering off by yourself."

"I know how to use a sword. I can defend myself."

"Against pirates?" asked Marcus.

"They didn't hurt me," she pointed out. "I scared them off."

"Hah!" laughed Marcus. "Believe me, Cousin, if they had wanted to hurt you, you'd be dead right now. Don't think holding a sword up to pirates had them running in fear."

"Well, mayhap you're right," she admitted, knowing it was only because of the pirate named Stitch that she was even alive right now. "But still, I know how to protect myself."

"And I now regret giving in to your whim, and teaching you how to wield a blade," said Marcus as they rode for home.

Amethyst put her arm around Matilda, pulling her closer. "I was so scared when we realized you were missing and then we found you with those ruffians. I don't want to lose you. You are family, Matilda, as well as a good friend. You mean so much to me – to all of us at Montclair Castle. Please, don't do something as foolish as this again."

Matilda fingered the empty spot on the goblet that was meant for the heart stone. She looked at the green and white stones still there, as well as the ornate etchings. There was no doubt in her mind that this was the same cup. Her heart felt empty now, just like the empty spot on the vessel that should hold the missing stone. All her thoughts of losing her parents and brothers came crashing down on her at once. She held the goblet to her heart, never wanting to let it go.

"You all mean a lot to me, too," she said, having accepted Amethyst as her family since Amethyst was married to her cousin. They'd always gotten along nicely. Truly, they were much like sisters. "I never want to lose you, or Marcus, or Uncle Gilbert . . . or this." She brought the cup to her mouth and kissed it, before hugging it once again. "It is all I have left to remember my family by."

"Then you'd better guard it closely," said Amethyst. "An ornate, expensive goblet such as that has got to be worth a lot of money. It'll catch the eye of every noble this side of the border."

"It will?" Matilda suddenly felt hope in her heart. After what she'd been through these past years, she thought she'd never marry again. Being a twenty-five-year-old widow, and with her baggage and tarnished reputation, she figured she'd eventually end up in a convent. Mayhap this cup wasn't just a memory of her father, but also a beacon of light for her future as well. "Yes, I suppose it will catch every nobleman's eye," said Matilda, realizing just how important this goblet was going to turn out to be after all.

CHAPTER THREE

NORTH LED THE way on horseback as he, his brother, and his friends arrived in a small town just across the border. They had thankfully not had any trouble from the English . . . yet. Four men in plaids, dressed to the hilt with weapons were starting to get some very odd looks from the commoners. He couldn't even imagine what would happen the first time they came across nobles.

"I'm hungry. Can we stop now and get somethin' to eat?" complained Cam from behind him.

"I dinna think I want to stop here. This place looks to be crawlin' with whores and thieves," Nash pointed out.

"God's eyes, did ye have to mention whores?" groaned Cam. Cam was more familiar with whore houses than anyone since he'd spent a good part of his life in them.

"Dinna tell me ye're goin' back to yer old ways," said Gavin. "Ye're a married man now, Cam."

"I assure ye, that is in my past. I only have eyes for Yvaine now," Cam told him. "But bein' around all these whores is only goin' to bring out my needs for my wife."

"Then ye and Gavin stay here on the high streets and Nash and I will take the low ones," said North. "Be sure to ask everyone ye see about the chalice."

"Now, wait a minute, Brathair, I didna say I would go down Grope Lane with ye," said Nash, reading off the sign that marked one of the seediest streets in town. Although there were signs, most of the commoners couldn't read or write. Therefore, each of the establishments also had a brightly painted sign in front of their shop depicting what they sold.

The tavern had a barrel and some grapevines in front of it. The butcher's shop had a cleaver and bone. The chandler had a candle on its sign, and the cordwainer's shop depicted a big shoe.

"Ye're comin' with me, Brathair," North told him, not taking no for an answer.

"I dinna ken. It doesna look . . . guid," said Nash, making a face, peering down the street that was covered with litter, food scraps, entrails, dung, beggars, thieves, and whores. Several men were sleeping right on the ground next to the buildings, making the ground their beds. The tavern had loud music coming from it, as well as shouting. Two doors down by the butcher's shop, there were several men engaged in a fist fight.

The roads were unpaved, and full of ruts. The streets were extremely narrow. Since the upper stories of the buildings jutted out over the bottom floors, it made shadows, blocking any sunlight from ever reaching the street. Pigs and geese roamed the area freely, picking at the garbage spewed everywhere, as the animals foraged for food.

The smell of the tannery at the end of the street was enough to turn anyone's stomach. Not to mention, the stench of feces and urine assaulted North's senses, making him want to retch. Still, he knew he had to go down here to ask if anyone had seen the thieves who stole the chalice. Their only clue right now was that it was seen in this area. North would do whatever it took to bring back Storm's silver cup so he would no longer be considered an outcast of the clan anymore.

"Just hold yer nose and follow me," said North, leading the way down the street. He saw an old woman sitting behind a table selling things. There was a copper bracelet on her table, as well as hair combs and things that looked like they were stolen from nobles. This was a good start. He hopped off his horse. "Excuse me," he said, meaning to confront her. The old woman looked up at him and her eyes opened wide when she saw that he was a Scot. Quickly, she went about packing up her belongings, acting as if she thought he were going to steal them.

"Do ye ken where I can buy an ornate silver goblet?" North asked her.

"Nay, and I wish people would stop asking me that. Now leave me alone, you stinking Scots, before I have someone gouge out your eyes."

"My brathair was bein' polite, but I canna promise I will be." Nash dismounted his horse and drew his blade.

"Nash, nay," said North, his hand going out to still his brother's arm. "We are no' here to cause trouble or to harm anyone."

"First, the lady with her blade, and now you with your sword," mumbled the old woman. "I'm going to stop selling altogether if this keeps up. I never had to fear for my life as much as I have these last few days."

"What lady?" asked North. "And what did ye mean when ye said people keep askin' about silver cups?"

"I don't know nothing." The woman's mouth turned down into a frown.

"Please. Tell me about the woman ye mentioned," said North, thinking a lady on this street was surely an unusual occurrence.

"All I know is that a noblewoman who always comes down here pretending to be a commoner, keeps trying to find a man with a scar on his sword hand."

North chuckled. "Well, that's an odd choice for a lady to want to marry a man like that."

"And to look here for him," added Nash.

"Nay, you fools!" spat the old woman. "She doesn't want to marry him. She wants to kill him, I'm sure." The woman scooped the last of her belongings into her bag and was preparing to walk away.

"Wait," said North. "Forget about the lady. Can ye tell me if anyone here has been tryin' to sell a silver chalice?"

"No one but those pirates a few days ago," said the woman. "A silver chalice isn't what we usually buy or sell on Grope Lane."

"Did ye say pirates?" asked Nash. "Actually, that's who we're lookin' for."

"Where are they now?" North wanted to know.

"How the hell do I know? Probably gone back out to sea by now." The woman headed off, making North feel as if he were too late and out of luck.

"Damn," spat North. "If we were only a few days earlier, we might have caught them." He looked down to the ground and, in a stray bit of sunlight, thought he saw something reflecting back at him. It oddly looked . . . pink.

"Well, that's it, then. Let's go find Gavin and Cam and tell them we failed." Nash got back on his horse.

"Wait a moment," said North, bending down and picking up what looked like a pink stone. It had part of a rotten apple on it. He brushed it off and wiped the stone on his tunic, hoping to take a better look at his find. Then he brought it to his mouth and blew on it, continuing to shine it on his plaid.

"What in the devil's name are ye doin', North?" complained Nash from atop the horse. "If ye're that hungry, we'll buy some food. Please, dinna pick it up off the ground to eat it."

"Nay, I'm no' eatin' anythin'. I found somethin'." North blew on the stone once more and wiped it on his sleeve. "It looks like a pink heart made from some fancy gemstone."

"Nice find," said a man from a stall next to where the old woman had been and left.

"Where did this come from?" asked North, holding it up for the man to see.

"I'd say it was mine, but you'd probably slit my throat and keep it anyway if I tried to take it."

"I'm no' handin' it over. I just want to ken who dropped it," said North.

"It was probably that lady."

"What lady?" asked Nash from atop his horse.

"The noblewoman who pulled a sword?" asked North.

"That's right," said the man. "And I heard you asking about a silver goblet, too."

"Did ye see one? Do ye ken anythin' about a silver goblet?" North started to get excited, thinking mayhap this man had it. "Did ye buy it from the pirates, perhaps?"

"Nay, I didn't," said the man. "Although they wanted to dump it quickly. I knew if I took it that it would only bring me trouble."

"What trouble?" asked North.

"Well, you Scots are here, aren't you? I'm sure that means trouble of some sort."

"I told ye, we dinna want trouble. Just tell me where I can find the silver cup." North was becoming impatient with the man.

"I don't have it."

"Who does?" asked Nash.

"Do the pirates still have it?" North hoped to hell that wasn't the case, or he would have no chance at all of retrieving it.

"Nay. It was stolen from the pirates before they had a chance to sell it."

"Stolen?" asked Nash. "By whom?"

"That lady," said the man. "Now, please leave. You are attracting attention, and I'm going to be in trouble for even talking to you at all."

"We'll leave, as soon as ye tell us who this lady is and where to find her." North finally felt as if he were getting somewhere. "Do ye ken her name?"

"I might know," said the man, not offering any more information.

"Well, what was it?" asked North.

The man hesitated and looked down the street in the opposite direction. North pulled a coin from his pouch and slapped it down on the table. The man's eyes trailed downward. This action seemed to interest him. "What was her name?" North asked once again.

"I thought I heard them call her Lady Matilda." The man snatched up the coin and shoved it into his pocket.

"Where can I find this Lady Matilda?" North asked.

"Well . . . I can't be sure." The man's eyes roamed back to North's money pouch.

North let out a deep sigh and slapped another coin down. "How about for that price? Can ye be sure now?"

"She's at the castle." The man greedily scooped up the coin and slipped it into his pocket with the other.

"Which castle?"

No answer.

"Damn it," spat North, slapping one more coin down. "Now tell me, because the next thing I pull from my side is goin' to be my sword."

"All right, all right," said the man, reaching out for the last coin. North's hand slammed down atop it before the man could take it.

"My information, first."

The vendor looked up at North and then over to Nash before answering. "She's from . . . Montclair Castle . . . on the border."

"Montclair Castle?" asked North, thinking it sounded familiar. His hand remained covering the coin.

"Aye. I'm surprised you don't know it, since Lady Amethyst has a brother that is Scottish."

"Wait a minute," said North. "Is her brother's name Onyx MacKeefe, by any chance?"

"Could be," said the man, looking down at North's hand.

"Bid the devil, forget I even asked." North picked up the coin and tossed it to the man who caught it eagerly. Not wanting to waste any more of his money on this swindler, North hoisted himself up into the saddle and he and Nash headed back up the street.

"What did he say?" asked Nash. "I thought I heard ye mention Onyx's name."

"Aye," said North. "We're in luck. The lassie who has Storm's silver goblet is at Montclair Castle. That is where Onyx's sister, Lady Amethyst, lives. I believe it is also where Renard and Hawke were visitin' when they heard the gossip about the silver chalice in the first place."

"Well, then we really are in luck," said Nash with a smile. "We should be welcomed there with open arms since we're MacKeefes, too."

"Aye," said North, feeling a sense of relief wash through him. "This is goin' to be even easier than we thought. I'll tell this Lady Matilda that the goblet is ours, and she'll hand it right over to me. Then we'll be on our way back to the Highlands first thing tomorrow."

North said the words but, deep in his gut, he had the feeling that it wasn't going to be that easy after all.

◆•◇•◆

CHAPTER FOUR

"I NEVER BELIEVED I'd ever hold this in my hand again." Matilda sat at the dais with her four-year-old son, Robert, on her lap and the silver chalice held high in her free hand as she moved it one way and then another, inspecting it.

Her son had been named after her late father. Matilda's dead husband, Lord Alaric Lumley, never would have permitted it, had he still been alive. He wanted a son named after him. Then again, Alaric had died right after Robbie had been conceived. Matilda thought it was a blessing for all involved. Her marriage hadn't been a happy one at all. Alaric had a gambling problem, and left Matilda with nothing but an unearned wretched reputation when he died. "Isn't it beautiful?" she asked to no one, other than herself.

"I want to play with it," said her son, reaching out for it.

Matilda pulled it away from him, feeling possessive of the cup. "Nay, Robbie, it's not a toy. This is something very dear to my heart and it is not to be touched. Do you understand?"

The boy pouted.

"Go on with Genevieve and Jeremiah to play with the new puppies in the kennel," she told her son, putting the boy on the ground. Genevieve and Jeremiah were Marcus and Amethyst's nine and seven-year-old children.

"I'll take him, my lady," said the nursemaid, hurrying up the stairs to the dais, taking Robbie by the hand.

"Thank you, Beatrice." Matilda smiled at the old nursemaid, who had once been a nursemaid to her when she was a child. Beatrice was the only servant who had stayed with Amethyst after the night Matilda's family was slaughtered. Thankfully, Beatrice had been away visiting a relative at the time or she may have died that night as well. Matilda trusted the old woman with her life.

"Matilda, you weren't but a few years older than Robbie when your father gave you that goblet, if I'm not mistaken," said her cousin, Marcus. He leaned back on his dais chair, stretching his legs out under the table as he cradled his tankard of ale in his hands.

"Aye, it was on my sixth birthday," she said, smiling, running her finger over the etchings on the cup.

"Well, Robbie is almost that age. Would it harm anything to let the boy touch it?"

"Marcus, you don't understand," she told her cousin. "I have been searching for this for almost twenty years now, and have finally found it. I had almost given up hope. I don't want anything to happen to it."

"What is that indentation in the cup?" asked Amethyst, leaning around her husband to see the vessel better. "It looks like something is missing."

"Aye," Matilda said sadly, running her finger over the area with the missing heart stone. "It was a pink stone, shaped like a heart. It fell out of the goblet that horrible night, and I picked it up. However, I think I dropped it on Grope Lane. Your husband wouldn't let me look for it."

"Oh. Sorry," said Amethyst.

"That cup looks expensive," stated Marcus. "How did your father ever come by it to begin with?"

"I don't know," she told him.

"And he gave something that valuable to a child?" Marcus shook his head. "It doesn't make any sense, Matilda."

"It does to me," she answered. "I was my father's only daughter. I'm sure he wanted me to have it as part of my dowry for when I was old enough to marry."

"Hrmph," mumbled Marcus. "How much did you pay for it on Grope Lane?" He raised his own cup to drink, looking at her in a suspicious manner.

"Pay?" she asked. "Why should I pay for something that is mine to begin with? It was stolen from me, and I simply took it back. I don't know how those pirates got it, but they shouldn't have had it at all. I will not pay for stolen goods that really belonged to me in the first place."

"Oh, Matilda, how could you steal it? Especially from pirates?" asked Amethyst, sounding shocked as well as disappointed in her.

"I don't want to talk about it." Matilda's words were clipped. She stood up, taking the cup with her. Right when she was about to leave, she decided there was something she needed to say to her guardian – her cousin. "Marcus, I want to marry again," she blurted out. "Robbie needs a father."

"What?" Marcus jerked in surprise, almost falling off his chair. He'd been drinking, and spilled ale on his tunic. Sitting up, dabbing a cloth against his tunic, he answered, "Matilda, we've been over this time and time again. I want you to forget all about getting married. It's not going to happen."

The meal was over, and the servants cleared away the trenchers while the knights helped to disassemble the long trestle tables, making room to dance.

"I can't forget about it. I no longer want to be a single mother. Robbie needs a father."

"Robbie has me to look up to. As soon as he's old enough, I'll teach him everything he needs to know."

"Nay. He's going to start asking questions about the man who sired him, and I want to be prepared. I want to marry again so he will have a real father. I need to. I have to."

"Now, Matilda, you know as well as I that your husband left you penniless and with a tarnished reputation."

"How can I forget?" she said with a sigh. "I only wish Uncle Gilbert could have found that hidden money at our manor house that I heard my father speak of."

"Your manor was burned to the ground," Marcus reminded her. "There is nothing left but ashes, I assure you."

"Uncle Gilbert said he'd take care of me but, instead, he left you as my guardian when Alaric died. And neither of you have even let me return to my home to look for the money myself."

"You told us you never wanted to go back," answered Marcus. "Besides, my father always thought it best you didn't return. Not after what you witnessed."

"I can handle it now, Marcus."

"Nay, Cousin. My father said there was nothing there. Besides, it would only be too disturbing for you to return."

"Mayhap if I ask Uncle Gilbert to take me, he will."

"Forget about my father, Matilda. He is hard-nosed and doesn't have patience with women – not even his own family. That is why I took you in. I'm not like him at all."

Amethyst cleared her throat and smiled.

"Well . . . I'm not like him anymore. I've changed," Marcus corrected himself.

"I appreciate everything you've done for me, but it just isn't enough," Matilda told him. "I have to think about my future, and about Robbie's future as well. I've been a widow for nearly five years now. It's been too long."

"Matilda, I've tried my best to find you another husband, but no man wants to marry you." Her cousin sat up straight, getting agitated now. "Perhaps, it is best just to accept the fact, and go to the nunnery and live there from now on."

"Husband! How can you even suggest that?" scolded Amethyst, glaring at Marcus. "Matilda is your cousin and you are her only family now. Nay, you'll stay right here at Montclair Castle, Matilda. No matter if you ever marry again or not, you and Robbie are family and are always welcome here."

"Thank you," said Matilda in deep thought. "But now that I

have this goblet again, it'll catch the eye of every nobleman in England, just like you said, Amethyst."

"Amy," said Marcus in a low voice, looking over to his wife and shaking his head. "Did you really tell her that?"

"Well, that's not what I meant, but she's right," said Amethyst, always playing the optimist. "I mean . . . it couldn't hurt, and would be a good addition to a dowry for Matilda."

"She has a child. A boy," Marcus reminded her, right in front of Matilda. "No man will want to claim Robbie as his own. He'll want a blood heir."

"Well, she can have more children. More heirs. All boys," said Amethyst, smiling.

Marcus scowled at the women. "Both of you need to come to your senses. Matilda is twenty-five years old, and not in her prime for bearing many more children, if any at all. She was lucky to finally conceive the one she has."

"Marcus, please," said Amethyst under her breath.

"Nay, he's right," said Matilda. "That is why this is so important to me."

"I give up!" Marcus threw his hands in the air and pushed up from the table. "Matilda, live here as an old maid the rest of your life if you'd like, I don't care. But I won't spend any further time trying to find you a husband. And I warn you, I will have no more of your shenanigans with this insane idea of hunting down your family's killer. It has been nearly twenty years now, and you need to let it go. It'll only bring you trouble, and bring us strife. Just like that cup you stole. Trouble is sure to follow." His eyes went to the chalice again.

Matilda smiled proudly. "It's all right, Cousin, don't worry. This cup has renewed my faith that my future will have a positive outlook after all."

"I need a drink," said Marcus, leaving the women, flagging down some of his knights to join him. Marcus had never been patient with Matilda, but Amethyst was like a sister to her.

"Thank you," said Matilda, reaching over and squeezing

Amethyst's hand. "I know Marcus doesn't believe it, but this cup will gain me a husband, I know it. Just like you said."

"Matilda, I never said that! Marcus has tried for years to find you another husband, but Alaric ruined that for you. I'm not sure what possessed him to tell all his friends that you were mad, not to mention barren, and broke."

"Since I have a child, that should prove that I am not barren after all. And this chalice will show that I am no longer broke."

"What about the mad part?" she asked with a smile. "After all, it isn't normal for a lady to purposely wander down Grope Lane unescorted."

"I told you why I did that."

"Well, what about when you wear braies and spend so much time in the practice yard learning to fight like a man? Surely, that is not ladylike and makes you look a little crazy."

"Really?" Matilda smiled slyly. "And wasn't it your eldest sister, Ruby, who did exactly the same thing?"

"Well . . . yes, but I mean –"

"Don't worry, Amethyst. At tomorrow's masked ball, I am going to do a little fishing. After all, this is a grand event and every eligible bachelor in England will be attending."

"Fishing?" Amethyst gave her an odd look.

"For a husband. A father for poor little Robbie."

"Oh, Matilda, please don't get your hopes up. You know, Marcus has already approached most of the single nobles at my insistence, but they all turned down his offer to betroth you."

"It's only because your husband is stingy. He didn't offer enough of a dowry for me. But now that I have this cup, I'll have no trouble at all attracting a man." She held up the goblet proudly.

"Are you sure that it's a good idea?" Amethyst looked very uncomfortable. "After all, it's stolen. Even if it wasn't, don't you think it might tempt dishonest people to try to steal it from you at the dance?"

"Hmmm. I hadn't thought of that." Matilda lowered the cup

and frowned. "Mayhap you're right. I'll have to give this matter further thought. I'll need to find a good way to protect it from thieves." Matilda got up, leaving the dais, stopping as she passed by Marcus who had just been approached by the barbican guard.

"There are four Highlanders at the gate requesting entry, my lord," the guard told him.

Matilda stopped in her tracks, heading back to Marcus. "Nay, don't let any Scots in," she begged him, still feeling afraid of them since the attack on her family.

"Matilda, stay out of this, please," said Marcus. He looked back to his guard. "Who are they?"

"They say they're from the MacKeefe Clan."

"Really?" Marcus seemed concerned. "The MacKeefes were just here recently. Why would they come back again so soon?"

"I'm not sure, my lord. However, they said they are here to collect some kind of silver goblet that was stolen from them."

"What?" gasped Matilda, hiding the chalice against her gown.

"I warned you about that," growled Marcus. His hand shot out. "Give it to me."

"Nay! They're lying. It doesn't belong to them. It's mine, and they can't have it. Please, do not let them enter."

"What are their first names?" Marcus asked the guard.

"I believe the one who spoke to me said his name was . . . West?"

"That sounds phony," said Marcus. "Perhaps Matilda is right. I'm not sure we can trust these Scots. I don't know all of the MacKeefes, of course, but I don't recall any of them having the name West. That, I would have remembered."

"They're imposters," blurted out Matilda. "They're here to steal from us and cause trouble. Send them away." She gripped the cup with two hands now.

"Matilda, take that goblet to your room, and keep it there," said Marcus. "If they say they are MacKeefes, then I believe I should talk to the Scots myself and see what this is all about."

"Nay, don't. I'm frightened." Tears streamed down her

cheeks as she relived the horror of the attack in her mind once again. Her body shook and her teeth even chattered. Sometimes, she had these anxiety issues, and she felt as if she were reliving the event over and over again. She couldn't do anything to stop it.

"Lady Matilda, what's wrong with you?" asked the guard. "Are you ill?"

"Marcus, I beg you. Send them away." Matilda couldn't have Scots within the castle walls. Especially not when they were after her prized possession. "I've been through so much today that I cannot have any further upsets. Please." The last time her thoughts took hold of her like this, it had taken her a week to get back to normal. It hadn't helped the rumors that she was insane.

Marcus let out a sigh, putting his arm around Matilda's shoulders. "I don't like to see you like this, Matilda. And now you see why my father and I never wanted to let you return to your home. I know how hard it must be for you. I'm sorry. You have been through a lot. Not just today, but ever since you were a child."

"Thank you, Marcus," she answered with a sniffle.

"Ask them to come back at a later date," Marcus instructed his guard.

"Aye, my lord." The guard turned and headed away.

"Cousin, you need to rest," said Marcus. "Will someone please take Lady Matilda to her chamber at once?"

"What is going on?" asked Amethyst, rushing to her side. "Matilda, why are you so upset? Your body is shaking like a leaf."

"There are Scots at the door and Marcus is going to let them in to hurt me," cried Matilda, feeling her legs quaking beneath her now.

"Marcus?" asked Amethyst, rubbing her hand over Matilda's back.

"Take her to her room, Amy. I've already taken care of the Scots."

As Matilda walked away with Amethyst, she heard Marcus talking in a low voice to some of his men.

"Ever since childhood, my cousin tends to have these spells where she get a little . . . addled at times. I'm sorry for the disturbance. Shall we have our drink now?"

"I know what they are thinking, but I'm not crazy," Matilda told Amethyst, upset about all this. "However, I am angry. I'm going to give my cousin a piece of my mind." She started to turn back, but Amethyst stopped her.

"Nay. Don't." Amethyst took her arm and ushered her to the stairs. "Let's go to your chamber. I'll call for a hot bath for you. It'll help you relax. You have had a trying day and need to rest."

"My day was a good one," said Matilda, once again looking at her chalice as she climbed the stairs. "If my plans go the way I want them to, this cup will not only help me find a husband, but it might also flesh out the murderer I seek."

"WHAT DO YE mean the lord of the castle willna let us enter?" asked North from atop his horse. "I told ye, we are the MacKeefes."

"I'm sorry, West, but the answer is final."

"Why are ye callin' me that, ye fool?" spat North. "I am here for the silver cup that has been stolen from my laird. I willna leave until I have it."

"Please go, anon, before we are forced to make you leave." This guard was joined by two others who all drew their swords and held them at the ready.

"North, I think we'd better go," said Gavin from behind him.

"Aye," agreed Cam. "There is a crowd of Englishmen setting up tents, and I dinna want to have to fight them all."

North turned to see nobles approaching, pitching tents outside the castle walls. There were wagons with trunks, servants, hounds, and lots of horses. It looked as if they were gathering for some kind of event.

North turned back to the guard. "What's goin' on here? Why are these men pitchin' tents outside the castle?"

"It's for the masked ball tomorrow," the guard told him. "There are too many invited to house them all inside the castle. They arrive early to get good spots to be the first to enter."

"Really," said North with a smile. "It sounds intriguin'."

"It's by invitation only," snapped the second guard. "Now, please, remove yourself from the premises immediately."

"Come on, Brathair," said Nash in disgust. "It seems this isna goin' to be so easy after all."

"Aye," agreed North, turning his horse and riding slowly with his friends. Every English eye was on them. North even saw some of the nobles with their hands on the hilts of their swords as they rode past. "I promise, I'll find a way to get inside," he told his friends. "Now that I ken the silver goblet is in there, I willna leave here without it."

"How are ye goin' to do that?" asked Gavin. "Unless ye're blind, I'd think ye'd realize we are four Scots amongst a hundred English nobles."

"Aye," agreed Cam. "Ye heard the man. The dance is by invitation only."

"I'll get in, dinna worry," said North. He was already devising a plan that was going to not only get him inside the castle walls, but also make sure he was able to collect the cup and be welcomed back into his clan after all.

CHAPTER FIVE

I T WAS ABOUT midnight when North threw the grappling hook with the rope attached to it up to the battlements. In one try, it hooked on the wall with a clank.

"Shhhh," said Nash with his finger to his mouth. "If they hear us and catch us, we're goin' to end up in the dungeon."

"Dinna fret about it. No one is goin' to even ken we were here," North assured him, tugging on the rope to make sure it was secure. "We'll get in, steal the cup, and get back out again, before the sun even rises. This should be easy. By the time everyone awakes, we'll be back on the road to Hermitage Castle and I'll no longer be an outcast."

"I dinna ken. I dinna like this." Nash nervously looked one way and then the other. "I have a bad feelin' about this, Brathair. Couldna ye just wait until mornin' and find a way in then?"

"Nay. We need to do this now, under the cover of night. We're in luck that it is partly cloudy and the moonlight willna give us away." North took a second rope and grappling hook and threw that up to the battlements as well. He'd found the rope on the back of a supply wagon, probably being used for pitching the tents. The grappling hooks were on the back of a blacksmith's cart. "All right, we're ready," he said, testing the rope and handing it to his brother.

"North, why canna Cam or Gavin go with ye instead of me?" His brother tried to get out of this, but North wasn't about to let that happen. Not after he had helped Nash so much with his sentence.

"Nay, ye said ye'd help me," said North, picking up his rope and putting a foot on the castle's wall. "Gavin is too big to scale the wall easily, and Cam is too lazy. Ye're the smallest, and the least likely to be seen. It's got to be ye, Brathair."

Nash groaned.

"Gavin and Cam are keepin' watch for us and will alert us by whistlin' if they see any guards." North started to climb.

"Damn it, North, I swear ye're tryin' to get me killed." Nash grabbed hold of his rope and started to scale the wall as well. "If I die because of ye, Kellina will never forgive ye." He passed up North easily, making it to the battlements before him.

By the time North got to the top, Nash was already reaching over the wall to help pull him up. As soon as North's feet were on the wall walk, he looked over to Nash and smiled. "This is another reason I asked ye to join me. Ye are guid at climbin' since ye had all that practice thatchin' roofs at Kellina's camp. After all, ye were the one who said ye were as sure-footed as a goat!"

"Dinna remind me," groaned Nash. "Come on, let's go get this done. I dinna feel guid about breakin' in here. Besides, it is way too easy, and that worries me." He started pulling the ropes up after them so the guards wouldn't spot them.

"It's only easy since there are so many nobles camped outside the front of the castle walls, and no one is watchin' the back of the castle where we are. Let's go," he whispered, grasping the rope and hook, looking around, and sneaking across the wall walk. He stopped with his back against the wall, watching a guard in the distance.

"How do ye even ken where to look for the cup?" asked Nash in a half-whisper.

"I overheard a servant talkin' about Lady Matilda and how she took some silver cup up to her chamber in the turret." North looked up to the nearest turret. There were four of them, one at each corner of the castle. There was no telling which one held

Lady Matilda's room.

"The turret? Which one?" Nash gasped, a little too loudly, causing North to clamp his hand over his brother's mouth. Nash pushed his hand away, scowling at him. "Scalin' the wall is one thing, but I'm no' goin' to climb the turrets as well."

"Fine. Then dinna. Just stay here and keep watch for me while I do it."

"Which turret will ye choose first?"

North looked at each of the four towers, not knowing what to do. His eyes scanned one and then another, finally seeing something that told him exactly what he needed to know. "Look," he whispered, pointing to the turret that was the furthest away from them. Candlelight lit up the open window, and he saw a woman with long, red hair peering out. "I think I've just found Lady Matilda. I'll be right back. Keep watch. And dinna forget to whistle if ye think I'm in danger."

"Well, then, mayhap I should start whistlin' right now, since this whole lame idea is much too dangerous."

"Try to keep a positive attitude, Nash. Worryin' doesna become ye." He patronized his brother by patting him on the back.

"What I'd give right now to be back thatchin' roofs," whined Nash, as North sneaked across the battlements, stopping directly under the turret where he'd seen the red-haired lady looking out. By the time he got there, he could no longer see her in the window. The room looked dark now. Perfect. She must have gone to sleep. This was his big chance, and he had to take it. He was sure the silver goblet was up there, just waiting for him to bring it home.

Throwing the grappling hook with expertise, he managed to hook the sill of the turret window easily. He tugged on the rope, looking around, and then upward, thinking how close he was to being redeemed. By this time tomorrow, he'd no longer be a Highland outcast. Nothing could be better. This was going to be easier than he thought. What could possibly go wrong?

MATILDA LEANED OVER, blowing out the bedside candle. When she did so, she swore she heard a clanking noise of some kind.

"Beatrice," she called out to her nursemaid who had just closed the door, having left the room. Oftentimes, when Matilda had these anxiety attacks, Beatrice sat with her until she fell asleep. She even acted as her handmaid at times, although Matilda didn't need one. Matilda had insisted on being Amethyst's lady-in-waiting in exchange for staying at Montclair Castle with Robbie. While Amethyst let her do it, she really was more of a friend, and not a superior. Most of the time, Amethyst told Matilda not to bother. She was an independent woman and liked to do things herself.

"Aye, my lady?" asked Beatrice, poking her head back into the room. She held a lit candle.

"Did you just hear some sort of . . . clanking noise?" she asked.

"Nay, my lady. However, I suppose it is the nobles pitching their tents outside, getting ready for the masked ball tomorrow."

"Aye, perhaps you're right. I guess I'm just a bit jumpy after all the happenings of today. Will you stay with me a little longer?"

"I would, my lady, but I need to get back to watch Robbie. He is all alone. Plus, he is so excited after playing with the puppies today, that he'll never fall asleep unless I tell him a story. He loves those puppies. I wouldn't be surprised if he tried sneaking one into his room. I'd better check."

"Oh, yes, of course. It is best that you stay with him, then."

"Is the outside noise disturbing you? I can close the window."

"Nay, it's fine. I'm warm, so just leave it open so I can feel the breeze."

"Aye, my lady." Beatrice stepped back out the door.

"However, can you send in Lady Gert to spend the night with me?" she called out. "I am feeling very shaken, knowing those

Scots are outside the castle, wanting to steal my silver cup. I'd feel better not being alone."

"Of course. I'll send her right over. I'll leave the door open a crack since she knows the way."

"Thank you," said Matilda, watching as the light faded when Beatrice left the room.

Even though she was shaken, Matilda was so tired that she could barely keep her eyes open any longer. She tried to relax by breathing deeply, and it seemed to work. Closing her eyes, she hugged the silver chalice to her chest for comfort, thinking about her love for her family. Gert would be here to protect her, so she didn't have anything to worry about. That was her last thought before drifting off to sleep.

NORTH MADE HIS way to the top of the turret, feeling the burning sensation in his arms and legs. He wasn't used to climbing castle walls and turrets, and was only glad this would all be over with soon. He threw one leg over the sill, hoisting himself through the open window of the darkened room. Just as he did so, the moon broke through the clouds for the first time that evening. The moonbeams lit up the inside of the room enough to enable him to see a woman lying asleep on the bed.

Quietly, he dropped to the floor, taking a moment to look around. It seemed there was no one else here but the lass. He breathed a sigh of relief.

In the light of the moon, as if it were pointing his way, he saw Storm's silver chalice clasped in the arms of the sleeping woman. Her head was turned and he couldn't see her face. However, by her stillness he could tell she was asleep. Luck was on his side. He almost laughed aloud. It surely was too good to be true.

Two long strides brought him to the side of the girl's bed. He reached out for the goblet, but right as he was about to touch it, the girl moaned in her sleep, turning onto her side. Now, her back was toward him, and the chalice was on the other side of the bed. Damn.

He sneaked around the bed, not making a noise. Gingerly reaching out, he managed to secure the cup, slipping it out of the woman's fingers. She moaned again, flipping onto her back. His heart beat rapidly, but none of that mattered. He had the chalice in his possession. Now, all he had to do was shimmy down the wall and go back to join his friends. His punishment was over.

He heard Nash whistle, realizing he needed to leave quickly. Before he could move, the moonlight broke through the clouds once again, lighting up the room. This time, it bathed the woman's face in a soft, bluish-white glow. He stopped in his tracks. His eyes immediately dropped to the lassie's face.

She looked like an angel lying there in her white nightdress. Pale, smooth, white skin peeked out from under the vibrant red mass of hair that had fallen across her face. He couldn't see her mouth or nose, just one closed eye that had long red lashes curled upward.

North felt a need stirring within him. It wasn't a lustful feeling, but more one of desire. His downfall was that he always wanted more. It was something he hadn't been able to control ever since he was a child. Nash called it greed, but North liked to think of it as curiosity, and the willingness to have nice things in life. Things he normally wouldn't have – like the silver goblet in his grip.

"Nay," he said in a mere whisper, shaking his head, trying to get rid of the thought. All that mattered was to get this cup back to the MacKeefes. This girl was nothing to him. He heard Nash whistle again, and took a step toward the window but, once again, stopped. He turned his head, looking back at the girl on the bed. He wondered what her face looked like. Was her nose turned up, or bent like an eagle's? Were her lips shaped like a bow, or did she have teeth that stuck out like a horse? "It doesna matter," he told himself but, for some reason, he could not walk away.

He stared at the girl on the bed, feeling the overwhelming need to see and know more. If he was taking this cup away from the woman who held it so possessively even in her sleep, he didn't want to leave before he saw her full face. He had to know more about her. North hurried back to the bed.

Slowly reaching out, he used one finger to push her hair back behind her ear, exposing her entire face. His breath hitched when he saw her beauty. Part of him almost wanted her to look like a horse. Then he wouldn't feel so guilty stealing the cup from her while she slept. He couldn't stop looking at her. She seemed so perfect.

The girl had a petite nose that turned up slightly, reminding him of a wood sprite or possibly a fae. Her full lips were parted slightly, with a perfect little circle between them. She moaned again, and that's when he realized her eyes were moving back and forth beneath her closed lids. She was having a bad dream. Once again, she whimpered slightly, making him want to comfort her and put his arm around her. But he couldn't. He needed to get out of here before she awoke.

"North? North, are ye up there?" came Nash's hoarse whisper from outside the window.

North started to leave for the third time, but looked back at the bonnie woman lying on the bed once more. His eyes focused on her perfect mouth as her tongue shot out to lick her lips in her sleep. It was almost as if she unconsciously, but purposely tempted him while she slumbered. Once more, she moaned in her sleep, and became restless atop the bed. Her mouth turned into a pout, and her brows arched and then dipped as her nightmare continued.

"North? What the hell are ye doin'? Didna ye hear me whistle?" Nash's face appeared at the top of the window as he peeked into the room, hanging on to the sill. North looked up, and waved his hand through the air.

"Go on, Brathair. I'll be right behind ye," he said in a soft voice.

"Ah, ye found the chalice. Nice." Nash's frown turned into a smile. "Hurry, we've got to go."

Then his head disappeared as he descended down the turret wall. North walked around the bed, but stopped when he got to the window. He heard Nash give a sharp whistle from below, letting North know they were in trouble.

Nash looked up and waved his arm. "We have to go right now," Nash urged him on, in a frantic manner.

North raised one foot to the sill, but something made him look back at the girl again. His want . . . his need grew stronger. She was still asleep and hadn't even realized he was in the room or that he was stealing the cup from her. Such an innocent little thing. His heart went out to her. By the way she'd coveted the cup in her sleep, it reminded him of a child with a favorite toy. What was she dreaming that would make her so restless, moaning in her sleep? It made him wonder. He had to know. Or at least comfort her before he left.

He crept back to the bed, thinking there must be something he could do to make her bad dreams cease. He bent over, placing his lips on hers, giving her a gentle kiss. Then he stood back up and smiled down at her. "Mayhap that will help ease yer bad dreams, my angel," he whispered, realizing her moans had actually ceased.

He turned to go, but stopped dead in his tracks as he saw the shadow of a huge beast standing before him, and heard a long, low growl.

The girl moved on the bed. "Lady Gert, what is it?" came the girl's soft, sleepy voice. Then she screamed loudly, bolting upright to a sitting position in bed.

"Relax, my lady, I am no' goin' to harm ye," said North, talking over his shoulder, trying to keep an eye on the huge dog at the same time that was holding him prisoner there. It was ugly and big, brindle-colored with a black mask around its eyes. He tried his best to step around it, but the thing wasn't about to let him leave. Damn. Now he regretted staying so long.

"You're a Scot!" she spat, as if saying it were naught but spewing out a foul curse. Her eyes fell to the goblet in his hands. "My cup. Nay!" The woman became frantic, slapping at the bedcovers, as if she were looking for it, even though she'd just seen it in his hand. She still seemed to be half-asleep and confused. Mayhap she thought he was part of the nightmare she'd been having. Mayhap he was, now.

"Calm down, my lady," he commanded, looking over his shoulder at her. Then something hit him like a brick wall, knocking him to the ground. The large dog that in the moonlight looked to be an English Mastiff, had him pinned to the ground. He was unable to move. The damned thing had to weigh more than him! "Stop it. Get off of me, I say!" He closed his eyes and turned his head, trying to push the hound off his chest, but to no avail. When he'd hit the floor, he'd dropped the goblet, and it went rolling under the bed. He turned his head, trying to see it. "Damn it, get off of me. Now." Somehow, he managed to push the dog off of him and get to his feet . . . only to feel the undeniable prick of the sharp end of a sword at his back.

"Don't move, or I'll cut out your heart right where you stand," snarled the woman, not sounding at all like the angelic lady he'd just kissed atop the bed a moment ago. Now, she was his nightmare coming true.

"My lady, I highly doubt that you'll really hurt me." He sidestepped his way toward the bed, hoping to be able to retrieve the chalice. He also hoped his assumption that she didn't know how to use the damned sword was true. His hand sank lower, getting closer to the hilt of his own blade hanging at his side.

"Someone help me," the girl cried at the top of her lungs. "I am being attacked by a bloody Scot!"

"Bloody Scot?" He made a face. "Attacked? Come now, that's a bold-faced lie, and ye ken it. Ye are the one holdin' a sword to me. However, that is all about to change," he spat. Unsheathing his sword in one move, he hit her blade with his, sending hers skidding across the floor.

The girl's big green eyes opened wide, and her hands went up in the air as she backed away from him. "Gertie. Get him," she said in a shaky voice, looking as if she were frightened out of her mind. The dog growled lowly, stalking him.

"Call it off, or I'll be forced to kill it," he warned her.

"Nay! Dinna hurt my hound. Please, I beg you."

"Call it off. Now!"

"Gertie, it's all right. Let him be," she said, seeming to confuse the dog. It looked at her and then back at North, and began to bark loudly.

"I dinna want to hurt ye or the hound," North told her. "Ye are the one who forced me to draw my blade."

"You are in my room at night. You are obviously here to attack me. Or possibly rape me, you bastard."

"Nay! That's no' true," he protested. "I didna do anythin' but kiss ye, I swear." North sheathed his blade, not wanting to scare the girl more. Something inside him felt bad for her, and he didn't want her to think the worst of him – even if he was now naught but a thief in the night. "I only came for the cup. Give it to me, and I'll leave anon."

"Never," she spat, her eyes going to the floor where the cup was sticking out from under the bed. She shot forward to grab it, but North clasped his hand around her wrist to keep her from getting it before him.

"Let me go," she cried, pounding her other fist against his chest as they struggled in the dark. The dog laid down next to the bed in the moonlight, blocking his means to get the cup with its damned big body being in the way now. "Don't kill me, you bastard. I hate you! Let me be."

The woman was acting mad, as if she were delirious or something. She needed to be calmed again, and there was only one thing he could think of doing that would shut her up before she called every guard in the castle to her chamber. He pulled her into his arms and pressed his mouth against hers in a long, passionate kiss.

Her struggling stopped and her body went limp in his arms. This time, her moan sounded like one of pleasure rather than from a nightmare.

"That's better, my angel," he said after breaking the kiss, running one finger over her bottom lip.

"I heard a scream," came the cry of a guard from out in the corridor through the partially opened door.

"Lady Matilda's in trouble. Someone, help her," came the voice of a woman next.

"Guards, this way. Fast."

"Damn it," North ground out, realizing he had no more time to retrieve the goblet now. Plus, he could never get to it with the dog blocking the way. He released the girl and ran to the window, scurrying down the rope quickly. North had to leave the silver goblet behind, and this bothered him immensely. He'd ruined his big chance, and now he had to fear for his life. He ran for the next rope to scale the wall to the ground. Looking over the edge, he saw Nash halfway down the rope.

"Hurry," he called out. "They're on my arse."

"I'm goin' as fast as I can," Nash called back.

North wished for the second rope and grappling hook that he'd had to leave hanging from the girl's bedchamber window. They only had the one now, and it wouldn't hold both him and his brother at once.

"There he is," cried a guard from the end of the battlements, running toward him.

North didn't have time to wait for his brother to descend. He climbed over the wall and started down the rope, hearing Nash's voice from below him.

"What the hell are ye doin'?" asked Nash. "This rope is no' strong enough to hold us both."

"Well, I dinna have the luxury of waitin' for the sure-footed goat to make his way to the ground." North was only about halfway down when the rope broke. He dropped through the air, and landed in a heap right atop his brother.

"Ooooh, ye fool! Get off of me."

"Sorry," said North, rolling off of his brother. Nash was on the ground, holding his foot. "I think ye broke my ankle," Nash grunted.

"Nay, it's no' broken, now get up, quickly. Haud yer wheesht and run!" North looked back up to the battlements to see several guards with lit torches peering over the edge. "Let's go, Brathair." He started to run, but stopped when he realized that Nash was still sitting there and not moving. "Come on," he said, running back to see his brother wincing in pain. Nash pushed up to his knees and then to his feet, but almost fell over.

"Och, nay. I canna run, let alone walk," said Nash.

"Bluidy hell." North realized his brother was going to cause them to be caught and possibly arrested. "Hold on tight," he said, bending down and scooping up Nash, throwing him over his shoulder.

"Well, now I'm goin' to retch for sure," complained Nash, sounding as if he really would.

"Ye vomit on me, and I'm no' goin' to be a happy man. Now, hold it in until we're back with the others." North took off at a run, trying to get lost in the sea of tents, hoping he could outrun the guards.

"North, what is it?" Gavin rode up on his horse, and quickly dismounted to help him.

"It's Nash's ankle."

"Is it broken?" asked Gavin.

"Hell if I ken. Help me hoist him atop yer horse, will ye? I've got English guards on my arse."

"What the hell is goin' on?" Cam rode up on his horse, bringing Nash and North's horses along with him.

"This is what I get for tryin' to help my brathair. Ooooooh," moaned Nash as Gavin and North flipped him up into the saddle.

"Can ye ride?" asked North, looking over his shoulder. The castle's gate was open and a half-dozen men on horseback rode out.

"It's my ankle that hurts, no' my arse, ye fool," said Nash. "Of course, I can ride. Let's get the hell out of here."

"Right," said North, mounting a horse.

Gavin did the same. "I dinna fancy bein' thrown back in prison."

"What happened?" asked Cam.

"Things didna go as planned," North answered.

"Did ye find the cup?" asked Gavin.

"Well, aye," North answered, not offering more information, nor wanting to tell them the whole story just yet.

"Guid. At least ye got the goblet," said Gavin. "Let's take the quickest road back to Hermitage Castle. We should be able to make it home by sunrise."

"Aye, let's go," said Cam leading the way.

"Nay. We canna." North rode up to Cam's side.

"Why no'?" asked Gavin, right next to him now. Nash was up ahead, leading the way, but slowed down to hear what they were saying.

"Because even though I found the goblet . . . I dinna have it." North hated to admit it, but his friends needed to know. "We canna leave yet."

"What in the clootie's name are ye sayin'?" asked Nash in surprise, joining in the conversation. "North, I saw ye standin' next to the lassie's bed with the goblet in yer hand. Where is it?"

"Ye see, I did have it. But . . . I dinna have it . . . any longer."

"God's eyes, I dinna believe this," said Cam, as the four of them rode fast and furious, trying to get as far away from Montclair Castle as they could.

"I dinna believe it either," said North to himself, not able to stop thinking about Lady Matilda. What was it about the woman that was so alluring to him? If he hadn't gone back to kiss her, he'd have the goblet right now and would be heading home. He'd no longer be an outcast. But because of his greedy nature, and his mistake of wanting to see her face, now he might end up as a prisoner of the English instead.

Then again, if he had never kissed her, he never would have known how sweet her lips tasted. He smiled, smacking his lips together, savoring her essence upon his tongue. It was something he would never forget for the rest of his life – and unfortunately, that might not be as long as he'd hoped.

CHAPTER SIX

"MATILDA, YOU ARE being a fool!" growled Marcus the next morning. He was walking on one side of Matilda while Amethyst was on the other as they left the castle's keep, heading for the blacksmith's shop in the outer ward. Matilda's dog, Gert led the way. "A Scot snuck into your bedchamber last night and attacked you. My men searched the area and even the woods but we didn't find him. It's difficult with such a crowd outside the castle. He could be hiding anywhere. We need to call off the masked ball."

"Nay, don't do that!" Matilda stopped in her tracks. "The Scot didn't attack me. I told you that."

"Then what did he do?" asked Marcus.

"He . . . was just there to steal the cup." She had the silver goblet in her hands. "There is no need to cancel the dance. All the nobles are camped outside the gate and will start to enter in the next hour."

"I will not purposely put you or anyone else at risk," said Marcus. "I wish we could have found those bloody Scots. I don't agree with this idea at all."

"Well, I do," said Amethyst, sticking up for Matilda. "It would be a shame to turn all those people away after they came from so far to be here."

"It's not safe," said Marcus. "My men couldn't find any trace of the Scots."

"Then I'm sure it means we scared them off and that they won't be returning. There is no need to continue with the search." Matilda couldn't forget about the Scot who had sneaked into her bedchamber last night. While it scared the daylights out of her, the man's kiss was remarkable, and she couldn't stop thinking about it.

He was different from the Scots who had attacked her family and killed them. She was sure of it. This one, although she never even saw his face clearly in the darkened room, seemed kind. He could have killed her dog or even raped her, yet all he did was kiss her. He said he meant her no harm, and she believed it somehow. The only thing that put doubt in her mind was that he had tried to steal her silver goblet.

"Matilda, what in heaven's name is the matter with you?" asked Marcus. "You didn't want me to let the Scots in the gate last night. You begged me not to, even though they said they were our allies. Now, you want me to call off the search, even though one of them was in your bedchamber, managing to get past all my guards? You make no sense at all."

"I have to agree with Marcus. Your behavior is a little odd, Matilda," said Amethyst. "Are you feeling all right this morning?"

Matilda stopped in her tracks, staring at her cousin and his wife in disbelief. "You two think I'm mad, don't you? Just like the rumors Alaric started about me years ago."

"Nay, no one thinks that," said Marcus.

"I heard you talking to your guards last night," she accused him.

"Well, that's different. I was talking about . . . now." Marcus ran a hand through his hair and looked the other way. "You do have nightmares, and act stranger than normal at times."

"No one said you are crazy, Matilda. That is not what Marcus meant." Amethyst reached out for her, but Matilda stepped back, not wanting to be touched.

"I might have nightmares about that awful night my family was killed, but I assure you I am in my right mind."

"We know that." Amethyst exchanged silent looks with her husband. "We just want to make sure you're safe, that's all."

"I am safe, I assure you. The only thing the Scot wanted was this." She held up the goblet to show them.

"Why didn't the hound protect you?" asked Marcus. "That dog has always been worthless, I swear."

Gert whined and laid down with her nose between her paws, as if she knew Marcus was speaking badly of her.

"Gertie did exactly what I told her." Matilda smiled at her pet and reached down to pat the dog's head.

"You . . . called off the dog even though there was a strange man in your room?" Amethyst was looking at her again like she thought Matilda was daft.

"I – I was half-asleep and thought it was a dream." Matilda fiddled with the cup. "Amethyst, will you walk with me to pay a visit to the blacksmith, please?"

"Why?" asked Amethyst, once again looking over at her husband in silent conversation.

Matilda continued. "Because after last night, I realized that this cup is coveted by many. I don't want anyone trying to steal it during the masked ball tonight, like you mentioned."

"What does the blacksmith have to do with all this?" asked Marcus. "I don't understand."

"I am going to ask him to make me a strong belt of chain. On the end, I'll secure this silver goblet. That way, I can still use it to attract a husband to me . . . or possibly my family's killer . . . and not have to worry about any further attempts to steal it."

"Now I know you've gone mad," mumbled Marcus under his breath.

"Marcus, I'll go with Matilda, and then see to finalizing plans for the dance afterwards," Amethyst told him. "Mayhap you can send a missive to the MacKeefes asking if they sent anyone from their clan here. Anyone named West."

"I'm sure they didn't, but I'll do it just so the two of you will stop pestering me." Marcus turned and left in a huff, not liking to be told what to do. Especially by a woman.

"Matilda, what really happened last night?" Amethyst asked her, once Marcus had left.

"I'm sure I don't know what you mean." Matilda looked down, running a finger along the rim of the cup, smiling. She couldn't stop thinking about the Scot's kiss and wondered if she'd ever see him again.

"If nothing happened, why are your cheeks blushing? And why are you smiling like a woman with a secret?"

"What?" Matilda's head popped up. Gertie looked up and whined again, and then put her nose back between her paws. "Oh, all right, so I lied. But I didn't want my cousin to know."

"Know what?" asked Amethyst. "You are acting very strange this morning."

"The Scot kissed me," she said, feeling the heat rise to her cheeks. "He didn't hurt me, Amethyst, I swear. All he wanted was this cup, for some reason."

"He kissed you?" Amethyst had a look on her face that was a cross between bewilderment and amusement. "Are you sure you didn't dream it?"

"Nay, I'm serious. He said he wouldn't hurt me or Gertie, and he didn't. He was actually trying to calm me down. I think he almost seemed to care about me. It was as if he didn't want to see me hurt."

"Then he shouldn't have been trying to steal the cup."

"Aye, I do agree." Matilda smacked her lips together and looked down at the goblet. "When I found this again after so long, I had no idea what it was going to bring into my life."

"Trouble. With a capital 'T', that's what," said Amethyst in a knowing manner. "Mayhap you should give the cup to Marcus for safe keeping until the ball is over."

"And miss the opportunities that this cup will bring me? Never." Matilda turned on her heel and marched to the blacksmith's shop, eager for the events of the night to begin. If she enjoyed the kiss of a Scottish Highlander so much, then mayhap she really was ready to marry an English noble again. Mayhap this time, she would even be lucky enough to fall in love.

⫷⫸

"WELL, YER ANKLE'S no' broken, but it is sprained," said Gavin, finishing wrapping up Nash's foot with a long strip of cloth.

"So much for the sure-footed goat," mumbled North under his breath.

"Dinna make me come over there and punch ye out because, right now, I'm so angry with ye, that I have half a mind to use my dagger on ye as well, Brathair," snapped Nash.

"Calm down, Nash. I'm sure North didna mean to crush ye under his massive body." Cam stretched out his long legs in front of the fire, resting his back against a stump. They'd outrun the English last night, only doubling back and camping in the woods when they were sure they were no longer being chased.

"I dinna understand why ye just dinna tell them what ye want," said Nash. "Wouldna that be easier than all this sneakin' around?"

"I did tell them," said North, popping a berry into his mouth. They'd had to forage the land for food this morning. "I told them I wanted the goblet, and that is when they refused us entry."

"Now, we'll be lucky if we dinna all end up in the dungeon, thanks to yer little episode last night," said Cam, raising a wineskin to his mouth.

"I'm confused," said Gavin, brushing off his hands. "North, if Nash said he saw ye with the goblet in yer grip, then why dinna ye have it now?"

"I – I lost it when the hound knocked me to the ground." North poked at the fire with a stick.

"A hound?" Gavin raised a brow. "I have the feeling there is more to it than just that."

"It was a big hound," added North. "Almost as big as me. And heavy."

"Mayhap it really has somethin' to do with the lassie that Nash said he saw lyin' on the bed," Cam interjected, knowing more about women than all of them put together.

"Tell us the truth, North." Nash rubbed his ankle. "After all, I almost died for a cup that ye were careless enough to lose, no' once but twice now. Why didna ye just follow me out the window?"

"Damn it, all right. I'll tell ye why." North threw the stick into the fire. "It is because the lass was havin' nightmares, and I didna like seein' her so agitated. I wanted to comfort her."

"Huh?" Nash looked at him and wrinkled his nose. "That makes no sense. There must be more that ye are leavin' out."

"I wanted to see her face in the moonlight, also. I mean . . . I was stealin' the cup she had clutched in her sleep. I just wanted to ken what she looked like before I left her."

"Och, nay," said Nash, shaking his head. "I hear that word *want* again, and we both ken that means trouble. Ye wanted somethin' that wasna yers and that ye couldna have. Just like ye always do, right?"

"So, I kissed her. What's the big deal? I mean . . . I just did it to shut her up so she wouldna call the guards."

Cam chuckled. "Well, I ken the feelin' of lust more than the rest of ye, but I must say, this action even surprises me, North. What were ye thinkin'?"

"I agree," said Gavin, taking a seat by the fire. "Usually, ye want things ye canna have. However, this is the first time I can ever remember that the thing ye coveted was a lassie. And an Englishwoman at that!"

"Her lips tasted like honey." North smiled, thinking of the beautiful girl.

Nash picked up a stone and threw it at his brother.

"Ouch, what was that for?" North rubbed his elbow.

"That was to bring ye back to reality. We are here for the cup, and no' the lass. That is all. Do ye hear me? Leave the wench alone."

"I canna," said North. "She is no' only bonnie, but fearless, too. She drew her sword and threatened to carve out my heart." He smiled thinking of it.

"What?" North's three companions said together.

"And that makes ye like her?" asked Gavin. "How can ye say that and smile at the same time?"

Cam cleared his throat and sat up straighter. "I canna say that I ever had a lass do that to me, and neither would I want one to."

"North, yer greed almost got us killed last night," Nash reminded him. "Ye've got to keep yer mind on the mission. The rest of us are here to help ye, but I, for one, canna wait to go home."

"Ye're right." This time, North cleared his throat. "I'll keep my thoughts on the job at hand. I want to go home just as much as the rest of ye. Plus, I canna wait until I am no longer an outcast. I need to be accepted back into the clan and will go to any extremes to make it happen."

"Then, ye'd better come up with a plan quickly," suggested Gavin. "They'll be on high alert now after last night."

"That's right," said Cam. "There is no way we'll ever get inside the castle's walls now."

"No' so," said North, putting his hand to his chin in thought. "There is a way inside, and we're goin' to take advantage of it."

"Ye're daft," spat Nash, rubbing his sore ankle with two hands now. "They'll never let us even enter their courtyard, let alone allow us to roam their corridors freely lookin' for the goblet."

"They will, but they willna ken it."

"Huh?" Nash made a face. "Brathair, ye make no sense."

"I have a plan, and it'll no' only get us into the courtyard, but inside the castle walls as well."

"Explain," said Gavin, losing patience with him. They all looked like they wanted to wring his neck right now.

"We're goin' to be in costume so they willna ken we are Scots."

"Costume? What costumes?" asked Nash. "We dinna have any."

"Leave that to me," said North, devising the plan in his head, feeling a thrill of excitement rush through him. "I guarantee, by tonight we'll be minglin' with the English nobles, and none of them will be the wiser."

CHAPTER SEVEN

"That should do it," said Matilda later that day, standing in her bedchamber getting ready for the masked ball. Over her costume, she had a silver chain wrapped around her waist twice, serving as a belt. A clasp locked around the stem of the silver goblet, securing it, while letting it dangle freely from her side. "That should keep anyone from trying to pilfer my goblet during the dance, but yet let me show it off at the same time. Don't you think so?" she asked Beatrice, who had helped her don her costume.

Matilda wore a sleeveless long, green velvet tunic over black leggings. She had a frilly long-sleeved white tunic underneath the green. A short, black vest covered it, lacing up the front. It was so tight that it gave the illusion of her breasts being bigger than they really were.

"I'm not sure who is going to be looking at the goblet, when they will all be staring at your cleavage instead, my lady." Beatrice fussed with the bodice, pulling it upward, but Matilda boldly reached out and yanked it back down.

"Beatrice, it is important that I show what I have to offer if I'm to find a husband. This might be my last chance." She glanced over at Robbie, playing quietly by the hearth. The little boy always seemed so sad, even though he had other children to play with at the castle. "Robbie needs a father," she whispered. "He needs to learn things that only a man can teach him."

"Isn't that what Lord Marcus is doing?" Beatrice helped Matilda don her headpiece. It was a small, pointy, green velvet hat.

"My cousin is the last person I want raising my son," she said, fussing with her dress. "He'll teach the boy that women are naught but items to own or order around. I want Robbie to know that women are strong and powerful and to be respected."

"Hrmph," snorted the old woman, fastening the hat, and brushing out the end of Matilda's long, red braid.

"What did you mean by that?"

"I think you are the only one who can teach your son that."

"How so?"

"Well, look at you." Beatrice stepped back and held out her arms. "Tonight, instead of being dressed like Maid Marian, you chose to portray Robin Hood."

"What's wrong with that?" Matilda picked up a quiver of arrows and slipped it over her shoulder. Then she picked up the bow. "I helped Amethyst dress earlier, and she is portraying a fae queen."

"Aye. But her fae costume is feminine."

"Mayhap, but it's a queen, and a queen is powerful."

Beatrice tsked. "If you want to find a husband, a costume like this is only going to scare them all away."

"I don't think so. Besides, if they don't like my costume, then this will capture their attention instead." She picked up the goblet hanging at her side and smiled.

"I hope you're not playing too dangerous of a game, my lady," Beatrice said in a low voice, glancing back at the boy.

"Whatever do you mean?" Matilda didn't like everyone telling her she was being reckless.

"I know all about the night that chalice went missing when you were a child. Whoever stole it in the first place, might decide to look for it again."

"Nay. I don't think so, Beatrice. It's been nearly twenty years now and no one has come looking."

"Yet, you are still searching."

"All but one of my family's attackers were Scots, and no Scots will be allowed into the castle," explained Matilda. "Marcus will have his men watching closely for any problems. It should be quite safe."

"Yes, but remember, you said there was one English attacker as well. What if the Englishman you stabbed comes back to look for you?"

A shiver went up Matilda's spine at the thought. Then she tried her hardest to push that fear from her mind. "If he hasn't done so by now, I'm sure he won't." Hearing this put a knot in Matilda's stomach. While she was hoping to find a husband, she was also dangling the goblet like a carrot in front of a horse's nose, trying to find her family's killer as well. She'd sworn she would get vengeance, no matter how long it took. Something inside her would not let her rest until this horrible man was caught and sentenced to death.

"I would never be sure, my lady," said Beatrice.

Matilda reached out and took Beatrice by the arm. "Please, keep a close eye on Robbie tonight, and take him far away if there is any trouble."

"My lady, I don't like this."

"You don't need to worry. That is why I am wearing the bow and arrows, and will use them if I have to."

"You won't find a husband that way."

"Mayhap not. But if I find my family's killer, then all this won't have been for naught."

"My lady, it's been a long time. I'm sure the man is no longer alive. I am sorry I mentioned it. Please, just let it go."

"You've known me since I was a child, Beatrice. Have I ever let anything so important go?"

"Nay. I suppose not." Beatrice wrung her hands and looked over at Matilda's son.

"Everything will be fine," Matilda assured her. Then she bent closer and whispered to her, "Just keep your eyes open for a man with a long scar on top of his right hand."

"I will, my lady," said Beatrice, looking so unsettled that it made Matilda start to question everything she was doing. Then she started thinking again about the Highlander who had kissed her and said he wanted to comfort her. She'd felt safe in his arms, although she shouldn't have. Now, she regretted even telling anyone anything about the man in her room because, secretly, she was hoping to have the chance of seeing him again.

⫸⫷

"IT'S ABOUT TIME ye returned. So, what's yer plan,?" asked Gavin, taking the stick with roasted rabbit from the fire, blowing on it to cool the meat.

"Aye, ye've been gone a long time. Where were ye?" Nash inspected his ankle that was still swollen, and continued to wrap it up again.

The men stayed in the woods under cover, not wanting to get too close to the castle so they wouldn't be captured.

"Cam and I found us some costumes for tonight." North detached a travel bag from the horse and threw it down. "Luckily enough, I managed to get one of these, too." North took an invitation out from under his sash and waved it in the air.

"What is it?" asked Nash.

"It's an invitation for tonight's ball." Cam ripped it out of North's hand and quickly looked it over. "North, this is only for three people."

"Damn," spat North. "Mayhap I can go back and pilfer one more."

"Nay, it's too late. The dance is about to begin." Gavin took a bite of the meat.

"I'll stay here," Nash offered. "My ankle is still sore and swollen, so I should rest it." He got up and walked over to Gavin with a slight limp to get some food. North realized his brother wasn't as hurt as he was letting on, but didn't say anything.

"Well, let's see what we've got." North dumped the costumes out onto the ground, picking up one and then another. "It looks like St. George slayin' the dragon. I'll be St. George." He greedily took the best costume for himself, but didn't care. This was his mission and he was in charge.

"This looks like a damned dragon costume." Cam held up an obnoxious headpiece to inspect it. "I dinna want to be a dragon."

"What did I get?" Gavin gave the stick of meat to Nash, and wiped his hands on his plaid. He walked over and picked up the last costume, holding it up to see it. "It's a dress," he said. "For a damned wench!"

Nash laughed heartily. "Sure am glad I'm stayin' here. I canna wait to see ye dressed like a wench, Gavin."

"It's no' goin' to happen," said Gavin with a snort. "I couldna get into this without rippin' it to shreds."

"We need someone smaller to wear that," said North.

"This whole idea is lame. Dressin' like dragons and wenches. Bah!" Cam threw down his costume and went over by Nash to get something to eat.

Gavin picked up the dragon costume next. "North, I really want to help out, but I'm afraid I'm too big to fit in this costume, too." He eyed up the knight's costume in North's hands. "Let me try that one. I think I'd make a guid St. George." He reached out for it, but North yanked it away.

"Nay. This is my sentence, and it is only fair that I get first choice of the costumes. I'm goin' to be St. George."

"There's that greed of yers rearin' its ugly head again, Brathair," said Nash. "Ye always want the best for yerself, plus things that ye canna possibly get."

"I dinna care," said North. "I'm goin' to be St. George, and I dinna want to hear another word about it."

"Ye're right," said Gavin, shrugging his shoulders. He walked over and sat down by the fire. "Since I'm the biggest and dinna fit into the two costumes that are left, I guess Cam and Nash will have to wear them instead."

"Why dinna we send North by himself?" asked Cam. "Then we willna have to wear those ridiculous costumes at all."

"Blethers! I helped all of ye with yer punishments, and now ye're goin' to desert me at a time like this?" asked North.

"He's right again," said Gavin. "He did help us."

"And we promised to help him as well," said Nash.

"I suppose it's only fair," added Cam.

"Great! Then grab yer costumes, men, because it is time to go to the dance and retrieve Storm's goblet." North hurriedly removed his plaid and started dressing in the breeches and tunic that was the costume of St. George. There was a long cape with a dragon on the back of it as well.

Nash and Cam both looked at each other. Then they made a mad dash for the remaining costumes, but Cam got there first. Nash's swollen ankle had slowed him down.

"I've got the dragon costume," said Cam, snatching it up before Nash could even object.

"Naaaaay," whined Nash, holding up the gown of the wench. "I dinna want to be a wench."

"Ye are the smallest out of all of us, Brathair," North pointed out. "Ye've got the best chance of pullin' off the act of bein' a lass."

"But I've got whiskers," said Nash. "And I dinna have diddies. No one is goin' to believe it at all."

"Here are some rags to roll up to make diddies." Gavin dug into a travel bag and held up two pieces of cloth, and smiled.

"And I have a sure way of gettin' rid of that small scraggle of whiskers on yer chin, Brathair." North held up his dagger.

"God's eyes, I'm goin' to kill any of ye if ye ever tell Kellina about this." Nash donned the costume, putting the gown on right over his plaid, and then prepared to shave.

North chuckled. The first thing he was going to do when they got home was tell every lass in the MacKeefe camp that his brother had attended a dance dressed as a wench.

$$\text{·◇·}$$

CHAPTER EIGHT

"**L**ORD AND LADY of the Hills," announced the herald as another couple walked into the great hall dressed in costume. Since it was a masked ball, everyone's real identity was kept secret. The steward collected the invitations, and only he knew who everyone really was.

"I'd like to announce The Conqueror of the Kingdoms," called out the herald next as a man dressed in black leather with gloves, boots and a mask walked in.

"Finally, a man by himself," Matilda whispered to Amethyst. "I'm surprised there aren't more here. It seems most of the men are here with women. Probably their wives."

"I assure you, Marcus has invited many single noblemen," Amethyst whispered back. She looked out to the sea of people all in costume and made a face. "Just don't ask me which ones they are."

"My ladies," said The Conqueror, taking first Amethyst's hand and kissing it, and then he did the same to Matilda. "What's this?" he asked, spotting the silver chalice dangling from the chain at Matilda's side.

"Oh, this?" she asked innocently, picking up the chalice for him to see it better. "It was a present from my late father, and is very expensive. It's also part of my dowry."

"Dowry?" asked the man, sounding interested. "Are you looking to be married, my lady?"

"I am a widow, and would like to marry again, yes," she told him. "Are you here with your wife, Lord Conqueror?"

"Nay. I am single," said the man, making Matilda smile.

"Excuse me, I'd like to meet Lady Matilda," said another man dressed like a monk. "I am single as well, my lady." He kissed her hand, too. Two more men looked on from behind him.

"I might have to ask you to officiate the ceremony, Sir Monk." Matilda giggled.

"Me? Oh, nay, my lady, I assure you I am no holy man." Still holding her hand, he pulled her closer. "Although, I could always pretend to be, and drink wine from that chalice with you, if you'll let me."

"Move on, please," came Marcus' bellow, sending the men on their way.

"I think this cup is working wonders already." Matilda kissed the chalice and dropped it back to her side.

"St. George, the fair maiden, and the dragon," called out the herald as three more people entered.

"Now that's interesting," said Matilda with a smile. "I wish I could see St. George's face, or mayhap even that dragon without his mask."

"Matilda, you know the whole idea of this ball is to stay anonymous. If they took off their masks, it would defeat the whole purpose," explained Amethyst.

"Of course," she said as St. George and his entourage approached her.

"My lady," said St. George with a bow, kissing her hand. "My, this is ornate." He boldly reached out and picked up the cup. "Ye have it chained to ye. Why would ye do such a daft thing, lass?"

"Of course I have it chained, since it's almost been stolen from me lately. It is very coveted, you realize." Matilda rested her hand over the chalice in a protective manner.

"I ken."

"You ken?" Matilda looked at him from the corners of her eyes. "St. George, I don't remember the stories saying you spoke with a Scottish accent."

"He doesn't," said the dragon, stepping in front of St. George. "Our humble apologies, my lady. My friend was just trying new dialects for the ball and must have forgotten which costume he was wearing." The dragon scowled at St. George.

"I wish we all could forget our costumes," mumbled the wench, her voice sounding a little masculine. Matilda looked over to her, thinking she was a big girl. Ugly, too.

"You must be St. George's fair maiden. Are you?" asked Matilda, wanting to know if either of the two men were married.

"Believe me, I'm far from his fair maiden. I cannot stand him right now." The ugly wench pushed past them, followed by the dragon who stopped right in front of her.

"I'm not single, either, if that's what you mean. "Although, if I were, you'd be mine by the end of this dance."

"Get out of here," growled St. George, giving the dragon a push. "I'm sorry my friend was so rude, my lady."

"What about you?" Matilda asked, feeling brave dressed in this costume. After all, she was in no real danger with Marcus and his men there to protect her if she should need it. Plus, she had the bow and arrows on her back. She wasn't as skilled with them as with her sword, but she could still use them well enough to fend off any attacker.

"Me?" asked St. George. "Och, I didn't mean to be rude. I'm sorry."

"Nay, that's not what I am asking," said Matilda. "What I meant is, are you married?"

"My, what a bold thing to ask," said St. George, seeming shocked that she would ask a man this question to his face. "Not likely," he said. "Tell me, why do you want to know?"

"I'm looking for a husband," she explained. "My son needs a father."

"You have a son?" North asked in surprise, not expecting this to come from the lassie's mouth.

"Mother," called out a little boy dressed like a dog. "I brought my horse because she wanted to come to the dance as well."

North jumped back when he once again saw the ugly dog who'd jumped on him in the turret. The dog was wearing some odd-looking coat with a long horse's tail attached. It didn't need a mask since its colorings made it look as if it were already wearing a black mask over its eyes. It looked directly at him, lowered its head, and let out a low growl.

"It's all right, Lady Gert," said North, hoping to calm the dog. "Be nice."

"You know my dog's name?" asked Matilda in surprise, making North realize his mistake.

"Aye. Of course. Doesna – doesn't everyone?"

"So, you must be a friend of the family behind that mask." She leaned in closer, peering into his eyes. "Who are you?"

North felt his mouth go dry. Would she recognize him as the one who broke into her chamber? He hoped the hell not. If she knew a Scot was here, she'd most likely have him captured and thrown into the dungeon immediately. He needed to be more discreet.

He smiled widely, trying to remain calm. He had to think hard to choose the right words to sound like a Sassenach, and not a Highlander. "If I'm not mistaken, this is a masked ball, my lady. Therefore, we are meant to keep our identities hidden. You wouldn't want me to ruin things now, would you?"

"Of course not. How foolish of me to even ask."

The minstrels up in the gallery started playing a lively tune. Music from their harps, lutes and nakers filled the great hall. The visitors started to pair off and wander to the middle of the floor to dance.

"Would ye care to dance, lass?" North bowed and held out his hand. He hoped she wouldn't reject him, because he needed to get close to the cup if he was ever going to manage to steal it. Then again, Lady Matilda seemed very interested in landing a husband, so he was sure she would take the bait.

Matilda giggled. "Of course, I'd love to dance, St. George. But please stop using that silly dialect and talking like a Scot because I don't like Scots in the least."

North's heart lodged in his throat. Damn. Had he slipped back into his Scottish burr again? He hadn't even noticed, but she obviously had. "My apologies. It won't happen again, I assure you." He bowed again and once more held out his hand, waiting for her to take his arm. Success. She took it. He'd have to bite his tongue now, not to make the mistake again. He wasn't good at speaking like a Sassenach, but he'd do whatever it took to get that goblet and head back home as fast as possible.

Lady Matilda was an interesting girl. First, she'd pulled a sword on him and threatened to cut out his heart. Now, she wore the costume of a man. He chuckled inwardly, thinking it should be Nash dancing with her right now instead of him. With his costume of a wench, he would make a better pair to her manly attire.

"I find your costume an odd choice," said North as they danced together.

"Well, I like to portray that I'm a strong woman." She giggled again, turning a circle as he spun her around.

"So, do you know how to shoot an arrow as well as how to wield a sword?"

She stopped and looked up at him in question. Her green eyes twinkled from beneath her face mask. "St. George, what makes you think I know how to handle a sword?" She sounded suspicious of him, and he was already cursing himself inwardly for letting it slip. He needed to stop being so distracted by this unique woman, and instead concentrate and be more careful with his words. If not, he was going to ruin everything.

"I just assumed so. I mean, since you were wearing the bow and arrows." He flashed her a smile. "I didn't mean to offend you."

"Oh, that's all right," she answered. "You haven't offended me at all. Actually, you've assumed correctly. I do know how to wield a sword. I learned from a very early age. Now, St. George, it is my turn to guess something about you as well."

"Pardon me?" He held out his arm and they walked in a circle with the rest of the lords and ladies dancing. "I'm not sure what you mean."

"Your voice sounds familiar to me, but I can't quite place it. Give me a hint at least. Tell me, have I met you before?"

"Me?" North cleared his throat and tried to raise his voice a little. "Nay, I don't think so." He put his arm around her waist as they promenaded along with the others who were dancing. The scent of rosewater drifted from her bright red hair that was tied into a long braid, trailing down her back. Her body felt hot beneath his slight touch, and the swell of her curvy hip was more than enticing.

"Now I know you're lying, St. George, because I am sure we've already met."

"I really don't think so, my lady. This is the first time I've been to Montclair Castle, I assure you." North's heart started beating quicker. Could she really have recognized him, even with his face covered and with him wearing this ridiculous costume? If so, she was sharper than he had given her credit for being.

She giggled, sounding as if she were enjoying this cat and mouse game. "I assure you, I know exactly who you are. There is no need to keep up the pretense."

"You . . . do?" North's eyes swept the room for his friends, already planning an escape in his mind. Cam was over at the food table, and Nash was trying to reject a man who was asking him to dance. Neither of them were looking at North at all. If Matilda revealed his identity now to everyone, they were going to have to make a run for it. He needed to get the attention of his friends somehow or they were going to be in big trouble.

"You're Lord Ashdown, aren't you?" Her words made him breathe a sigh of relief. "I remember meeting you about five years ago, and you were fascinated with St. George slaying the dragon. That was all you could talk about at the time. Therefore, I know it must be you under that mask."

"Ashdown," he repeated, not knowing who that was, and neither did he care. As long as she didn't know he was a Scot, that is all that really mattered. Then he remembered seeing the name Ashdown on the invitation that he had stolen. This was perfect. He'd just go along with it, pretending that Ashdown was who he was. That should throw off any suspicion from him. "Shhhh. Ye must keep it a secret, my lady," he whispered, reaching out and gently touching his finger to her lips. They felt so full and lush, and he couldn't stop himself from thinking about the kiss they'd shared in the tower. He longed to taste those sweet lips once again.

Her eyes closed partially and her head fell back slightly, as if in silent invitation. He could feel her breath on his finger, and it excited him. Her breath came from between those perfectly parted lips, instead of from her nose. He half-expected to hear her moan with desire next. Or mayhap it was himself who would be moaning, since he felt such a strong attraction to her right now.

God's bones, she was naught but a distraction, and a bonnie one at that. Plus, she liked him touching her in this manner, that much was clear. The lass must be starved for the companionship of a man, he decided. If not, she would be acting coy right now instead of wanton. Her actions were not those of a normal lady. They were not proper, this much he could tell.

That got him thinking again. It made him wonder just how long she'd been a widow, or when the last time was that she coupled with a man. He shook his head, trying to clear his brain of these illicit thoughts, needing to chase away the curiosity aroused within him concerning this lovely lass. She was interesting and unique. She was brave and strong. North liked anything that was out of the ordinary, and this girl certainly was different from the rest.

North realized that he had her right where he wanted her now, so he needed to use it to his advantage before it was too late. No more distractions, he told himself. No more mistakes, like what happened in the tower. If he botched this up once more, his friends would surely leave him and head back to Scotland without him.

Things were going smoothly with his plan, and it was time to move it along. "Why dinna we walk out to the courtyard for some air?" he suggested. "It is rather noisy in here, as well as stuffy. Perhaps we could talk privately without so many people gathered around us."

He half-expected her to deny his request. After all, English ladies didn't accept invitations to be alone with masked men without an escort along for protection. Of course, he supposed this didn't worry her. After all, she did know how to use a blade, and had already proven that when she'd threatened to cut out his heart. He was certain she would not hesitate to shoot him with an arrow as well if he got out of hand.

"I'd be happy to go out to the courtyard with you, but only if you'll promise to drop that ridiculous accent. I'm sorry to say that you're not very good at it, Lord Ashdown. As a matter of fact, you don't even sound anything like a real Scot."

"Really," he said, a muscle ticking in his jaw as she so brashly accused him of being a phony Scot. She was naught but a fool and didn't even know it. He might be a phony Sassenach, but hearing her belittle his true self was unnerving. He wanted to tell her more than anything that she had no idea how a real Highlander spoke, or she wouldn't be saying such rude things to his face. He wanted to say even more than that, but he wouldn't. He couldn't. Instead, he just bit his tongue and smiled. Offering her his arm, he escorted her out to the courtyard, trying to act like one of those stuffed, rigid English noblemen that she was so used to.

"So, tell me about that silver cup that you have chained to your waist," he said, once they were outside and away from the crowd. He figured he'd get straight to the point and not waste any more time.

"This goblet was given to me by my father when I was a child," she told him, sounding so proud, and as if she really believe it.

"I doubt it," he mumbled under his breath.

"Did you want to see it?" She held it up in front of his face, tempting him like a siren of the sea. It called out to him with promises of no longer being an outcast. He was so close to getting what he wanted that he could taste it right now. It was even sweeter than this bonnie lass' lips. All he had to do was to take what was being offered.

As North took the cold, metal goblet into his hand, his eyes roamed downward to the base. It was clamped with a metal ring that was locked on it tightly. A blacksmith had to concoct this contraption. The ring was connected to a chain that was wound around the girl's waist. Twice. The only way he was going to steal it was to unclasp the belt and remove it from her. Egads, what was the matter with this wench? No one wore a cup chained to their waist. She had to be mad. This wasn't going to be easy after all. He would have to get her in more private quarters and distract her if he was going to try to take it off. He might even have to seduce her. If not, how was he going to have any reason for touching her waist, or attempting to disrobe her?

"Do you like it?" she asked.

"Aye. More than you know." He held the cup, and his finger flitted over an indentation in it that looked like the shape of a small heart. "What's this?" he asked, curiously.

"That is where the rose quartz heart used to be."

"Where is it now?"

"Sadly, I lost it somewhere on Grope Lane just recently."

"Really." North thought about the gemstone heart that he had in his travel bag. He'd found it on Grope Lane. It must have come from this goblet.

"What would a lady be doing on Grope Lane?" he asked curiously, although he already knew the answer.

"I was looking for this cup. It was stolen from me when I was a child. Attackers killed my family and burned down my father's manor house."

"Egads, you can't be serious?"

"I lost both of my parents, as well as two brothers that night. The only reason I survived was because I was in hiding."

"I'm sorry, lass," he said, his heart going out to her.

When she gave him a certain look, he realized he'd called her lass again.

"I mean . . . my lady. Who would do such an awful thing?"

"It was the Scots," she said, making him jolt in surprise.

"What Scots? Which clan?"

"I don't know. But I hate them all."

"I don't think it is fair to hate all Scots for something that was caused by a few bad seeds. It would be like a Scot hating all English, when I'm sure some of them are not that bad." He was thinking of her when he said it.

"That's an odd thing for an Englishman to say."

"I only said it, because I know that Lady Amethyst has a brother who was raised by the Scots."

"That's true," she said. "The MacKeefes. And there was one Englishman who attacked that night. He killed both of my parents, and I saw it."

"That is awful," he said, not sure how to console her. Now he realized why she'd been having nightmares, like the one she'd had when he had entered her tower chamber.

"The MacKeefes are a good clan. I'm sure they were not part of your family's attack."

"I suppose not," she answered. "And other Scots must know that. That's why there were some Scots recently who showed up at the castle gate, claiming to be MacKeefes. They were saying that, I'm sure, just to get in to steal my cup."

North decided it would do no good trying to defend the MacKeefes at this time, or to let her know he was the one at the door that she wouldn't let in. If he was going to accomplish his task, he had to gain her trust instead of making her more suspicious.

"How old are you, lass?" he asked, bringing the conversation back to her.

"I'm five and twenty years . . . laddie," she said with a giggle. "You never stop trying with the phony accent, do you?"

"I'm sure if I practice hard enough, I'll eventually get it right." He smiled at her sarcastically, but she just thought he was flirting.

"How old are you?" she asked in return.

"Four and twenty," he told her.

"So . . . it looks like I'm older than you." She sounded so heartbroken. "I'm sure you're not interested in me at all now."

"Nay, don't say that. I'm more than interested." He reached out and stroked her cheek. Her eyes closed again and he swore he heard a slight whimper at the back of her throat when he touched her. "Is there somewhere we can go to . . . be alone?"

Her eyes popped open. "That isn't proper, Lord Ashdown, and you know it." She said the words but, at the same time, didn't sound at all offended that he had asked.

"I just meant – to talk. To get to know each other better. You see, I'm in the market for a wife."

"You are?" This piqued her interest and it seemed to please her. "So, you wouldn't be opposed to marrying a woman older than you, and who already has a child?"

"Why would I be?"

"I'm talking about me."

"I know that."

"You don't mind?"

"Is there something about you that should deter me? I mean, is there a secret that you're keeping from me that everyone else already knows?"

Her mouth opened, as if to answer, but then she shut it quickly and smiled sweetly. "How about if we take a walk over to the mews?" she suggested.

He turned and looked across the courtyard. It wasn't crowded since everyone was inside the great hall. Yes, this could work to his advantage quite nicely.

"You're sure you wouldn't mind?" he asked, trying not to sound too eager to get her alone. If she thought he was going to take advantage of her, she might change her mind. "After all, I wouldn't want anyone to see us and get the wrong opinion of you." He threw in the latter part, just so she wouldn't try to flag anyone down.

"I don't mind at all. We're not doing anything wrong. But just to make sure no one starts rumors, we'll stay in the shadows and keep out of view."

"Good idea. But what about the falconer? Won't he be in the mews?"

"Nay, we will be alone. Our falconer died recently, and his assistant just got married and moved to his wife's family's castle. No one will be in there at this time. Actually, I've been looking after the birds myself until we can find a replacement."

"You know about birds, too?" Was there anything this woman could not do?

"Aye. And healing," she told him eagerly as he opened the door to the mews and she stepped inside. "I have an overwhelming urge to learn new things. I've been experimenting lately with herbs and their effects on the body if too little or too much is taken. It is all quite fascinating."

"I suppose so," he said, not even listening to her anymore. His mind was back on his mission now that they were away from everyone else. "Show me the birds." He saw a pair of nippers used to trim the birds' nails, and secretly picked it up, hiding it in his hand. He figured, he could use this to cut the chain. Now, all he had to do was distract her long enough to complete his task.

"My hawk is the one over there. Follow me, and I'll show her to you."

"Never mind," he said, taking her arm and pulling her back to him. "I'm more interested in seeing how you kiss."

"What?" she asked, seeming very startled.

"Don't take it the wrong way. I promise I am not going to accost you. I just meant, that if you're possibly going to be my wife someday, I'd like a little sample of what I'm receiving."

She reached out and slapped him across the cheek.

"I'm sorry," he said softly, realizing he was moving too fast. "I just thought you wanted your suitors to know what they'll get.

After all, you are exposing all that cleavage and waving the cup around, trying to lure every eligible man in."

"Is it that obvious?" she asked, suddenly looking as if she felt ashamed.

"Don't worry. I don't mind. It worked on me, didn't it?" He smiled, and this seemed to relax her. "What else are you offering as part of your dowry?" He didn't really care, but had to sound as if he did if he wanted her to believe him.

"I don't have much to offer other than the goblet," she said sadly. "But my late father hid away some money before he died. As soon as I find it, it'll be part of my dowry as well."

"He hid money? How much?" asked North, thinking this sounded like an odd thing for an English nobleman to do. It almost sounded as if he were mixed up in something dishonest. Otherwise, he'd have no need to hide it.

"I don't know," she told him. "But I'm sure it's a substantial amount."

"Mayhap I can help you look for it," he offered.

"I'm confused. Is this a proposal, Lord Ashdown?" She lowered her head and looked up at him, batting her eyelids, waiting for his answer. God's eyes, what was he supposed to do? He couldn't disappoint her. Not now. Not until he had the cup in his possession.

"It could be," he answered, continuing to play her little game. "Then again, it all depends on the kiss, I suppose." He pulled her into his arms, kissing her deeply. At the same time, he let his hands slip down her waist, fumbling for the chain. He had the nippers ready in his other hand.

"Mmph" she said, breaking the kiss. "Lord Ashdown, are you being improper with me?" She was smiling when she said it, giving him the impression she wanted him to act this way.

"I thought you liked the kiss."

"I did. But you have your hand on my ass."

"Oh," he said, putting his arms around her again, getting ready to clip the chain from behind her.

Shouting from outside was heard, and it sounded like a commotion of some kind.

"What's that?" Her head popped up and she broke away from him, hurrying to the door of the mews just as he'd been ready to cut the chain. He cursed inwardly, throwing the nippers to the ground and following her. People were running through the courtyard in a heated frenzy.

North had been so close to completing his mission, and some silly nonsense just ruined his chance this time. Bad luck seemed to follow him wherever he went.

"Lady Matilda, come back. I'm sure it is nothing." He ran after her, and they stopped just inside the door to the great hall. The music had ceased and Marcus was up at the dais, raising his hand to get everyone's attention.

"Mayhap we should wait outside," he whispered.

"Nay. Something is wrong and I need to find out what it is."

"It seems we have some imposters here today," Marcus called out.

North looked across the great hall. Cam was talking to several of the ladies, and Nash was with some man on the dance floor. Nash looked like he wanted to kill someone right now. Most likely, him.

"Imposters?" someone called out.

"Aye," said Marcus, motioning to two men and a woman next to him who were not in costume. "It seems someone has stolen not only their costumes, but their invitation as well."

"God's eyes, no' now," North mumbled, trying to signal to his friends, but neither of them were looking in his direction.

Marcus continued. "These people are Lord and Lady Ashdown and the lord's brother, Lord Henry. Their costumes were St. George, a maiden, and a dragon. So, those in their costumes are the imposters, and will be thrown into the dungeon immediately."

"WHAT?" GASPED MATILDA, turning around to face St. George, but the man who'd been with her was gone.

✦•◦◇◦•✦

CHAPTER NINE

MATILDA WATCHED IN horror as a fistfight started between some of the people on the dance floor. She saw the dragon throw down his headpiece. St. George pushed through the crowd, trying to get to the fair maiden.

"Run!" she heard St. George call out once the guards moved in. The two men fought their ways across the floor, but the maiden seemed to limp, and wasn't as lucky. St. George and the dragon ran out the door, but the maiden fell to the ground.

"Let me pass," called out Matilda, clawing her way through the crowd. She didn't want any woman being hauled away by guards no matter who she was. "Are you all right?" she asked, looking down at the maiden whose headpiece and mask had fallen off. "Oh!" she exclaimed, seeing hairy legs, and a Highland plaid under the maiden's gown. The woman was really a man.

"Leave me alone. I'm a MacKeefe," cried out the man on the ground. Two guards hauled him to his feet. By now, the fair maiden's gown had ripped down the front. The man pulled it off and threw it to the floor. "I am Nash MacKeefe, now unhand me," he shouted.

"Bring him to me," Matilda heard Marcus command. She followed the guards and the struggling Scot as they dragged him over to the dais.

"Who is he?" asked Amethyst.

"He's a bloody Scot," someone called out.

"He's a Highlander," ground out the real Lord Ashdown. "I should have known no Englishman would steal from me."

"Mother, I've never seen a Scot before. Is he really a Highlander?" Robbie ran up with Gertie on his heels.

"Don't get too close, Robbie," Matilda warned her son, pulling the boy to her, cradling him protectively in front of her. "You have no idea how dangerous they are."

"I'm no' dangerous, and neither are my friends," the man protested.

"Why did you steal from these people?" asked Marcus.

"I didna steal anythin'. That was my twin brathair that did that. I never wanted to be here at all, and especially no' dressed like a wench, I assure ye. I tell ye, I am yer ally. I am a MacKeefe."

"Do you know him?" Marcus asked Amethyst. "Is he from your brother's clan?"

"I – I can't be sure," said Amethyst, tilting her head and looking him up and down. "There are so many MacKeefes, and most of them stay in the Highlands and never even venture across the border. I'm sorry, I don't recognize this one, or even his name."

"Then take him to the dungeon and send troops out to look for the other two Scots," commanded Marcus.

"Nay!" cried the man named Nash as they dragged him away. "We're only here for the bluidy silver goblet. We were never goin' to hurt anyone. We're allies, I tell ye. God's eyes, listen to me. I am a MacKeefe!"

Matilda thought about the man in the mews. She realized now that he kissed the same way as the Highlander she'd caught sneaking into her tower room. By the rood, that is why he kept talking like a Scot. He was one! How could she have been so blind as to be fooled by his deception? She looked down to the cup hanging at her side. Was he really only kissing her to try to steal the goblet, she wondered? Her heart ached to realize it was true. She had thought for some reason the man actually liked her. She had been attracted to him, and had been willing to marry him as well. All her hopes shattered when she realized she had been naught but a means for him to get what he wanted.

"Marcus, he says he's a MacKeefe," said Amethyst. "Mayhap you shouldn't put him in the dungeon."

"Then, where do you suggest I put him?" growled Marcus.

"I don't know. Mayhap just lock him in a tower until we find out for sure who he is. My brother, Onyx, is a MacKeefe and I don't want to cause trouble with his clan. He's traveling right now, and I don't know how to reach him, or I would contact him immediately to find out. I don't think you should lock this one in the dungeon. It's just not right."

"We saw how that last Scot managed to climb the walls and get into Matilda's tower room. I am not going to give him the opportunity to escape."

"Still, we have to be sure."

"Is his plaid from the MacKeefe Clan?" asked Marcus.

"Aye, it is," answered his wife, knowing it well.

"They could have stolen that, too, just like they took our costumes and invitation," interrupted Lord Ashdown's brother. "Highlanders cannot be trusted."

"I'm sorry, my wife, but I just can't take the chance. Especially not with all these people here," said Marcus. "I have to protect them. Guards, take him to the dungeon and continue to search for the other men," he instructed. "The dance will continue for now."

"Let's get our costumes, or what we can find of what's left of them," Lord Ashdown told his friends. They headed out to the middle of the floor to look for the discarded costumes.

"Cousin, could they be telling the truth?" asked Matilda, picking up her son and walking up to Marcus and Amethyst. The guards hauled the Highlander away. "Could they possibly be MacKeefes? If so, it might cause a battle with the clan if we lock away their clansman. They really did nothing wrong."

"Yes, they did," rallied Marcus. "They stole from a nobleman and pretended to be people they weren't, just to get inside the castle. Who knows what else they'd planned to do. Stealing and lying is not right, Matilda. Something is going on here, and I intend to find the answers. You, of all people, should want the Scots removed after what they did to your family. Whatever it is these men want, it has to do with that blasted cup. Give it to me." Marcus held out his hand, but Matilda did nothing to hand the cup over to him.

"Go with Beatrice, Robbie. Stay with her until I get there." Matilda put her son down. "Gertie, stay with him as well," she instructed the dog. Once they left, Matilda continued speaking, her hand hovering above the cup at all times. "The man dressed like St. George took me out to the mews and kissed me," she blurted out.

"What?" Marcus' mouth turned down into a deep frown. "How could you let a strange man take you to the mews?" he reprimanded her. "And unescorted. Anything could have happened."

"I thought he was Lord Ashdown, and that he wanted to marry me. Remember, I am looking for a husband."

"Well, that's no way to find one. You'll only tarnish your reputation further by being so wanton."

"I am not wanton!" she snapped.

"Marcus, please," said Amethyst, trying to calm down her husband. "Did you ever send the missive to Hermitage Castle, like I asked you to do? That is how we'll find out once and for all if these men are truly MacKeefes."

"You don't know them, so that should be proof enough." Marcus was as stubborn as they came.

"I know some of my brother's friends, but I admit I don't know the entire MacKeefe Clan," Amethyst continued. "Especially, not the Highland sect. Did you send the missive or not?"

"I was going to do it first thing in the morning. After the dance. There is too much commotion tonight. Now, excuse me, I need to assist my men in looking for these Scots." Marcus left Amethyst and Matilda standing there, speechless.

"Amethyst, I don't think they meant any harm," said Matilda, thinking once again about the Scot who had kissed her. He hadn't seemed dangerous. He was so different from the Scots who had stormed her father's manor. This one had been polite in more ways than one, and was actually kind to her. He seemed to like her. That was more than she could say for most of the English noblemen. Since her late husband had sullied her reputation and died before he could correct it, none of the Englishmen were respectful or kind to her at all. She had felt unwanted and undesirable for many years now. This Highlander had made her feel alive and pretty again.

"Matilda, you need to be careful," Amethyst warned her. "Marcus is right when he says that the Scots can be dangerous. I don't have to remind you what happened to your family."

"I know," she said, feeling her knees shaking just thinking about the past. Anxiety started to course through her again, wracking her body with trauma that was long over with, but never forgotten. "Why do you think they want my goblet?" asked Matilda. "They seem so persistent."

"I'm not sure. But until they are found, you, as well as your goblet, better stay locked away in your chamber."

"Damn it all to hell," spat Cam, standing with North, watching from the back of the great hall as the guards hauled Nash away. Cam had removed his costume but North couldn't, or he'd be standing there in his braies right now. Instead, he managed to steal two hooded cloaks from a peg on the kitchen wall. They used them now to hide beneath and blend in to the crowd. "North, we've got to do something to help Nash," Cam said in a low voice.

"I ken. But what?" asked North. "Ye heard my brathair tell them no' only who he is, but also that we just wanted the goblet. That only seemed to infuriate them more."

"What should we do?"

"Nash will be safe in the dungeon for now," said North. "The one we need to worry about is Gavin. He's out there in the woods and has no idea the guards are searchin' for us. We need to get to him fast to warn him."

Ten minutes later, North and Cam were with Gavin in the woods, hurriedly packing up their belongings. They could hear the guards in the distance searching for them, as well as the hounds barking. They were moving in on them, and getting closer.

"How could ye two just leave Nash there?" scolded Gavin. "God's teeth, North, he is yer own brathair!" Gavin pulled the straps tight on the saddle, preparing the horses so they could leave. "We've got to go back and get him."

"And how would ye suggest we do that?" asked North, throwing a few last things into the travel bags. He still wore the breeches and tunic of St. George that he'd donned for the costume ball. "We do that, and we'll be captured and thrown into the dungeon with him."

"North's right, Gavin," Cam agreed. "Ye didna see how angry everyone was. There are too many of them for us to fight them all. Neither can we just walk in and demand his release."

"We've got to do somethin' to help him." Gavin hoisted himself atop his horse, tying the reins of Nash's horse to his.

"I have an idea," said North looking down at his costume.

"Nay, no' another of yer bluidy ideas, North." Cam hoisted himself up into the saddle. "After all, we saw how wonderfully that worked out already. Nash is goin' to kill ye for this. He didna even want to go, and couldna run because of his hurt foot that was yer fault to begin with."

North waved a hand through the air to dismiss the accusatory remarks about him. "Nash is fine. Dinna worry about him. I'm talkin' about how I can sneak back in to the castle."

"God's eyes, forget about the damned goblet," growled Gavin. "I'm goin' to the gates first thing in the mornin' and demandin' to talk to the lord of the castle. I'll tell him who we really are. I'll get Nash released."

"Nay," protested North. "I heard them talkin'. Lord Marcus is sendin' a messenger to Hermitage Castle askin' about us. Once the messenger returns, he'll give them the information that we are really MacKeefes and they'll let us go."

"Do ye really think so?" asked Cam.

"Aye," said North. "Just give the messenger a day or two to get back with word from our chieftain. Ye'll see."

"If so, our worries are over," said Cam.

"No' exactly," said North. "I still dinna have the goblet, and Lady Matilda is no' goin' to willingly hand it over to me."

"What are ye talkin' about?" asked Gavin.

"She told me it was a gift from her faither when she was a child. She's also usin' it as part of her dowry because she is a widow with a child and wants to remarry."

"So what?" asked Cam. "That doesna concern us."

"Wrong," North told him. "I am goin' to disguise myself as a Sassenach, and court the lass. She is very eager to marry. So eager that she willingly let me take her inside the mews and kiss her."

"Bid the devil!" Gavin threw his hands in the air. "No' again, North."

"The lass likes my kisses, I tell ye." North smiled with pride. "I'll convince her to take off that chain around her waist that holds the goblet. I'll take it off myself if I have to, but I promise ye, I'll get the cup."

"Wait a minute," said Gavin. "Back up the story a bit. She has it chained to her waist?"

"Aye. She's an odd wench, I agree. But I kind of like that. Besides, I ken what she wants now. As soon as she thinks she's gettin' it, she'll let down her guard, and bang, I'll steal the goblet before she kens what happened."

"I'm losin' faith in yer abilities to steal anythin' lately," mumbled Gavin.

"Aye, me, too," agreed Cam. "And how in the name of the

devil do ye think ye're gettin' inside the castle, even if ye can pull off bein' an Englishman, which I highly doubt."

"I'll get inside, dinna worry." North chuckled. "However, it willna be as a Scot."

"We ken. Ye're goin' to pose as a Sassenach," Cam said with a roll of his eyes.

"No' just a Sassenach, but more," answered North.

"Dinna even think ye can pull off the guise of a noble because we all ken ye canna do it," said Gavin.

"No' a noble. I'll be workin' for them, so I'll belong there and my presence will never be questioned again. Now, let's go and find a new place to wait this out. The guards are on our tail."

"Ye'd better be right about this," warned Gavin as they rode away. "Because I still dinna feel guid about leavin' Nash in the dungeon."

"Look at it this way," said North, smiling, thinking about all he had done for his brother when he was thatching roofs. "Nash needs to rest his foot, and now he'll get time to do just that. He has nothin' to complain about at all."

CHAPTER TEN

M ATILDA HADN'T SLEPT much at all last night. And what little sleep she did get was either filled with nightmares of her childhood, or laden with lustful dreams about kissing that blasted Scot. Why in heaven's name couldn't she get the Highlander out of her mind? She didn't even know the man's real name. He was here only to steal her goblet, she reminded herself. That didn't sit right with her. After the fiasco last night, she hadn't even had the desire to look for a husband anymore. She'd left the dance early and spent the rest of the night in her room, peering out the window, hoping to see the kissing Scot.

She walked out in to the bright sun of the courtyard this morning, yawning.

"It looks like someone didn't get much sleep last night." Amethyst greeted her with her everlasting smile. Marcus' wife was a smart woman, and also one who seemed to find good in all things, even out of bad happenings.

"Nay, I didn't sleep much," she admitted. "A messenger came to my door this morning to tell me that someone is here to apply for the position of falconer. Is that so?"

"Aye, that's right," said Amethyst. "I've convinced Marcus to let you choose the new falconer since you have been the one caring for the birds lately and know the most about them."

"Where is my cousin?" Matilda yawned again, and looked around the courtyard.

"Here he comes. Marcus," called Amethyst, holding out her hand to her husband. "Where have you been?"

"I sent a messenger as well as a few guards to Hermitage Castle," explained Marcus. "When they return, they'll have our answer and I'll know for sure if the Scots are MacKeefes. If not, I'll have to decide what to do with the man in the dungeon."

"Is he causing any trouble?" asked Matilda curiously.

"Nay," answered Marcus. "However, he keeps talking about killing someone named North, so that concerns me."

"Well, never mind about that. Where is the man applying for the position of falconer?" asked Matilda.

"Actually, there are two men applying for the job," Amethyst informed her. "They are both in the mews waiting for you. Shall we?"

"I'll make the final decision, but I'd appreciate your input, Matilda," said Marcus. It didn't surprise Matilda at all, since Marcus had problems in the past giving any woman authority. It wasn't seen or even heard of, even amongst the nobles. Amethyst had changed Marcus over the years, but he still fell back on his old ways and beliefs at times.

"Hmph. I thought it was too good to be true that you'd let a woman decide anything," remarked Matilda as they made their way to the mews.

Once there, Matilda saw two men. One was older, mayhap the age of her Uncle Gilbert, and the other looked to be about her age. The younger one was very handsome. He had long, brown hair tied back behind his head. He wore a tunic that buttoned at the top, very tight breeches, and a pair of boots. She couldn't keep from looking at his legs. It was as if he wore a second skin, and she had to take another look to make sure he wasn't without breeches since they were light in color.

"Good morning," said Matilda.

"Gentlemen," said Marcus with a nod. "We only have one position to fill, so I'd like you to both introduce yourselves and tell me why you think you would be good for the position of my falconer. You first," he said to the older man.

"I am Walter Ballard, my lord," the man told him. He had graying hair, and a tall build. He was dressed like a falconer with the proper attire, including a hawking glove made of black leather on his right hand. "I have served as falconer to Lord Dunlap in Ireland for the last twenty years, and have just arrived in England. Have you heard of him, my lord?"

"Nay, I haven't," said Marcus. "But twenty years of service is more than qualified."

"Why don't you speak like an Irishman?" asked Matilda, curiously. "You sound more like an Englishman to me."

The man cleared his throat before he answered. "My last lord insisted I speak like an Englishman, and so I learned. He was infatuated with England and wanted to move here someday. I suppose it's habit that I speak in this manner, now."

"Where is your last lord now?" asked Matilda.

"He's dead, my lady. Died with a bad fever, right in my own arms, I'm sad to say."

"That's a shame," said Marcus, looking over to the next man. "And whom might you be?"

"I, my lord, am Nor . . . Norton."

"Norton? Do you have a surname?" asked Marcus.

"Aye. It is . . ." he looked around, and then cleared his throat again. "Birdwhistle. Norton Birdwhistle at your service." He bowed slightly.

"Birdwhistle?" Matilda giggled, and the man's silver eyes swept over to her.

"It is a dying family surname, my lady. To my knowledge, I am the last Birdwhistle left in England."

"Really." Matilda thought this man to be jesting, or possibly daft if he believed they were going to buy his ridiculous story.

"Aye, I've heard of the Birdwhistles," said Marcus, surprising her.

"You have?" If Matilda didn't know her cousin better, she would have thought he was jesting as well. However, Marcus didn't have a sense of humor, so he had to be serious.

"The Birdwhistles have years of falconry experience behind them. I suppose you have learned the skill as well?" asked Marcus.

"Well . . . I . . . I have to admit, I might not be as experienced as my ancestors," he told them.

"Really," said Marcus. "And why not?"

"Well, I . . . I was in training for something else, but it didn't work out. But now, I've decided to follow in their footsteps after all."

"Training for what?" asked Matilda, having to know more.

Lady Gert ran into the mews, followed by Robbie.

"Mother, I was playing ball with Gertie, but she wanted to come here," Robbie told her.

"Shhh, Robbie. Not now," said Matilda, picking up her son. "Go ahead, Mr. Birdwhistle. What were you trained in?"

The man looked down at her hound, and then answered. "Kennel groom. I was trained as a kennel groom," he answered, dropping to his knees and petting Gertie. The hound gave a low growl.

"Kennel groom, you say?" Matilda looked the man over. "The dog doesn't seem to like you much. For being a kennel groom and all."

Norton jumped to his feet. "Like I said, it didn't work out." He brushed off his hands, looking at the floor.

"Well, we don't need a kennel groom," said Marcus. "And since Walter has more experience, he has the job."

"Marcus," said Matilda. "I thought you said I had a choice in the matter."

"That's right, dear, you did tell her that," agreed Amethyst.

"Well, there is no choice here," Marcus answered. "Walter has experience and Norton really doesn't. There is no question who gets the job."

"Our last falconer had an assistant," Matilda pointed out. "I think Mr. Birdwhistle deserves a chance. He can be the assistant falconer." Matilda liked the looks of this one, and she wasn't about to let him go. Handsome men were hard to come by lately. Even if she couldn't marry a commoner, she would enjoy looking at him in the meantime.

"Fine," said Marcus, throwing his hands up in the air. "You both have the job, then. Matilda, you tell them what to do. I have to meet my men in the practice yard, and I'm already late."

"Excuse me, my lord," Walter said, causing Marcus to stop in his tracks. "I heard there was a search going on. For some Highlanders? Did you ever find them?"

Matilda noticed Norton shifting back and forth all of a sudden. He was either nervous or needed to use the garderobe.

"Nay, they managed to elude us," said Marcus. "We only have the one we caught and put in the dungeon."

"In the dungeon?" asked Norton. "Did the man do something wrong?"

"Aye, he did," Marcus answered. "But I don't think I need to explain anything to either of you. You two are being hired to take care of my birds, not interrogate me about my decisions. Now get to work."

"So sorry, my lord," said Walter, bowing with respect.

"Och, aye." Norton jerked. "Me, too," he said, bowing as well. When he did, Matilda heard the ripping of material.

"Was that . . . your breeches splitting?" Matilda almost laughed aloud.

"They shrunk. The last time I washed them," said Norton, putting his hand to his backside, seeming very embarrassed.

"Then you'd better change at once," Matilda told him.

"I – I'm afraid I don't have a change of clothes. Not with me, I mean."

"Don't worry. I can find you another pair of breeches to wear while the ladies in the solar repair yours," Amethyst offered. "Come with me, Norton."

"I'll take him." Matilda put Robbie down on the ground and eagerly stepped forward. "I mean . . . I have to bring my son to the garderobe anyway, so I don't mind showing him where to go."

"I don't care what any of you do. I need to get to the tiltyard to practice." Marcus hurried off.

"Amethyst, would you mind showing Walter around the mews until I return?" asked Matilda.

Amethyst got that knowing look on her face. "I'd be more than happy to. And be sure to hurry back."

"Right this way, Norton." Matilda held her son's hand and Norton followed her out of the mews. As soon as they were outside, Gert started barking playfully. Several children showed up with a ball.

"Can we play ball with your dog, Robbie?" asked one of the boys.

"I want to go play, too," said Robbie, looking up at his mother. "Can I?"

"Go on, Son. Have fun. I see Beatrice by the well. Go to her if you need anything. She will be watching over you." Matilda waved to the nursemaid who waved back.

NORTH LOOKED AT Matilda from the sides of his eyes as the boy ran off with the dog and other children. "I thought the lad needed to go to the garderobe."

"Lad?" She looked at him suspiciously.

"I mean boy. I've been talking to Walter, and I suppose his accent is catching. I mean – with the way he talks and all."

"Interesting you should say so, since Walter speaks like an Englishman. I haven't noticed him slipping into any other dialect at all."

"Mayhap we'd better get another pair of breeches quickly." North held his hand behind him, and leaned over to speak in a softer voice. "I think the rip is widening."

"I'm not surprised they ripped since they were so tight that it was almost indecent."

"You noticed my breeches were tight? You were looking at my body?" he asked, liking the fact she was interested in what he had.

"I was not looking, but couldn't help notice. From now on, you need to wear breeches that are looser."

"Whatever you say, my lady."

"I'm surprised you don't have other clothes with you." Matilda continued to walk toward the castle.

"I didn't have any because . . . I wasn't sure I'd get the job."

"You can thank me for that. I could tell my cousin, Marcus, has no use for you." She stopped and turned to look at him.

North drank in the woman's beauty. Her long, red locks cascaded over her shoulders in waves, while part of her hair was tied back at the top. She had fresh flowers woven into her locks that made her smell sweet . . . and enticing. Her body was curvy in all the right places. He couldn't stop thinking about all the cleavage she'd displayed at the dance. Even though she wasn't showing it today, he knew it was under those clothes and that only made him randy.

"Is something wrong?" She looked up at him, her big, green eyes staring into his. She blinked her eyes twice, waiting for him to answer.

"Not at all," said North, taking her hand, bending down and kissing it. "Thank ye, so much." A ripping sound was heard again, making Matilda giggle.

"I'd suggest we move quickly. This way, please."

North was surprised when instead of going to the ladies' solar, Matilda led him to her tower bedchamber. She opened the door and stepped inside, but North stopped at the threshold.

"What's the matter?" she asked. "Why are you standing there like a dolt in the doorway? Come inside quickly, and close the door."

North cleared his throat, looking around. No one was watching. While he didn't want to be caught in the lady's bedchamber, he also didn't want to waste a perfect opportunity to possibly steal the cup.

"Of course, my lady," he said, stepping into the room and

closing the door behind him. Everything looked different in the daylight. He didn't realize how quaint the room was the other night when he'd entered in the dark. A four-poster bed took up the center of the room. It had long, purple curtains hanging down, tied back, exposing the lush pallet and several overstuffed pillows. It looked very inviting.

He saw the open window where he'd climbed in. He strolled over to take a better look, trying to find the rope and grappling hook he'd left, but they weren't there.

"Looking for this?" she asked, causing him to spin on his heel.

Matilda stood there holding out the rope and grappling hook. She no longer looked friendly, and her mouth was set in a straight line.

"What . . . is that?" he asked, trying to sound innocent.

"You know damned well what it is." She threw it down under the window and picked up her sword that was on a side table. She pointed it right at him.

"Now, wait a minute." North instinctively reached for his own sword but, of course, he didn't have it. He couldn't wear it and have them believe he was only a falconer when he applied for the job, so he'd left it in the woods with Cam and Gavin. Wearing a sword would have given himself away. "I don't know who you think I am, but I assure you that you're wrong."

"Am I?" She smiled and took two steps forward, all the while holding her sword at the ready. "I know you're that Scot who sneaked into my room and kissed me. You slipped several times back into your native tongue, and you don't fool me. Now, take off your clothes."

"What?" he asked, shocked to hear her say that, although the idea of being naked with her was not at all unappealing to him. "Ye want me bare-arsed and in yer bed?" He raised a brow. "Lassie, I rather like the idea of it, but are ye sure it's proper?"

"That's not what I mean," she spat. "This time, I am not taking any chances. I highly doubt you'll try to escape from a tower window while you're naked. Now strip, I tell you. I'll not ask again."

"Dinna fash yerself, lass. I'm more than happy to show ye what I've got to offer."

"Offer?"

"That's right." He removed his tunic, watching her eyes travel lower, down his chest. "I mean, I'm sure ye want to test out the guids before ye make the commitment to marry me."

"Marry you?" she gasped. "Don't be absurd. I would never marry a Scot."

"Highlander," he told her, kicking off his boots. His breeches were split, and his manhood was hardening quickly as he thought of bedding the girl. It poked out under the cloth making things even worse. The breeches were much too tight to remove them the normal way, so he took hold of them and ripped them right off his body, throwing them at her feet. "So, what do ye think?" he asked, standing there naked, and as straight as an arrow.

⬥•◇•⬥

CHAPTER ELEVEN

MATILDA NOW WISHED she had thought this plan through more thoroughly before bringing the Highlander to her bedchamber, and then demanding he remove his clothes. She was so sure it was the man who had kissed her, both the night he climbed in her window and also at the dance, that she wanted him to pay for what he had done.

She figured she'd make him strip at the end of her sword, then lock him in the room while she brought Marcus back to show him she'd caught the intruder. But now that he stood there naked, she could barely breathe.

The sword in her hand shook as her eyes scanned down his remarkable body. His chest was sturdy and strong, just begging her to touch it. His upper arms showed bulging muscles that would be the envy of any man. A thin trail of chest hair caught her interest, and her eyes followed its ragged path down past his taut stomach, and to the beginning of a thatch of brown, curly hair just below his waist.

She should have looked away, but she couldn't. She was so mesmerized by his manly beauty that she had to see and know even more. Curiously, she looked just a bit lower. When she did, her jaw dropped open and she gasped. Now she knew exactly what it was that this Highlander had to offer. His manhood was stiff, and thick and very long. It was most amazing. She couldn't stop the moan that lodged in the back of her throat when she drank in his physique, longing to reach out and touch him.

She had been without a man for years now since her husband died. Even when Alaric was alive, he wasn't half as big or as enticing as this rugged Highlander standing before her. Matilda had needs, just like any woman. Alaric had never satisfied them. This Highlander was well endowed, and had more than his share of male sex appeal. Just looking at his erection had her thoughts spiraling out of control and caused a tingling vibration between her thighs. Bid the devil, she couldn't help herself for wanting him. Her knees shook and she felt excitement deep in her core as her body became warmer and warmer.

Matilda lifted her eyes back to this handsome face, and her thoughts went to his kiss. It had felt so passionate that she'd never forget it as long as she lived. It had made her feel hot inside, and well-protected. But seeing this . . . this made her feel downright naughty. Oh, what was the matter with her? She was a lady! This was so wrong. She shouldn't feel lust for a man who had sneaked into her bedchamber window and a man she didn't even know.

Why had she even brought him here? She asked herself that question over and over. Marcus was always calling her daft, and now she realized why. She found herself in the midst of a very dangerous situation, and had no one to blame but her herself.

"Like what ye see, lass?" He waggled his brows, making her feel even more nervous.

"Stop it," she commanded in a breathy voice, not able to speak and breathe at the same time. This desirable Highlander seemed to fill the room and suck the air right from her lungs just with his presence. Her cheeks became very warm now, and she felt a little faint. "I didn't expect you to not be wearing undergarments, or I would never have told you to strip. You could have mentioned it."

"Ye should have asked. Besides, it's even more reason to get a pair of breeches for me that are no' ripped. Dinna ye agree?"

"Who . . . are . . . you?" she asked, breathing heavily. It was getting hard just to speak. Her eyes traveled downwards again and, this time, she swore she saw his manhood move on its own. "Oh!" she exclaimed. Her eyes snapped back up to his face and she heard the rapid pounding of her heart drumming in her ears. He had beautiful silver eyes, a strong nose, and chiseled cheeks. His long oaken hair was tied back, and she couldn't help but wonder what he would look like with it falling over his shoulders. Would it be soft or coarse? How did it smell? Her breath hitched again, and her eyes started to close.

"Who am I?" he repeated. "Well, lass, I can be whoever ye want me to be."

"Aye, I've already seen you prove that, St. George. Or is it Norton?" Damn, why did he have to say that to her? He was being playful in a lusty manner, and his words only excited her even more. She had always wanted Alaric to use foreplay in the bedroom, but the man never had. He'd always finished bedding her before she ever even got excited. She had never known satisfaction or even found her release. This Scot already had her excited, as he seemed to hold some sort of power over her, making her want to give herself to him freely and completely.

He chuckled, his low voice reverberating in her ears, but thankfully bringing her back to her senses. She pushed all thoughts of lust from her mind, and tried to be as mean as she could.

"Tell me!" she snarled, raising the tip of her sword, holding it in both hands now. She couldn't let him control her. She wouldn't. She had to show him who was in charge.

"Losh me, ye can put down the blade, lass. I'd be happy to tell ye who I am, but do ye really need to keep threatenin' me? After all, I'm naked, and have no weapon or means of escape. Ye hold all the cards now."

"Tell me your name," she spat, trying to sound threatening, even though it was the last thing she was feeling at the moment.

"I'm North MacKeefe. I'm a Highlander, but my clan also owns Hermitage Castle in the Lowlands," he explained.

"Why are you here?" she demanded to know.

He looked at her and the side of his mouth turned up into a slight grin. "I thought I was comin' for a new pair of breeches, but it seems ye have somethin' else on yer mind, lass."

"Quit calling me lass!" Every time he called her lass, she felt special and it made her want him even more. She liked it, though she knew she shouldn't. God's eyes, what was this she was feeling? It was a new experience and she'd never felt anything like it before.

"Well, what do we do now?" he asked with a shrug. "Did ye want me spread eagle on the bed?" He walked over to the bed and plopped down, lying on his back with his manhood sticking straight up, and his legs spread apart.

"Have you no shame?" she retorted. Her lips were dry and her tongue shot out to wet them.

"Nay, I guess I dinna. However, I think ye like it."

"I do not!"

"Then why are ye lookin' at me and lickin' yer lips, lass?

Damn, he did it again. He called her lass, and he also noticed how much his nakedness was affecting her.

"Ah, this is nice," he told her, looking up at the curtains. "I suppose it could be very private if two people wanted to make love." He yanked at the cords holding back the bedcurtains, causing them to close, hiding him from sight.

"Nay!" she shouted, thinking he was doing this as a means of escape. "I demand you open those curtains so I can see you." She ran over to the bed, pulling open the curtains with one hand, still holding her sword with the other. The bed was empty. "Oh, no! Where are you?" she cried.

Her sword was knocked out of her grip from behind, and she was pushed down on the bed.

"Ooomph," she exclaimed as she hit the pallet hard, face down. She flipped over to see the Highlander standing there holding her sword to her chest now.

"Never trust a Highlander no' to try to escape, even if he is bare-arsed and randy."

"Go ahead, then," she told him, scooching up to a half-sitting position on the bed. "Leave, if you want to, I won't stop you." She was testing him, to see if he was just as interested in her as she was in him. Secretly, she hoped he decided to stay.

"Leave?" There was that deep, sexy chuckle again that was driving her mad. "I'm naked, lass, unless ye've forgotten."

Forgotten? Like that was possible! The things she'd just seen she'd never forget for the rest of her life. "There are some of my late husband's clothes in the foot trunk," she told him. "Take them, dress quickly, and go."

He paused for a moment, looking over at the trunk. Then he looked back at her. "Nay," he said, throwing down the sword on the floor behind him. "No' until I get what I came for."

"W-what do you mean?" Her heart beat rapidly in her chest. Did he come for her? Did he want her in a sexual manner? She became frightened now, because she had acted reckless and might not be able to get out of this situation. She wished she had thought this out clearly before attempting to capture the Scot. While she was interested in coupling with the man, she didn't want him to force himself on her. Besides, if they did anything and it was discovered, she'd be ruined for life. Then again, wasn't she already ruined? Mayhap it didn't matter. She'd made a mess of things, and didn't know what to do.

"Ye have somethin' I want and have been tryin' to get but havena been able to do so." He kneeled on the bed and came toward her like a lion stalking its prey. It frightened her, but excited her at the same time. She always wished for a man who looked and acted like him in the bedchamber. It was crazy to want him, especially since he was a Scot. Then again, perhaps she was mad, just like the rumors said.

"If there is something you want, then why don't you just claim it as yours?" she challenged him. If she was going to be taken by the Highlander, she wouldn't let it be said that it was against her will. Already, no man wanted her. If word got out that this man forced himself on her, she would surely be doomed.

What little hope she had left of someday finding a husband would be over. Matilda would surely end up spending the rest of her life in a convent.

On the other hand, if it was said that she was the one who initiated a tryst with the Highlander, things would be different indeed. She'd be looked upon as a loose woman, but at least this way, she wouldn't end up with the nuns. They wouldn't want her if they thought she gave herself freely to a man although she wasn't married to him. It was the lesser of two evils in her mind. Plus, if this was the last time she'd ever couple with a man, she wanted it to be with North MacKeefe.

"I dinna mind if I do," said North, leaning over, kissing her gently. Her eyes closed and her breathing labored.

"Just be quick about it, and don't make noise," she told him.

"Really?" He chuckled under his breath. He kissed her again, this time slipping his tongue between her lips and into her mouth. It was so sensual that it made her squirm beneath him. She fought to keep her mind on the matters at hand.

"Afterwards, I want you gone from here, and I never want to see you again," she told him.

"All right, that can be arranged," he said, kissing her once more. She felt his hardened form poking at her, as well as his hand caressing her cheek. She moaned and leaned in to his touch, her eyes once again closing. Then his fingers skimmed down her body, cupping one breast, making her back arch up off the bed. Lower and lower, his hand slid, stopping at her waist. Then she felt him fidgeting with her belt, preparing to undress her. Matilda kept her eyes closed even when she heard the sound of the rattling chain that secured the cup around her waist.

One deeper kiss, and she had started to relax. By now, a fire burned hot between her legs. This was crazy, but she welcomed the Highlander's touch and wanted to know how it felt to make love with a man like him. It was something she had longed for her entire life.

Just when she was sure he was going to push up her gown

and enter her, she felt him pulling away. He got up off the bed. Her eyes opened to see him digging in the trunk for clothes.

"What are you doing?" she asked in confusion. "North MacKeefe, talk to me. Why did you stop?"

"I'm findin' some clothes so I dinna have to run through the courtyard naked," he told her. He stood up with a tunic and a pair of breeches in his hand.

"What do you mean?" She scooted to the edge of bed, looking at him over the top of the open trunk. "You said you wanted what you came for. So why don't you take it? Why did you stop?"

"Huh?" He pulled the tunic over his head, and stepped into the breeches. "I'm no' sure what ye mean, lass. I didna stop. I got what I wanted."

"You did? So, all you wanted was to kiss me? That's it?" She stood up, walking around the bed, feeling sorely disappointed and rejected. Perhaps her fantasies of making love with him were only fantasies indeed. He was no better than Alaric.

Then she noticed something that she hadn't before. He stood there with her silver goblet in his hand. Her head snapped back to the bed where her empty belt chain lay on the floor. "Nay," she said, unable to believe this man had just taken advantage of her in a way that was worse than if he had bedded her against her will. "Give that to me! It's mine." She rushed over to him and tried to grab the cup.

"Nay, it's no' yers," he said, holding it high above his head, trying to put on one boot at the same time. "It is the goblet of my laird, Storm MacKeefe. It was given to him years ago by the Scottish king."

"That's a lie!" She jumped up, trying to touch it, but he was tall and held it far from her reach. "It is the goblet my father gave me as a child. It was stolen from me when my family was attacked by the Scots and killed."

"So ye say. However, it is my guess that yer da stole this from the Scots to begin with."

"Nay!" She was crying now, tears rolling down her cheeks.

"My father was a good man. He only wanted to show me how much he loved me by giving it to me. No one has ever given me a thing, except this. It means the world to me. Please, give it back."

North didn't like to see lassies cry. His heart went out to her and he lowered his hand enough that it enabled Matilda to take the goblet. She cradled it possessively in her arms, kissing the damned thing, and then backing away from him, toward the bed.

"Och, I'm sorry, lass," he told her, knowing he couldn't return to his friends without the cup again. "Hand it over, please." He frowned as he donned the second boot.

"Nay. Never!" She held it tighter. Her whole body seemed to shake now. He'd never seen anything like it.

"I need that goblet," he told her, moving slowly toward her across the floor. "If I dinna bring it back to my clan, I will remain an outcast, and I canna let that happen."

"I don't care. I will never give up this cup. It is my only hope for a good future. Without it, no man will ever want to marry me, because my late husband spread rumors about me, and I have a wretched reputation."

"I'm sure things will work out, and those rumors will die in time. Now give me the goblet."

"I don't have a dowry big enough for anyone to overlook my horrid reputation."

"I'm sure that reputation comes from actin' like anythin' but a lady." He moved closer.

"What do you care? You're not interested in me. You only kissed me because you wanted the cup."

"That may be so, but I assure ye I am enthralled by ye, lass." He looked down to his hardened form poking out under the breeches to prove his point.

"Please don't take the cup from me," she begged, moving backward as he moved forward. "I also want to use it to flesh out my family's killer."

"Ye said it happened when ye were a child," he told her,

obviously having listened to what she'd said after all. "Dinna ye think it is ridiculous that ye believe ye'll find yer family's killer all these years later?"

"Nay, I don't." She stopped when the back of her legs hit the bed.

"Well, I do. Besides, if they were Scots, then why would ye think they'd show up here? Especially when yer lord has forbidden any Scot to enter?"

"One of them was English, I told you. He is the one I am really looking for."

"Give it up, lass," he said, so close to her now that it tempted him to kiss her once again. Instead, he reached out and snatched the goblet from her, turning and heading toward the door, knowing what he had to do.

"North!" she cried out, causing him to stop in his tracks. "Turn around," she told him.

North turned around, ready to hear the girl beg him again not to take the goblet. He opened his mouth to speak, but turned speechless when he saw her standing there . . . stark naked. Her breasts were nicely rounded, and her pink nipples were so taut that there was no mistaking she was aroused. That thought only made him randier than he already was. His eyes swept down her body, and rested on the thatch of bright red curly hair nestled between her shapely thighs.

"I . . . I . . ." North's mouth became dry and his mind went blank. He didn't move, and neither could he seem to speak. He wanted this girl right now more than he'd ever wanted any woman in his life. She truly was a siren, and he had been entrapped by her silent song of the sea.

"Like what you see?" she asked playfully, rolling her hips as she padded across the floor in her bare feet. Next, she reached up and unpinned her hair, letting it all fall down loose around her shoulders.

He planned on turning and running from the room, but when she shook her hair out, he felt his manhood straining against his breeches even more. Her lips were parted slightly, and she had a look of desire on her face that could not be mistaken for anything else. She raised her hands and flipped her hair, making those voluptuous breasts jiggle even more. His eyes focused on them. They were begging to be suckled.

"If you're going to leave with my goblet, at least give me something to remember you by." She moved closer, as if she were stalking him now.

"Y-ye mean ye . . . want to couple with me? For real?" This was too good to be true.

"Would I be standing here naked, offering myself to you if I didn't?"

"But I . . . I dinna even ken ye, lass. No' really."

"What better way to get to know each other?" She smiled, reaching out and rubbing her hands down his chest. Then she hooked her fingers at the waist of his breeches, pulling them down, sinking to her knees as she did it.

MATILDA HAD ONLY meant to distract North enough to grab the goblet, and then her sword. But her act of playing a seductress suddenly took on a life of its own. When she pulled down his breeches, his hardened manhood popped out, almost hitting her in the face. Her eyes fastened to it. It was so long, so big . . . so delectably hard. She had to know how it felt in her hands.

Reaching out, she wrapped her fingers around his hardened form, reveling in the feel of silk over steel.

"Och, lass, ye dinna ken what ye are doin' to me." His voice was low and sultry.

She heard the goblet fall from his hand and hit the floor with a loud thunk. She was about to grab for it, when his hands cupped her head and he pulled her face closer to him. Matilda opened her mouth to object, but when she did, his manhood pressed between her lips.

"Open wider, lassie," he said. Before Matilda knew what was happening, she was pleasuring him with her mouth and then her tongue. It was the first time she had done something like this, but it was easy and exciting. She liked the way he moaned and fondled her head. Still, a part of her felt like she was acting like a whore and she knew this had to stop.

She pulled back and stood up. "I don't think I should have done that. I'm sorry."

"Losh me, ye're right." He scooped her up into his arms and carried her over to the bed. He put her down on the edge and got down on his knees.

"What are you doing, North?"

"I am the one who should be pleasurin' such a bonnie lass as ye. No' the other way around." He slid his hands up her legs little by little, getting closer and closer to her womanhood. Before she knew what was happening, his head was between her legs and he was using his mouth and tongue to arouse her in her most private place.

"Oh, my!" she gasped, holding on to his head this time, breathing heavy as her body came to life. "Oooooooh," she moaned, her eyes closing and her head falling back. Nothing else in the world mattered right now. This felt so naughty, but oh so good that she couldn't bring herself to make him stop.

"Ye have me so excited that I can barely wait." North got to his feet, laying her back on the bed. Matilda's eyes opened and she saw him removing his tunic and kicking off his boots and breeches that were pulled down to his knees. "Are ye sure ye want this, lass?"

All Matilda could do was nod. The Highlander had awakened a part of her that no man had ever done before. He aroused her so much that she could not stop now even if she tried. He awakened her femininity that she thought was dead. It was the best thing that could ever happen to her because it gave her hope. All those times with Alaric when she'd never gotten aroused was not because she couldn't. It was just because it was with the wrong man.

All Matilda could wonder now was what else he could do.

And how much better could he possibly make her feel.

"All right, then." He straddled himself over her, using his knee to push apart her legs. She was already wet from his foreplay, and her body vibrated, wanting more. His mouth came down on hers and he kissed her hard. She liked it. It felt as if he were claiming her as his lass.

Then his kisses trailed downward, until he'd covered one nipple with his mouth. He tugged at it, using his tongue in circles to arouse her even more.

She moaned and felt her back arching on its own. She gripped his head, pushing herself further into his mouth. "This feels so good," she cooed.

"Ye act as if ye have never had someone do this to ye before."

"I haven't," she admitted.

"But ye were married, lass. Ye have a child."

"I was married to a cur who never thought to please me. Only himself."

He lifted his head and looked at her as if he didn't believe her. "So, ye are sayin' that ye've never . . . found yer release?"

"I have never found anything with a man other than frustration," she replied.

"Och, lass, that is no' guid. I think I can do somethin' to remedy that. But let me ask ye once again . . . are ye sure ye want to do this?"

"I am more sure of this than of anything in my life. Please, North. Don't stop now. Don't turn me away." Matilda squirmed beneath him, feeling herself climbing that precipice that she'd often heard other women speak of. She wanted to feel that excitement for herself, for the first time in her life. She wanted to be pleasured and also to find her release.

"I'll be gentle," he promised, slowly slipping his length into her a little at a time, making her gasp. "It's too much, isna it? I'll pull out," he said, but Matilda gripped his shoulders, not allowing him to leave.

"If you leave me now, like this, I swear I'll hunt you down

and have your head."

"Well, that's no' the head I want ye to have." He grinned evilly now, and entered her fully. "Work with me," he told her, taking her hips, helping her to find a comfortable rhythm between them as he entered her and pulled back out and entered her yet again.

Matilda felt like she was in heaven. Her body cried out for this man, and everything he did only seemed to excite her more. It didn't take long before they both reached their peaks and she cried out in elation to have finally felt that special feeling that happens when a man and woman make love, bringing each other to completion.

They lay together in each other's arms, not talking, just breathing for a few minutes.

"That was . . . amazin'," said North.

"I agree," she said, giggling, thinking how crazy this whole thing was. She had been reckless and naughty and, honestly, she didn't care.

"My lady, are you in there?" A voice was heard from the corridor, and then pounding resounded on her door.

"My guard!" Matilda bolted upright. "Stay here and be quiet," she told North. She sprang from the bed, throwing his clothes to him and hurriedly closing the curtains around the bed. Then she quickly dressed.

"I'll see if she's in there," came Amethyst's voice from out in the corridor.

Matilda picked up her chain belt and wrapped it around her waist. "Just a moment," she called out, running to the door. Her foot hit the silver chalice that was no longer attached. She bent down and picked it up, securing it to the belt as the door opened and Amethyst walked inside.

"Matilda, we've been looking everywhere for you. Where have you been?" asked Amethyst.

"Why, I've been right here all along." She smiled, her eyes darting back to the bed.

"I thought you were going to take Norton to the ladies' solar so they could mend his breeches. My ladies tell me that neither of you were ever there."

"Right," she said, licking her lips. Her eyes traveled back to the bed. "I decided to come here. Instead." She cleared her throat.

"And do what?" asked Amethyst, looking at the bed. "Take a nap? I see your hair is all disheveled, and the bedcurtains are closed. You know that Marcus will have your head if he thinks you are sluffing off again." She marched over to the bed and yanked open the curtains.

"Wait!" screamed Matilda. "Amethyst, I can explain!" Matilda ran after her, but to her surprise, North was not on the bed.

"Will there be anything else, my lady?" the guard asked Amethyst from the door.

"Nay, you're dismissed," she answered with a wave of her hand. "Just please don't mention to my husband that his cousin was in bed in the middle of the day."

"Of course not, my lady." The guard bowed and closed the door.

Matilda's eyes scanned the room, but she didn't see North anywhere. Little did Amethyst realize that when she said Matilda was in bed in the middle of the day, she was more accurate than she thought.

"This room is a mess, Matilda." Amethyst walked over and slammed down the lid of the trunk. "What are these?" She bent down and picked up the boots that North had taken off.

"Oh, those," said Matilda, feeling a fluttering in her stomach. She really didn't want anyone to know what she had done. "I gave the Scot – I mean Norton some of Alaric's clothes to wear. I was going to give him those boots as well. The man is poor. He only had the clothes on his back. Or so he said." Her eyes looked downward. North must be hiding under the bed, she decided.

"Well, don't leave these out here where someone can trip over them. Keep them under the bed where shoes belong." Amethyst bent down, but Matilda rushed forward and took them from her.

"I'll do it." Matilda pushed the boots under the bed, looking for North. He wasn't there either. How could the man just have suddenly disappeared?

"Oh, Matilda, really." Amethyst marched over to the window next. "If Marcus sees that you never removed this rope and grappling hook from your window, you know he'll have a fit. Any thief in the night could use it to climb up here." She leaned over and pulled the rope up, rolling it into a coil and handing it to Matilda. "Now, please go down to the mews and instruct our new hires of how Marcus likes things done."

"Of course," said Matilda, glancing out the window. She saw North hurrying across the courtyard to the mews . . . barefooted. She giggled, feeling a blush rise to her face. She couldn't stop thinking of the amazing time she'd shared with this Highlander who was nothing more than a stranger. He'd brought her back to life and she liked feeling alive once again.

Amethyst got to the door and stopped. "Oh, I forgot to tell you. Marcus has had several men from the ball inquiring about courting you."

"What? Me?" That took Matilda by surprise.

"Yes, you."

"Well, I'm not interested," she said, shaking her head. Her gaze darted back out the window.

"Matilda, you are acting odd again. What is going on?"

"Nothing." She ran her hand over the goblet and smiled. She hoped to look innocent, even though she felt very naughty for what she'd just done.

"Well, I'm sure one of the three men will be perfect for you."

"Three men? What do you mean?"

"For a husband," said Amethyst. "That is what you wanted, wasn't it?"

"Well . . . aye."

"Marcus said you will spend time with each of the three men who has shown interest in marrying you. Then you will decide which one to wed."

"But what if I don't want any of them?" asked Matilda, only wanting North right now.

"If you can't decide, then Marcus said he will choose for you."

"Wonderful," said Matilda sarcastically, feeling disheartened. A day ago, she would have welcomed these new suitors with open arms. But now . . . now, the only man she wanted was the one she could not have. That is, the sexy Highlander, North MacKeefe.

CHAPTER TWELVE

"I HAD IT right there in my hand and was headed out the door." North paced back and forth in his bare feet, talking to his friends in the woods.

"Let me get this straight." Gavin took a flask from the back of his horse. "Ye had the damned cup, and then ye went back into the room and left through the window without it? Why?"

"It sounds to me as if ye're leavin' somethin' out, North." Cam yawned and leaned back against a rock. "Why did ye go back into the room in the first place?"

"Why do ye think?" growled North, pacing again, and this time stubbing his toe. "Ow!" He jumped up and down holding his foot.

"By the looks of yer bare feet and disheveled clothes, I'd say ye were busy beddin' the girl." Cam smiled. "Tell me I'm wrong, but I willna believe ye."

"Ye're right," said North with a sigh. "But I swear it was she who promoted it. She removed her clothin' to distract me. The lass was a sly seductress, I tell ye."

"Nice," said Cam, sitting up and taking attention. "So, how was it?"

"It was the best damned beddin' of my life. Damn it." North kicked at a stone and then moaned and held his foot again.

"Ye'd better put on Nash's boots before ye hurt yerself," said Gavin.

"Speakin' of Nash – how long do we intend to let him sit in the dungeon?" asked Cam. "I'm sure he's furious by now."

"No' to mention, he's wearin' a pair of lassie's shoes and his ankle is still swollen." Gavin went and sat at the fire next to Cam.

"Aye, I do feel bad about that," said North. "I never meant for anythin' to happen to my brathair."

"Mayhap ye should have thought about that before ye got distracted with the lass and lost the cup . . . again." Gavin shook his head in disgust.

"We need to do somethin' to get him out of there." Cam was usually the most relaxed of the group but, right now, he sounded very tense.

"We will do somethin'. Eventually. When the time is right," said North. "I'm sure the messenger will return from Hermitage Castle today. Then Nash will be set free when the earl realizes just who we are."

"I dinna think we should wait," said Gavin, standing up and pacing now as well.

"Me, neither," agreed Cam. He threw a stick into the fire. "I'm tired of just sittin' here waitin' while ye keep foulin' up a simple task." Cam got to his feet as well. "I'm goin' in to get that blasted cup."

"What?" North's head snapped around. "Nay. Ye canna do that!"

"Why no'?" asked Gavin. "I agree with Cam. It's time for another one of us to try to retrieve the goblet, or we'll never be headed back home to our wives."

"How hard can it be?" asked Cam with a chuckle. "It's a damned cup."

"Harder than ye think." North sat down and buried his face in his hands.

"Ye need to get back to the mews," said Gavin.

"Why?" North removed his hands from his face. "I canna go back there. The lass kens who I am now. I've ruined everythin'."

"Do ye think she'll tell anyone? Because I dinna believe she will," said Cam.

Cam always thought he knew the most when it came to the lassies. Mayhap he did, but North didn't want to admit it. Cam's self-importance was already overflowing.

"Why wouldna she tell anyone?" asked North. "After all, I tried to steal from her again."

"Did ye bring her to completion?" asked Cam. His blatant question shocked North, even though it shouldn't have. Cam had no qualms at all about speaking openly when it came to intimate matters.

"Och, aye." North smiled. "She said it was the first time in her life, too."

"Oh, hell, then she's no' tellin' a soul," said Gavin.

"Nay, she's no'," agreed Cam. "If ye ask me, she's goin' to be eager to see ye again. Then, ye'll have another chance to get the cup."

"Losh me, I dinna think so. She's a lady," protested North. "She only offered herself up to me in the first place because she didna want me leavin' with her prized possession. And it worked."

"She sounds like a sharp one," said Cam, chuckling once again.

North continued his story. "She said her faither gave her the vessel when she was a child. Then it was stolen by the Scots."

"How can that be?" asked Gavin. "I've always heard that the chalice was made for our king. It belongs to the Scots, no' the English."

"I dinna ken," North answered. "All I care about is gettin' it back so I am no longer an outcast."

"Then force the girl to hand it over to ye," said Cam.

"Nay," North answered. "I like her. She's a fine lass, and I dinna want her to get the wrong idea about me."

"Here we go again." Gavin swigged down some whisky. "Go back to the mews, North, and be sure to sneak to the dungeon and check on Nash."

"How am I goin' to do that? I'm hired help," North told him. "I willna ever be invited back into the castle."

"Never mind," said Cam, jumping up. "I've got this handled. Ye just go back to the mews and wait for my word."

"Wait. What are ye goin' to do?" North looked at him suspiciously, not liking this idea at all.

"Somethin' ye should have done long before now," answered Cam.

North had a bad feeling about this. He felt it in his gut that something was about to go terribly wrong.

⟫⟫⟩✕⟨⟪⟪

"LADY MATILDA, THIS is Lord John Burroughs of Suffolk," said Marcus, standing out in the courtyard, introducing the first suitor to her.

"How do you do?" Matilda nodded. She had just visited the mews, leaving North's boots there for him to find them later. She had met Walter as she left the mews, but didn't see North anywhere and wondered where he was.

"I saw you at the dance, my lady, and was instantly fascinated by you." The man's eyes weren't on her face, but on the cup dangling from her side. "May I?" He held out his hand.

Matilda sighed, giving him her hand even though she figured he was asking to see the cup. He was already not to her liking. He was shorter than her and probably ten years her senior. He had a wiry mustache and such a thin chin that he reminded her of a girl. As he kissed the back of her hand, her gaze went over his head. She saw Walter standing by the mews, holding a falcon on his gloved hand, waiting for her.

"If you'll excuse me, my falconer requires my presence," said Matilda.

"Cousin, you'll take Lord Burroughs with you," scolded Marcus. "After all, he has expressed interest in your hand."

"You mean my goblet," she mumbled.

Marcus glared. He walked over and whispered in her ear, "You will choose one of the three suitors to wed. If you don't, I will do it for you."

"I think I've changed my mind," she whispered back. "Perhaps it isn't so important to have a husband after all."

"You're doing it for Robbie," he reminded her.

Matilda looked over to her son, playing with the children in the courtyard. Her heart went out to him. He deserved a father.

"Fine. Will you escort me to the mews, Lord Burroughs?" she asked.

"It's my pleasure." He held out his arm and she reluctantly took it. They headed over to the mews together.

"So, is that silver chalice part of the dowry?" He still hadn't looked at her face once.

"Yes, it is," she answered staring forward.

"What else does the dowry include?"

God's eyes, the man was greedy. It was already obvious that he only wanted her for her money. Too bad he didn't realize she didn't have any. Then again, mayhap he should know. Aye, Matilda decided to tell him.

"Oh, just the goblet is the entire dowry, and it doesn't leave my side. Ever. You see, I have no money, and a horrid reputation as well. Haven't you heard?"

"There's nothing else included in the dowry?" asked the man. She felt the muscles in his arm tighten. Funny how he never even seemed to hear her say she had a bad reputation.

"There's the cup, and the honor of being my husband. That's it," she said. "Isn't it enough?"

"I was told that the chalice as well as a suitable-sized dowry would accompany the betrothal, if I decided to take the offer."

"The offer?" Matilda started feeling like nothing more than a business deal. Of course, that is really all that betrothals were, marrying for alliances and not love. She'd married Alaric years ago just for an alliance. She'd been miserable every day of her life as well. Nay, she wasn't about to make the same mistake again. The next time she married, if she ever did, she would marry for love, she decided. "Lord Burroughs, I'm sorry to have wasted your time, but I can see that I'm not what you're looking for." She decided to turn things around and fan his male pride.

"Nay, I don't believe you are."

"You need a rich woman for a bride because that is what you deserve. I'm sorry if my cousin made this sound like something it isn't, but if you marry me, you'll be broke for the rest of your life."

He let go of her arm and cleared his throat. "I really need to leave now. I'd like to thank the earl myself for his generous offer, but perhaps you will do it for me, as I am in a hurry."

"Don't worry, I will let him know you didn't find me suitable," she said with a smile.

"Thank you, my lady." The greedy fool almost fell over his own feet as he left at a near run, just trying to get away from her.

"My lady," said Walter, the new falconer, coming to join her. "The earl asked me to bring you your falcon." The man held the jesses too tightly, and the bird fluttered its wings, trying to get away.

"Walter, that isn't mine, it is Lady Amethyst's falcon. My bird is a hawk. I highly doubt Lord Marcus told you anything, since he knows what kind of bird I have and just which one it is. Too bad I can't say the same for you."

The man looked at the bird and scowled. "Aye, I know yours is a hawk. What I meant was, Lord Marcus asked me to give his wife's falcon . . . some air. I'll go get your hawk now." He leaned far away from the bird and almost seemed afraid of the thing. Shouldn't a falconer be more at ease in the mews?

"Wait," she said as the man started away. "Have you seen your assistant, Norton, at all today?"

"That fool?" asked the man.

"What did you say?" She didn't like this man's attitude at all. He didn't seem to hold any respect for anyone, nor did he know as much about birds as he claimed to. Also, something about his voice unnerved her. She didn't know what it was, but when he spoke, she noticed her legs shaking.

"My lady, I saw Norton along with another man headed toward the keep earlier."

"You did?" She turned around and shaded her eyes but didn't see him. "Where were they headed?"

"I'm not sure. They were both wearing long cloaks with hoods covering their heads. I think they were headed toward the dungeon." The bird fluttered its wings again, and Walter held up his other hand to his face as if protecting himself. He almost looked scared if Matilda wasn't mistaken.

"Please put Lady Amethyst's falcon back. And do not hold the jesses so tightly. The bird doesn't like it."

"Yes, of course." He continued to lean away from the bird, heading back into the mews.

"Matilda, there you are." Amethyst hurried over to join her. "Where is Lord Burroughs?" She looked around. "Marcus told me you two were going to go with the falconer to fly your hawk. Are you finished already?"

"Hrmph. More than you know," she answered with a sniff. "Lord Burroughs asked me to inform Marcus that he is no longer interested in marrying me."

"Oh, I'm sorry." Amethyst took her by the hands. "I know how much you want a husband."

"Well, not him! He was only after my dowry. Never once did he even look at my face."

"I'm confused," said Amethyst. "Isn't that why you are dangling that silver chalice in front of all available men? To lure them in?"

"Mayhap I was, but I've changed my mind. If I marry again, I want it to be for love."

"Matilda, what are you saying? You know that marriages are usually done for alliances and have nothing to do with love at all."

"You're in love with my cousin, aren't you?"

"Well, yes."

"Then I want a man I can love as well."

"I hope one of the other two suitors will prove to be what you're looking for, then." Amethyst had a good heart and Matilda knew she would want her to be happy.

A guard approached and bowed before them. "Lady Amethyst, the messenger has arrived from Hermitage Castle with a missive from their laird regarding the men who claim to be MacKeefes."

"Oh, wonderful," said Amethyst. "I'll get my husband immediately. Tell the messenger to join us in the great hall right away."

"Aye, my lady." The guard bowed again, and left.

"Lady Matilda, I've sharpened and polished your sword as you've asked," said the blacksmith, approaching and using two hands to return her weapon.

"Thank you, Garth, that will be all."

She took a second to admire her sword, and then slipped it into the sheath on her weapon belt.

"You will scare away any potential husband wearing that," Amethyst told her.

"Good," she said, feeling as if that were exactly what she wanted to do.

"Pardon me, Matilda. I need to find Marcus and tell him about the missive," said Amethyst.

"By all means." Matilda was glad Amethyst chose to leave, because this would give her time to find North now. She picked up her skirts and headed toward the dungeon.

CHAPTER THIRTEEN

"YE KEEP A lookout," Cam whispered to North, stopping in front of the door to the dungeon. "I'll take out the dungeon guard and steal the keys and set Nash free."

"Hurry up about it," said North, nervously looking over the grounds to make sure they wouldn't be spotted. "And dinna kill the guard."

"What difference does it make?" asked Cam.

"I dinna want any deaths on our heads. Remember, until I have that goblet, I have to stay here. I'm still no' even sure if Matilda will give away my identity or no'. We dinna need any more problems."

"I ken lassies better than anyone, North. Believe me, she willna say a word about ye."

"Go," commanded North. "I think I hear someone comin'."

Cam disappeared inside, but North had the feeling he needed to follow his friend. After all, this was his brother they were trying to spring from the dungeon. He should be the one doing it, not Cam. Turning, he slipped through the door, following the lit torches to the guard post. When he got there, Cam was standing over a guard with his sword raised up. The guard was unconscious on the floor.

"Nay!" North shot forward, stilling Cam's hand. "I said, dinna kill him." North bent over and snatched the keys from the unconscious guard. "We have to hurry. Stay here and watch. I'll get Nash." He ran over to the door blocking the cells, unlocking it, and retrieving the key. "Nash? Are ye in here?" he called out.

"North, if that is ye, I'm goin' to kill ye," came his twin brother's reply from one of the cells.

"God's eyes, it is dark and dank in here and smells like piss." North used the key to unlock his brother's cell door.

"I canna believe ye left me in here to rot!" Nash swung at him but North grabbed him by the arm.

"Stop it. We can talk about this later. Right now, we need to get ye out of here."

"What took ye so long?" Nash ground out. "Do ye have the cup yet? Can we go home now?" He shot one question after another at North. Then he looked down. "Are those my boots ye're wearin' while I wear the blasted shoes of a wench?"

"They might be," said North, not wanting to explain more.

"Give me my damned boots before I wrestle you to the ground to get them."

"Calm down, Brathair. Here, take the blasted boots." North removed the boots and handed them over, standing there barefooted while Nash shoved his feet into them.

"Tell me what's going on," said Nash.

"The fool had the cup but lost it again," said Cam, over North's shoulder.

North spun around, pulling his sword out from under the cloak.

"Calm down. It's me." Cam's hands shot up in the air.

"I thought I told ye to keep watch," whispered North.

"I am watchin'. However, I'm with Nash on this one. I would have slugged ye, too."

"I meant for ye to watch the door, ye simpkin," hissed North.

"North? Are you in here?" called out a feminine voice from outside the gate.

"God's bones, it's Matilda," said North in a hoarse whisper. "What is she doin' here?"

"Why is she callin' ye by yer real name?" asked Nash, looking at him suspiciously.

"Never mind. I'll tell ye later. Just follow my lead." North hurried back to the guard room to see Matilda staring down at the prone guard.

"Oh!" she gasped, as North stepped out, followed by Cam and Nash. Matilda's head snapped around and North saw fear in her eyes. "Ye killed him?" She clutched something in her arms.

"Nay! It's all right, lass. The guard will be fine," North assured her.

"What are you doing in here?" she spat, eyeing up the other two. "Are you helping our prisoner escape?"

"Matilda, this is my friend, Cam, and my twin brathair, Nash." It was a strange time to do it, but North made the introductions. "They've done nothin' wrong, I assure ye."

"Your twin?" She glanced over at Nash. "He doesn't look much like you for being a twin."

"I agree. I'm the handsome one," said Nash flashing her a smile.

"Are those my boots?" asked North, realizing what she was holding.

"Aye. I left them in the mews, but when Walter told me he saw you coming this direction, I thought I'd bring them to you." She looked down to see his bare feet. "I can see you need them."

"Thank ye." North took the boots and put them on.

"Brathair, are ye goin' to tell us why she has yer boots?" asked Nash.

"Get back in the cell." Matilda surprised North by unsheathing her sword and holding it out toward them. He hadn't thought she'd even be wearing it around the castle.

"Why do ye even have that on right now?" asked North, nodding to her sword.

"I told you before, I can take care of myself, and this is how."

"I'll handle this," said Cam, stepping forward, but North, grabbed his arm to stop him. He unsheathed his sword as well.

"I've got it," said North. "Ye get Nash out of here before she alerts anyone."

"Whatever you say." Cam and Nash walked past Matilda as North kept her at bay with his sword. Once they left the dungeon and went outside, North reached out and grabbed her arm, slowly lowering her blade.

"Dinna give us trouble, lassie. We are no' here to hurt anyone. I just couldna leave my brathair in the dungeon."

"Why don't you just leave, North? What is keeping you here at Montclair Castle anyway?" she asked, raising her chin in challenge.

"I told ye, I willna leave without the cup."

"And I told you that I will never part with it, so you'll have to go home empty-handed."

"Mmph," he grunted, pulling her to him and kissing her, not able to stop himself from doing so. "The feistier ye are, the more I want ye. Now, stay here and tend to the guard and dinna tell anyone a thing."

He left her there, heading out after his friends.

MATILDA'S LIPS TINGLED from North's kiss, and her jaw ached from clenching her teeth since she was so angry with him right now that she could scream. Did he really think a kiss would shut her up? He was controlling her with her want for him, and she didn't like it. What bothered her even more was that his ploy seemed to work every time.

"Wake up." Matilda bent over and shook the guard by the shoulder. "Someone has released the prisoner, and you need to sound the warning bell."

"What?" The guard sat up and shook his head. Then he sprang to his feet, grabbed his sword, and ran out the door.

"RING THE BELL and close the gate! The prisoner has escaped,"

called out the prison guard, just as Nash and Cam got to the middle of the courtyard. North was a little ways behind them since he had stayed back to talk to Matilda.

"Damn," spat North, looking back over his shoulder. He had hoped for a little more time before Matilda ran off her mouth, exposing them. He could see Nash leaning on Cam, trying to walk with his twisted ankle. Cam was doing his best to help Nash, but it was really slowing them down. North wanted to run up and help him but, unfortunately, it was too late.

The portcullis could be heard lowering to the ground as the warning bell in the tower cried out. Everyone had been alerted of their attempt to release Nash.

"There they are," called out a guard from the battlements, pointing at Nash and Cam. North quickly dove into the mews so he wouldn't be spotted.

"What's going on?" asked Walter from inside the mews. He walked over to the door and looked out, donning his falconer's glove. North noticed an ugly scar running down the top of the man's hand, realizing why he kept it covered now.

"Dinna say a word," North warned him, still holding his sword in his hand. The man looked down at it and then back out to the courtyard.

"You're a Scot!" he said in an accusing manner. "And you have a sword. You're not a falconer's assistant."

"That's right," answered North. "And neither are ye an Irishman or even a falconer at all. Ye didna fool me for a minute. It is obvious that ye dinna ken the first thing about birds."

"You have no proof of that."

"Who are ye? Really? Tell me." North saw the man look down at North's sword.

"I am just a man out of luck, looking for a job, that's all."

"Ye are devious to try to fool these good people."

"And you're not?" the man answered with a cocky smile.

"If ye say a word to them about me, I'll tell Lord Marcus that ye are an imposter as well."

The man hesitated for a second before answering. "All right. I'll be quiet," he promised, stepping away from North.

North leaned against the door frame of the mews, still gripping his sword. He would fight if needed, because he wouldn't let anyone ever hurt Nash or Cam.

⟫⟫⟫⟪⟪⟪

MATILDA RAN OUT to the courtyard to find the guards holding Nash and Cam, but North was nowhere to be seen. Marcus ran up with his sword in his grip, followed by Amethyst and more of his men.

"Mother, what's wrong?" Robbie came to her, followed by Beatrice.

"I'm sorry, my lady, I tried to stop him," apologized the nursemaid.

"It's fine. I've got him," said Matilda, scooping up her son and holding him close to her chest.

"Release us," cried out Cam, trying to fight his way free. Marcus slammed his fist into Cam's face and knocked his sword to the ground.

"Get his weapon," Marcus ordered his guard.

"What is going on?" asked Amethyst.

"Two men tried to release the prisoner," the dungeon guard reported.

"Two men?" asked Marcus. "I only see one. Is there another?"

"Nay, he meant one," said Matilda, hurrying over to them.

"Nay, there were two," protested the guard.

Matilda had to do something to keep them from finding North. "I was there and found this guard lying unconscious on the ground. I'm sure he's just confused."

"Well, mayhap," said the guard, rubbing his head, looking embarrassed.

"Who are you, and why are you trying to steal my prisoner?"

asked Marcus.

"I am Cam MacKeefe and this is my friend, Nash. We have done nothin' wrong. I demand that ye release us at once."

"I just received an answer to my missive that I sent to your chieftain at Hermitage Castle." Marcus held up the parchment to show them.

"Guid," said Nash. "That'll prove that we tell the truth of who we are."

"On the contrary, it's just the opposite," said Marcus. "Your chieftain claims there is no MacKeefe named West, and that they didn't send anyone here to Montclair Castle."

"What?" both Nash and Cam said together.

"Why would ye ask about anyone named West?" Nash shook his head, frustrated.

"That is what my guard told me that one of your names was," answered Marcus.

"None of us are named West," scoffed Cam. "Of course they wouldna ken us by that name."

"Still, they should have realized it was us here," said Nash. "We were sent here on a mission by the chieftain's grandda."

"Sorry, but your chieftain didn't seem to even know that," answered Marcus. "And I highly doubt the man's grandfather is still alive. It is clear you are lying."

"Nay. That isna true," said Nash. "I canna believe our chieftain would deny us."

"Me, neither," said Cam. "Plus, he would ken that our friend's name is North, not West."

"Friend?" asked Marcus. "So there are more of you then. That's right. I thought there were three of you imposters at the dance. Is that all, or are there even more?"

The Scots didn't answer.

"Let me see that missive," said Matilda, handing her son to the nursemaid and taking the message from Marcus, scanning it quickly. "He's right. Ian MacKeefe swears not to know you men."

"Ian MacKeefe?" asked Nash, followed by a groan.

"No' Storm?" asked Cam, looking like he'd lost all hope.

"My messenger said Storm was in the Highlands so he spoke to your other laird, Ian instead," Marcus relayed the information.

"But Ian is sick and losin' his mind," Cam told him. "Lately, he wouldna ken his own name half the time if ye asked him."

"Didna the messenger talk to Lady Clarista or Lady Wren?" asked Nash. "They would vouch for us."

"I'm sorry, he just spoke to Ian and came right back with the message, as I instructed," said Marcus. "Men, take these two to the dungeon."

"Now wait a minute," said Cam, as the guards hauled both Cam and Nash back to the prison cells. "I just got married. I canna be shoved into a nasty cell."

"I kent this was too guid to be true," complained Nash. "North, I'm goin' to kill ye, Brathair," he shouted at the top of his lungs.

Matilda watched as they escorted the men back to the dungeon. Her heart went out to North's brother and friend. Now, she wished she would have given them a little more time to get away. She'd been sure the missive from Hermitage Castle would have cleared them, but it had only seemed to make things worse.

Matilda looked around the courtyard, trying to spot North. He was nowhere to be seen. Perhaps she needed to apologize to him. But she was never going to get to do that if she couldn't even find him. Right now, she wasn't even sure she'd ever see him again.

✦•◦◇◦•✦

CHAPTER FOURTEEN

"I STILL CANNA believe that both Cam and Nash are in the dungeon now!" Gavin was still griping about this the next morning, and it was getting hard for North to even think with all his complaining.

"I told ye, I'll take care of it," said North for the tenth time now.

"Just like ye've done so far?"

"It was Cam's lame idea to storm the dungeon and get Nash out. I told ye both that Nash was better off there until I can collect the cup."

"This shouldn't be such a hard task, North. What is it that's keepin' ye from doin' it?"

North didn't want to admit to Gavin that he wasn't in a hurry to get the chalice anymore, because he liked being around Matilda. If he had the cup and they managed to free Cam and Nash, then they'd have to go back to Scotland. His heart ached thinking about leaving the lass behind. He'd grown fond of her since they'd been intimate. He couldn't stop thinking about her, and even dreamed of her at night. And in the morning, he woke up with a hard-on. Egads, he'd never thought he'd be in this position. Why was this happening to him?

"I still canna believe that Ian said he didna ken us." It wasn't the first time this morning that Gavin said this either. He was becoming redundant.

"I can," North answered. "After all, Ian is losin' his mind. If Storm had been there, or even Clarista or Wren, things would be different right now. Cam and Nash would be free to go and the earl would gladly hand me the goblet."

"Do ye really believe that? About the goblet?" asked Gavin with a raised brow. "It seems to me by what ye've said that the girl will never release it. I just dinna understand this at all."

"She told me part of her story, but I need to get closer to her to learn more."

"Then do it," snapped Gavin.

"Really?" North smiled, getting this approval from his good friend.

"Ye just do whatever the hell ye have to do, but I am no longer goin' to sit around waitin' for somethin' to happen."

"Gavin, I'm no' sure I like the tone of yer voice. What does that mean?"

"It means I am goin' to figure out a way to get into the castle and get that damned cup so we can go home."

"Remember, that was Cam's intent, too, and now he sits in the dungeon along with Nash."

"Well, I dinna have a choice. The longer they are there, the bigger the risk. Since Ian said he doesna ken us, Lord Marcus could decide to behead them both tomorrow."

"Nay. That canna happen." North paced back and forth at their camp in the woods, running his hand through his long hair. "I'll talk to Matilda. I'll get her to convince Marcus to send a missive to Storm at our Highland camp instead."

"Dinna be daft, North. No Sassenach is goin' to take a missive all the way to the Highlands and ye ken it."

"Well, then mayhap they can take a missive to Callum at the Horn and Hoof instead. Callum will vouch for us. After all, he's the one who sent us on this doitit mission."

"Ye do that," said Gavin, getting atop his horse.

"Where are ye goin'?"

"I'm headed to the village to hire a lad to watch our horses while I retrieve the cup."

"And just how do ye plan on doin' that?"

"I have a few tricks up my sleeve. Ye just get back to the mews and convince Matilda to have the earl send that missive to Glasgow. I will take care of the rest."

"TAKE THE SAGE potion twice a day for cramping, but discontinue its use as soon as your courses are over. Too much of anything for too long of a time will only cause problems." Matilda reached into her basket and handed a vial of liquid to one of the ladies of the castle.

"Thank you so much," said the woman, smiling and walking away with it.

Matilda had been working with herbs her whole life and was considered the healer of the castle. She liked being useful. It made her feel as if she were pulling her weight.

She turned to go, gasping as she bumped into someone. She dropped the basket, the vials clinking together as they hit the ground. Thankfully, they didn't break.

"Sorry about that, lass."

"North!" Matilda's heart fluttered when she saw him standing before her in his falconry attire. "I was afraid you left the castle after yesterday."

"I told ye, I wouldna leave without my brathair or my friend." He hunkered down and picked up the spilled vials, perusing them curiously. Then he gently placed them back into the basket and handed it to her. "I heard ye talkin' to that lass."

"That was a private conversation. You shouldn't have been listening."

"This sage ye speak of. Is it guid for anything else?" he asked.

"Like what?" She wondered just what he was up to now. "Are you ailing from something?"

"Nay, no' me. But our chieftain has been ill lately. He seems to be losin' his memory. Can any of those herbs possibly help him?"

"Well, yes, mayhap. Sage is good for the brain and the memory in general."

"Guid. I'll take some." He started to reach into the basket but she slapped his hand away.

"Nay, you can't just start giving someone an herb without knowing what is causing their ailment in the first place."

"That's just it. No one kens."

"What are some of his symptoms?" she asked.

"I'm no' sure, but he is irritable and sometimes gets dizzy and falls. He canna walk right. Sometimes he even hallucinates. All this, and he's been said to be losin' his mind as well."

"Hmmm," she said. "I've heard the same thing said about me at times." She looked down at her basket, organizing the vials.

"Ye have? Are ye ill?" he asked, sounding truly concerned.

"Nay, just reckless. And sometimes very stupid."

"Dinna say that about yerself, lass. Ye are brave and smart, as well as very allurin'." He placed his hand on her arm, wanting more than anything to touch her again.

Her eyes darted back and forth. "You need to let go of me before someone sees you. It isn't proper to be touching a lady. You'll end up in the dungeon if you're not careful."

"Sorry," he said, releasing her. "I canna help myself when I'm around ye. I want to touch ye, and do so much more."

"Don't apologize." She let out a deep sigh. "I'm the one who is sorry," she told him. "I didn't mean for your friends to get into trouble. I wish there was something I could do to help them."

"There is," said North. "Ye can convince the earl to send another missive askin' about us."

"What good would that do? Ian MacKeefe already said he didn't know you."

"That's because he's losin' his mind, I tell ye." He seemed to be losing patience with her. "This time, have Lord Marcus send the missive to Old Callum MacKeefe at the Horn and Hoof Tavern in Glasgow."

"Callum?" she asked.

"Aye. That is Ian's faither. He's also the man who bestowed this punishment on me, requirin' me to retrieve the chalice I lost or be an outcast forever."

"Ye had my chalice?" she asked, confused

"Well, nay. No' really. It was Storm's, but I borrowed it. And then it was stolen by thieves."

"Those pirates," she said, thinking back to the pirates she'd had the confrontation with on Grope Lane.

"Aye, that's them. But at least they dinna have it any longer. Now that I found the goblet, there is hope I can be redeemed and welcomed back into my clan."

"I'm not handing the cup over, if that is what you're hinting at."

"Nay, lass. I'm no' askin' ye to do that, although I wish ye would. I'm only askin' for yer help concernin' my brathair and my guid friend right now. Ye see, it is my fault they are in this position and they dinna deserve it. They both just got married and need to be home with their new wives."

"Oh, they have wives," she said, wondering now if she should consider his request. It made her sad to think that the men couldn't be with their new brides. It made her even sadder that she didn't have a husband. "I'll think about it," she told him, still not convinced she should give up her possession.

"Lady Matilda, will you come with me to the mews?" Walter walked up, interrupting them.

"What's the matter, Falconer? Is something wrong with one of the birds?" asked Matilda.

"Nay. I just wanted to go over a few things with you. After all, I am new here and need to know how you want things done."

"Oh. Of course." She was hesitant to go, because she didn't like this new falconer. Something about him made her feel cautious. "Norton, you'll come with us, of course. It's best if you learn at the same time."

"Nay, my lady. There's no need for him." The falconer scowled. "I had hoped to talk to you alone. In private."

"Well I . . ."

"Lady Matilda has requested my presence, Walter," said North, back to his English accent again. "Do you have a problem with me being there? After all, I am your assistant."

"That's right," said Matilda. "I want Norton there as well."

Walter hesitated, and then scowled at North. North gave him an odd look back. Somehow, Matilda got the distinct feeling there was something going on between them that she knew nothing about.

"Matilda," called out Marcus just as they were about to enter the mews. She turned to see her cousin heading over with another man she figured wanted to marry her.

"Oh, nay," she groaned. "Go on into the mews and I'll meet you there, Walter. There is something I have to take care of first."

"I'll come with ye," whispered North, once the other man left. When they were alone, North went back to talking like a Scot.

"Nay, North. This is a suitor who my cousin has chosen for me. I don't think it would be proper for you to be standing at my side when I meet him."

"Suitor? As in, a possible husband?" asked North.

"That's what it means. There are three of them, and Marcus has told me to choose one to marry, or he'll do it for me."

"Ye're goin' to marry?" This seemed to upset North for some odd reason.

"Well, yes, of course I'd like to marry again someday. It is important that Robbie has a father to guide him while he's growing up. He needs a strong male to look up to who will someday teach him how to be a man."

"Isna that why nobles usually send their sons away to be fostered when they're about seven?"

Matilda didn't want to think of her son possibly leaving her.

Robbie was all she had. "He's only four," she retorted. "And I don't see that it is any of your concern. So, please, stay out of this."

"Oh. I see."

"Go now," she said, sending him away.

NORTH WATCHED FROM the shadows as Marcus introduced the suitor to Matilda as Lord Ralph Danneville of Devon. He was an older man, and North didn't think he would even know what to do with a young boy like Robbie. North loved children, and now wished he had told Matilda that earlier. Not that it would make a difference. Still, he wanted her to think of him as a strong male who might someday be a good influence on her young son.

He pretended to be busy fixing the wattle and daub on the side of the mews, but he was actually straining his ears to listen to Matilda and the old suitor. He had to know what they were saying.

"IT'S MY PLEASURE to meet you, Lord Danneville," said Matilda, noticing North watching from the shadows and most likely listening to every word she said. It pleased her, actually. That told her that, perhaps, he was jealous. And if North was jealous, that meant he had feelings for her after all. Still, being a spy was not an honorable trait. If he was going to watch, then she decided she'd give him something to see.

"I'll leave you two to get acquainted," said Marcus, nodding and walking away.

"Do you like children, Lord Danneville?" Matilda spoke loudly so North would be sure to hear.

"Children?" the man asked, glancing at the cup dangling at her side. Then, he looked back up to her face. "Oh, yes, I adore them. I have six of my own," he told her. "Of course, they are all grown now. I believe a few of them are even older than you."

"Your children are older than me?" she gasped. That struck a note of fear in her heart. Now she wished North hadn't heard that part. Glancing over her shoulder once again, she noticed he was still watching her. "Oh, that's wonderful," she told Lord Danneville. "Mayhap your grown children will want to help take care of my son, Robbie." She didn't know what else to say. However, by the grouchy look on Lord Danneville's face, she could tell he wasn't pleased at all.

"You have a son?" he asked, becoming fidgety. "No one told me this." He glanced down at the silver goblet again – probably the only thing keeping him there right now.

"Yes, Robbie is four years old now, and a very bright boy. Would you like to meet him? After all, it is important that he takes well to the man I'm to marry since the man will also be Robbie's father. Don't you agree that his opinion is important in this matter as well?"

"A four-year-old boy? Having an opinion on the man you marry?" The man seemed outraged now.

"Uh huh," she said, picking up the chalice hanging at her side, running her finger around the rim. His eyes focused on it again.

"Well, I . . . I suppose so," he finally answered, almost choking on the words.

"Robbie," Matilda called out, turning around to call her son to her.

"I've got him," said North, walking up with Robbie in his arms. She almost moaned out loud – with desire. The Highlander looked good holding her son. He looked so masculine, and so protective. Robbie was smiling and seemed to like North. That made her feel even better. Lady Gert followed at North's heels, wagging her tail. Even the dog seemed to like North now. Matilda's heart about burst from her chest. Why did this look like the perfect image of a family to her?

"Why, there you are, Robbie," she said with a nervous giggle. "What are you doing with Norton?" She quickly looked back at her suitor, feeling the need to explain before rumors started. "Norton is my assistant falconer."

"North is going to play ball with me and Gertie," said Robbie happily. "He said he's going to teach me and Gertie how to play hide and seek, too. I like him. He's funny and makes me laugh."

"Does he, now?" she asked, her heart racing since her son just called the Highlander North. "His name is Norton, Son," she said, her eyes flashing over to North when she said it. North was smiling from ear to ear. She wondered just what kind of game he was playing. "And you and Lady Gert shouldn't be bothering him, he has work to do."

"Who is Lady Gert?" asked Lord Danneville. "And why on earth would a lady want to play with a child? A lady's place is in the solar, or tending to her husband's many needs."

"I play ball with my son, and I am a lady," said Matilda, despising his attitude toward women and wanting to set him straight. Her cousin, Marcus, had been just like this at one time until he met Amethyst. Thankfully, Amethyst managed to change him. "For your information, Lord Danneville, Lady Gert is my dog."

"And what a fine hound she is," said North, shifting Robbie to his other hip and reaching down to pet the dog on the head. "You'll never find one better. She's a terrific watchdog, too." The dog looked up at North, and Matilda saw North drop some food into the hound's mouth. Gertie then licked his hand.

Well, now Matilda realized why Gertie had finally stopped growling at him. North was a clever one at getting what he wanted, she'd give him credit for that.

"Yes, Gertie is very devoted to those who pamper her." Matilda glanced up at North and gave him a sarcastic smile.

"Do you like hounds, Lord Danneville?" asked North. "Lady Matilda sleeps with this one in her bed."

"I do what?" Matilda gasped, too shocked by his words to deny them, even though they weren't true. The dog was much too big for her bed and slept at the side of the bed on the floor instead.

"That dog sleeps in her bed?" Lord Danneville looked flustered.

"That's right," said North, tickling Robbie and making him giggle.

"And tell me – how would you know that, as the assistant falconer?" Lord Danneville crossed his arms over his chest, glaring at both Matilda and North now.

"Yes, I'd like to hear the answer to that as well," said Matilda through gritted teeth.

"Well, you see, Lady Matilda shares *everything* with me," answered North, stressing the word everything, making Matilda cringe even more. "We're very close, I guess you could say."

"I guess so!" snapped Lord Danneville, his jaw dropping open, and his hands falling to his sides.

"Stop it," Matilda whispered to North, feeling her face flushing right now from embarrassment. She wished North wouldn't say these things in front of her suitor or her son. She would have to have a word with him in private about it later.

"Pet the hound," North persuaded Lord Danneville. "Get to know her since she'll probably be sleeping between you and your wife. I mean . . . if you marry Matilda. Lady Matilda," he added quickly, using her title.

"Well, I don't know." The man backed away instead of moving forward. Matilda could tell he didn't like dogs in the least. She also wasn't so sure he really liked children.

"Go on, Gertie. Say hello to Lord Danneville." Matilda took the dog's collar and pulled her over to her suitor. "You can pet her. She won't bite," she told the man.

"Nice dog," said Lord Danneville, keeping his distance, and using short slaps atop the dog's head. Matilda was certain the man had never even touched a dog in his entire life.

Gertie growled at him and showed her teeth, the same way she did when she'd first met North after he'd sneaked into her bedchamber through the open window. When the dog moved her head quickly, her slobber splashed up on the suitor. And then, to Matilda's surprise, the dog snapped at him as well.

"God's eyes, put a muzzle on that beast!" Lord Danneville pulled his hand away quickly, holding it to his chest. "The thing almost bit me, and soiled my clothes with its drool."

"Gertie!" Matilda cried out. "That wasn't nice. I'm so sorry, Lord Danneville," she apologized. "I don't know what got into her."

"Why don't you see if Lord Danneville wants to play ball?" asked North, putting Robbie down. As soon as the boy walked over to the man, North threw a ball to him, purposely aiming too high, if Matilda wasn't mistaken.

Gertie loved to play ball so, of course, the hound lunged for it. Robbie screamed and ran to Matilda, and the dog came down atop Lord Danneville, knocking him to the ground.

"Lord Danneville," cried Matilda, glaring at North. "Help him up, Norton."

"Aye. Of course." North's smile was most aggravating right now. "Let me give you a hand. Ooops," said North, letting his hand slip, causing the man to fall back on the ground a second time. "Sorry about that. The dog's slobber on my hand is a little slippery." The dog ran over, dropping the ball on Lord Danneville's chest and drooling in his face.

"Bid the devil, get this wretched thing away from me." Lord Danneville swiped at the hound with one arm.

"Allow me to help you," said Matilda, stretching out her arm but, of course, a man would never take help from a woman.

"Lord Danneville, are you all right?" called out Marcus, running over and helping the man to his feet. "What is going on here?" he asked, glaring at Matilda.

"It was my fault," North interrupted, stepping forward. "I never should have thrown the ball to the dog. My aim was too high."

"I apologize, my lord," Marcus told the man. "I'm sure you'll want to join me for some ale in the great hall to calm down."

"Nay, I won't! I don't want to stay here another minute, and I want nothing to do with this woman. Ever," spat the man, wiping dirt from his clothes. "I will leave now," he said, huffing and puffing as he turned and headed for the gate.

"Of course. Let me see you out," called Marcus with his hand in the air. He glanced back over his shoulder and scowled at Matilda once more. She smiled and shrugged her shoulders.

"Goodbye, Lord Danneville. I had a ball," Matilda shouted to the man.

As soon as they walked away, North started laughing. "Had a ball. I get it. Ye are too funny."

"Go play, Robbie," said Matilda, sending her son and the dog away. Then she looked up at North. "I was angry at you but, actually, I have decided I'm glad I don't have to marry that wretched man after all."

"I hope he didna break a hip when he fell." North grinned again.

"I don't think he likes children or dogs much. Plus, I can't believe he really has six children of his own."

"Who are probably all twice as old as ye," North made sure to mention.

"Thank you, North, for your help in sabotaging that. However, I really do want to find a father for Robbie."

"Robbie is a fine boy." North turned and smiled at her son who was playing with the dog. "Mayhap I'll take him for a ride on my horse. He was askin' about it."

"You have a horse?" This surprised her, since she hadn't seen one.

"Well, aye. Although I dinna bring it here. Would ye like to come with us?" he asked. "Mayhap we could ride down to the river and spread out a blanket and have some wine and cheese."

North's words were like magic to her ears. She wanted this kind of treatment for her and her son from a man, but had never had it. Her last husband wanted nothing to do with her. She doubted he would have ever wanted anything to do with Robbie, either. This felt nice. She'd been meaning to sneak out anyway, because she wanted to visit her old manor. She thought it was time and that she could handle it now. Even though Marcus and her uncle thought it would be too disturbing for her, she had to try. Matilda wanted to search the ruins for the money her father said he had hidden there. "All right, I accept," she said shyly. "However, there is something I have to take care of first. I'll collect Robbie and Gert and meet you by the gate in a half-hour."

"Willna it be odd for the others to see me leavin' with ye?"

"You're right. I'll take the wagon instead. I'll have the stable boy leave it down the road for me, and then return on foot. I'll sneak out the postern gate with Robbie and meet you there."

"Unescorted? I dinna think yer cousin will allow that."

"I'll manage it. Don't you worry." Matilda smiled to herself, humming a little tune as she went to find Marcus to ask him to send a missive to the Horn and Hoof Tavern in Glasgow.

◆•○◇○•◆

CHAPTER FIFTEEN

NORTH STOOD IN the shadows outside the castle, waiting for Matilda to arrive with Robbie. He stayed hidden from the stable boy who had brought the wagon. He glanced around nervously, hoping no guards would spot him. If so, there was a good chance he'd end up in the dungeon for attempting to spend private time with a lady of the castle and her son.

"Where is she?" he mumbled to himself, worried about more than just this. When he'd headed back to his camp in the woods earlier, he'd discovered a village boy watching over their horses, but Gavin was nowhere to be found. The boy said he didn't know where Gavin had gone and, to North, that only meant trouble. Gavin wasn't a patient man. North was sure he was devising a plot to spring Cam and Nash from the dungeon.

"Damn," he spat, feeling like a traitor for not doing anything to help his friend and his brother. He supposed he had been a little distracted with Matilda lately, but he had to be. He needed that goblet in order to be accepted back into the clan.

Guilt ate away at his soul. Was that really the reason he'd been hesitant to try to free Nash and Cam from the cell? He wanted to believe it, but if he was honest with himself, it was so much more than that. He needed everything to remain calm for now, and prisoners breaking out of the dungeon was only going to cause more trouble.

North selfishly wanted to spend more time with Matilda. He

supposed he could have been forceful and demanded that the lass hand over the goblet while he held her at bay at the end of his sword. Nay, he couldn't do that. She had been through so much already and didn't deserve such treatment. He only knew the vague story of her childhood, but just hearing it had touched his heart. He felt something for Matilda, and didn't want to hurt her in any way. Of course, stealing the goblet from her was going to hurt her, he was sure. She treasured that damned cup more than anything in life besides her son.

"Just a little more time, and I'll have it," he told himself, although he wasn't sure he believed it any longer. Too much time was passing and his brother and friend were in grave danger. God's teeth, why did this have to be happening to him? He was even starting to like that big, slobbery dog of Matilda's. North had grown fond of her son and, somehow, it felt right. Like they were a family.

"I canna get distracted," he told himself, pacing back and forth. "I have to convince her to give me the cup. If no', I have no choice but to steal it from her. I have to do this." He paced some more. "I canna remain an outcast. I also canna let down my brathair and friends any longer."

He'd just decided that he was going to use this time alone with Matilda to steal the goblet, when he heard Matilda's sweet voice calling out to the stable boy. He looked up and his heart skipped a beat. There was his bonnie lass, coming down the road holding her son's hand. The wind blew her hood down, and her long, red hair lifted around her shoulders making her look like a goddess.

"Thank you, and please don't say a word," Matilda told the stable boy, slipping him a coin. "I'll leave the wagon outside the gate later where you can collect it."

"Aye, my lady. Thank you," said the stable boy, running down the road back to the castle.

Matilda was dressed in green today, which made a striking vision with her bright red hair. Her son was with her, as well as that big, ugly, but loveable hound. Lady Gert sniffed him out, running over and sitting at his feet, waiting for another treat. Her ears flapped in the breeze, and her tongue hung down as her mouth was wide open. He swore the hound was smiling.

"Well, none of them will be smilin' when I am finished with this mission," he mumbled, stepping out into the open to make his presence known.

"Matilda, I'm here," he said, walking out to greet her. "I was startin' to think ye werena comin'."

"I'm sorry it took so long," she said, reaching over the side of the wagon and placing a covered basket inside. "It took a while to get the food and then sneak out the postern gate. Not to mention I had to walk down the road."

"Hi, North," said Robbie, smiling at him excitedly. "Are we on a secret mission?"

"Somethin' like that," he mumbled, ruffling the little boy's hair. If only they knew what mission he had planned.

"I also went to Marcus and convinced him to send a missive to the Horn and Hoof Tavern in Glasgow, asking Callum MacKeefe about all of you."

"You did?" Now, he felt even worse. "Thank ye. But I hope you didna tell Marcus too much about us. If so, he will become suspicious."

"Don't worry," she told him in a singsong voice. "I was very vague."

"Cam and Nash are no' in any danger for now, are they?" asked North.

"Nay. Marcus won't do anything to them until he hears back from Callum, I'm sure."

"Guid," said North. "I dinna want to let my brathair and my friend down." He picked up Robbie and slid him onto the bench seat, and then helped Matilda climb up as well. "Get in the back, Gertie," said North. The dog jumped in. "And keep yer slobbery nose out of the food basket." Once they were settled, he climbed up on the seat and took the reins.

"Where is this other friend you spoke of?" asked Matilda.

"Gavin?" he asked. "I wish I could tell ye. I'm afraid he's goin' to do somethin' stupid."

"Well, let's not worry about that now. I am looking forward to our little outing."

"Me, too," said Robbie, getting up on his knees and reaching back to pet the dog. "So is Gertie."

"Robbie, sit down before you're thrown from the wagon," Matilda scolded. "This road is very bumpy."

"I've got him," said North, taking the boy onto his lap. "How would ye like to drive the wagon, Robbie?"

"Would I!" exclaimed the boy.

"North, I'm not sure that is a good idea."

"Ye dinna have to worry. I'll be holdin' the reins along with him," he assured her. North put the reins in the boy's hands, and then covered his hands with his own. "Now ye'll ken what it feels like to be in charge of a horse, Robbie."

"This is fun!" exclaimed the boy. "Mother, look at me. I'm driving the wagon."

"You sure are, Robbie," Matilda answered.

MATILDA'S HEART SWELLED with love when she saw North with her son on his lap. He'd taken the boy under his wing and was teaching him to do something that she never would have done herself. It made Robbie smile, and that made her happy. Her son needed this time with a man instructing him. He needed a father.

Thoughts filled her head about North. Crazy thoughts that she never should be having. What if she married North? What if he became Robbie's father? She had no doubts that the man could protect them. After all, he was a Highland warrior. Even though Amethyst's brother, Onyx, was raised with the MacKeefes as a Highlander, she was sure Marcus wouldn't be happy to let a MacKeefe live there with them at Montclair Castle.

If not, Matilda would have no choice but to live in Scotland with North. That scared her immensely. After all these years, she was still having nightmares about the night the Scots slayed her family. She could never live amongst them. She hated Scots. Didn't she?

"Matilda, is there anywhere special ye'd like to go?" asked North, dragging her from her daydreams.

"Yes. I want to stop by the ruins of my old manor house. It's not far from here," she told him.

"I dinna understand," said North. "I thought ye said it burned down."

"It did. But the night my family was murdered, I heard my father say that he hid money somewhere inside the manor. I want to find it. I need it. Especially if I'm never going to marry again. I'll need money for Robbie and me to live on."

"But that was so long ago. Why havena ye gone to look for it sooner?"

"My cousin and uncle never allowed me to go. Uncle Gilbert looked for the money but couldn't find it. They thought if I went, it would be too devastating, considering what I've been through."

"Well, willna it?"

"I'm not sure. I think I can handle it now."

"But do ye think it's wise? Especially with the lad along? Why dinna ye let it go?"

"Nay. I want to go there. It's not far from here, and we'll go to our outing right afterwards. It shouldn't take long."

"If ye insist. Show me the way."

North stopped the wagon in front of the ruins of a burned-out manor. It wasn't a pretty sight. Over the years, vines and weeds had covered the crumbled ruins, but the place still smelled like death to him. Even after all this time.

"Mother, what is this place?" asked Robbie.

"It is where I grew up," said Matilda softly, looking as if she were going to be ill. Her face became pale.

"Ye dinna look so well, lass," said North. "Perhaps it is time to go on our outin'."

"Nay. I have to do this," she said, slowly sliding off the wooden bench seat and getting to the ground. "I didn't think it would be this hard." Her lips trembled. "It is almost as if I can still hear the sound of the clashing blades, and the screams." She held on to the side of the wagon, wavering back and forth.

"Robbie, stay in the wagon with Gertie and dinna come out." North helped the boy climb to the back. "Gertie, stay! And watch the lad."

The hound whined and laid down in the wagon with its tongue hanging out.

North hurried around to the other side, taking hold of Matilda's arm.

"If ye really need to do this, then I am comin' with ye, lass. However, I can tell ye right now that if there was hidden money, bandits would have found it and stole it long before now. It willna be here."

"Mayhap not. But I needed to come here to see for myself."

"Where do ye want to look?"

"This way," she said, holding on to North and leading him to a certain place in the ruins. "I think this is where the solar was, but it is hard to tell." Her breathing labored and this seemed to be taking a toll on her.

"I really believe we need to leave."

"I can't, North. Not yet."

"Then let me look for any hidden money for ye. If it's here. I'll find it."

"Mayhap I'll just sit down for a minute." Matilda's body shook as she lowered herself atop part of the broken stone wall.

"I'll be fast. Call me if ye need me."

"I will," she said, biting her lip and looking the other way.

North searched the ruins thoroughly, but couldn't find anything that was worth salvaging. There was no hidden treasure or coins anywhere. Finally, he headed back, only to find Matilda on her knees, crying. She had a small velvet pouch in her hand that she fingered.

"Matilda," he called out, running to her, gathering her into his arms. Her body shook and she reached out and clung to him, as if she never wanted to let him go. "Did ye find somethin'?" he asked, pulling back to look at the pouch.

"Nay. This was the pouch with the coins my father gave my mother before he made us hide. I have had this all these years, although I spent the money long ago."

"I'm sorry, but I didna find anythin'. There is nothin' here, Matilda."

"It was right here that it happened," she said, nodding with her head to a small enclosure at the bottom of one of the ruined walls. "I hid in there with my mother. I was so scared." Tears trailed down her cheeks.

"I think it's time to go now, lass.

"Nay. I want you to look inside the enclosure."

"Look inside?" He glanced over at the small burned space and shook his head. "Nay. There is nothin' in there, lass. We need to leave. This is too hard for ye to bear."

"Please," she begged him. "Take me over there with you. I have to see it one more time."

"All right." He took her by the arm and guided her to the hiding spot where she'd been that horrible night. She fell to her knees and cried some more. "Search inside, North. Please."

He didn't fight her. North hunkered down and looked into the space. It was small and dirty. He couldn't even imagine what this poor girl had been through. He reached out and ran his hand inside, just to make her happy. He never expected to find anything, but his hand did come across something. "I found somethin'."

"What is it?" she asked, hope resounding in her words. "Is it money?"

"Nay," he said, holding up a dirty, rusty eating knife. "It's just a knife," he said, brushing it off. "It has bloodstains on it, lass."

"Nay!" She started crying in hysterics. "Put it back," she said, jumping to her feet as if she were scared. "Throw it down. Don't touch it. I want to go now, North. I want to leave this place and never return here again."

They made their way back to the wagon, and North pulled away. Robbie was sleeping in the back and Gertie was watching over him.

North headed to the creek for their outing, but he didn't know if it was a good idea at this point. Matilda was pretty shaken.

"Do ye want to go back to the castle instead and mayhap lie down?" he asked.

"Nay." She sniffled and blew her nose in a hand cloth and then wiped the tears from her face. "I'm glad Robbie is sleeping though. I don't want him to ever see me that way."

"What was that knife?" he asked her. "Did someone . . . kill yer family with it?" He hated asking, but thought she needed to talk about this so she wouldn't keep things inside forever.

He didn't think she was going to answer, but she finally spoke. "I stabbed my attacker with that knife," she told him. "I gave him a long scar on his hand. It was the Englishman who killed both of my parents."

"So, then, Scots werena solely to blame."

"Nay. They weren't."

"I canna even imagine how hard this is for ye. Mayhap we never should have come here."

"It's all right," she told him. "I had to come here, North, and I thank you for bringing me. My cousin and uncle would never allow it and will be furious if they find out I came after all."

"I can see why. It is a horrible place and must bring back bad memories for ye."

"The memories will be with me forever. I wanted to come to look for the money, but like you said, bandits probably looted the place years ago. I didn't think it would affect me so much, but you were right in saying I should have never come back. I don't need to do that anymore, North. Never again."

"Remember the guid things about yer family, lass. No' the way they died, but the way they lived instead."

She scooted over to him as they rode, and rested her head on his shoulder. He put his arm around her.

"I think I need to stop looking for my family's murderers, too. I am ready to let that go now, North. You are more than right. I should have listened to you. I don't need to keep putting myself through this. It's not right."

"It's time for a new life, lass. Start over with Robbie. Make guid memories and leave the bad ones behind."

"I agree," she said, sniffling once more.

"Let's start with an outin' in the woods near the creek then." North stopped the horse near the creek and dismounted. He came around to the side and held out his arms. "Let me help ye, my lady."

WHEN HE CALLED her my lady, it made Matilda feel anxious. It only pointed out how different from each other they truly were. He reached under her arms and lifted her, placing her down in front of him, and leaned close to whisper in her ear. "Ye smell so guid it makes me want to eat ye." He nibbled at her neck, making her breath hitch.

This only made her think of the intimate time they'd spent together and how much she wanted to do it again. She started to feel randy, so she pushed him away.

"North, please," she whispered, looking over to her son who had woken up and was standing in the back of the wagon. "We have to behave ourselves in front of Robbie."

"Aye, of course. Ye're right," he said, reaching into the wagon, and helping the boy to the ground. Gertie jumped out after him. "What did ye bring to eat?"

"I have cold beef and bread, along with fresh fruit and some sweetmeats."

"Sounds guid. I'm starvin'." North picked up the basket and also the blanket. It was a sunny day, and there was barely a cloud in the sky. The summer breeze smelled sweet, and the air was warm. It felt good to be away from the ruins, and the feeling of death that surrounded the manor. Here in the woods, she felt life. That is what she needed right now.

"I also found and brought along a special treat I think you'll like," she told him, starting to feel so much better.

"I'm already lookin' at that," he told her in a sultry voice with a dangerous hunger in his eyes.

"Stop it, North," she said, playfully hitting him on the arm. She reached over the side of the wagon and picked up a wineskin.

"Wine?" he asked.

"Nay. Take a taste." Matilda uncorked the wineskin and handed it to North. He took a long draw, closed his eyes and swallowed. With a satisfied sigh, he opened his bright silver eyes, looking ever so happy.

"Mountain Magic," he said excitedly. "Where did ye find this?"

"I know all of my cousin's hiding places for the good wine and whisky he doesn't want to share."

"Thank ye," he said. "But I dinna think ye, and especially no' Robbie, should drink this. It's much too strong."

"I have some spiced mead as well," she said, reaching for another wineskin. His hand atop hers stilled her action. She looked up into his eyes. "What is it?" she asked.

"I just wanted to tell ye, that whatever happens, I want ye to ken that ye mean a lot to me, Matilda. I never want to hurt ye or Robbie."

She smiled at him, reaching up and stroking his cheek. "I know that. I trust you, North. If I didn't, I wouldn't be here alone with you right now, would I? I never had any doubt in my head that I was in danger being around you."

"Nay?" he said, looking back into the wagon. He pushed aside another blanket and pulled out her sword that she had hidden there before she'd ever left the castle. "Then, what's this?"

"That is for protection, but not against you." She took it from him and put it back in the wagon. "I never go anywhere outside the castle walls without it."

"It's a guid idea, I suppose. Ye never ken what kind of danger is lurkin' around in the shadows. Robbie, help me set up the meal," he called out, heading to the creek with the basket, the wineskin, and the blanket.

Matilda watched Robbie run over to North. Gertie ran circles around them. North picked up a stick and threw it for the dog. Then he put down the things and scooped up Robbie, holding him high over his head before dipping him upside down, pretending he was going to drop him. Robbie laughed and squealed, enjoying every minute of it.

"Mayhap it could work between us," she said softly, wanting to believe it. Matilda had never felt these feelings for any man before, not even her late husband. She came to life with excitement around North. Even though he'd tried to steal her goblet, she didn't think ill thoughts of him anymore. He'd been good to her son, and even the dog seemed to like him. He was also kind to her. Matilda had never felt so satisfied before in her life. If only he wasn't a Scot. If only he were an English noble.

"Matilda, are ye goin' to join us for a bite to eat?" North called out.

"Hurry, Mother," cried Robbie, jumping up in down in excitement. "North told me that he'd teach me how to fish as soon as we're done with our meal. I want to catch a fish as big as me."

"As big as ye?" North laughed, handing the boy some food. "We're no' in the ocean, lad. This is only a creek. Ye'll be lucky to catch a fish any bigger than yer hand."

"Sit down and eat, Robbie," said Matilda, sitting down next to North. "And remember, you have to call him Norton when we're back at the castle. No one can know he's a Scot."

"Why not?" asked Robbie, plopping down and shoving a piece of bread in his mouth. Gertie stood next to him, her nose so close to his food that it was almost touching.

"Gertie, this is for ye," said North, handing the dog a chunk of meat. The hound eagerly wolfed it down.

"Let's show my mother how Gertie can play hide and seek," said Robbie, jumping up.

"All right," said North, reaching out and covering the dog's eyes with his hand. "Go on and hide, Robbie."

"What are you doing?" asked Matilda with a giggle.

"Ye'll see. All right, Gertie," said North once Robbie was out of sight, hiding behind a tree. "Find him. Go on and find Robbie."

The dog barked twice, then ran off sniffing the ground. Then it ran behind the tree where Robbie was, and barked like crazy, jumping up on the boy.

"She found me!" Robbie ran back with Gertie on his heels.

"Guid job, Gertie." North reached out and scratched behind the dog's ears. Then he gave it a crust of bread and Gertie took it and ran down to the creek to lay down to eat it.

"Did you see that, Mother? Gertie can play hide and seek. North taught her how." Robbie was bubbling over with excitement. It was a fine sight indeed.

"That's nice, Robbie," said Matilda. "But remember, don't call him North in front of anyone."

"Why not?" the boy asked her again.

"Robbie, yer mathair doesna want ye to tell the others at the castle who I am because it might put me and my friends in danger."

"Ye mean the men in the dungeon?" asked Robbie, chewing with his mouth open.

"That's who I mean," he said.

"Are your friends Highlanders like you?" asked Robbie.

"Aye," said North.

"I want to go to the Highlands," said the boy.

"Well, mayhap ye'll have a chance to do that someday, lad." North looked over at Matilda and winked.

Her heart skipped a beat. She wondered what he meant by

that, but didn't dare ask him.

"Why are you here?" asked Robbie.

"We're havin' somethin' to eat. And we're goin' to fish," North answered.

"Nay, I mean why are Highlanders at our castle? Lord Marcus says most Scots are no good."

"Robbie," Matilda said. "That's not nice."

"Nay, it's fine," said North, munching on some food. "The boy has a right to ken. I came here for that goblet yer mathair has chained to her waist."

Matilda's hand automatically went to the silver cup. A tinge of doubt crept into her mind, and she didn't like it. Still, she had to remember his true purpose for being here.

"Why do you want her cup?" Robbie handed a chunk of bread to the dog since it had come back to beg.

"I'm an outcast of my clan," North explained.

"What's an outcast?" asked the boy.

"It means he is no longer welcome," explained Matilda.

"Why?" The boy was full of questions, and it made Matilda feel a little uncomfortable. She didn't want anything to ruin this special time they were sharing and wished they could talk about something else instead.

"Robbie, eat your meal and stop asking so many questions."

"It's fine, lass," said North, not at all hesitant to answer. "Robbie, that goblet yer mathair has belongs to my chieftain, Storm MacKeefe."

"Nay, it's mine." Her hand clasped over it possessively.

North continued. "I was drinkin' at the Horn and Hoof Tavern with my friends, when it was stolen by thieves. It was kind of my fault since I used it without permission."

"Why did you do that?" asked Robbie curiously.

"I dinna ken." North turned and looked deeply into Matilda's eyes. "I suppose it's because sometimes I want things that are no' mine, and that I can never have." His gaze lingered. Her hand slid off the goblet. Matilda's heart ached. Did he mean he wanted her, but that he could never have her?

"Well, I think the fish will be bitin' about now." North stood up and brushed off his hands. "Robbie, we need to find some long sticks to use for poles. I have some hooks in my pouch I carry along with me since I fish a lot."

"I have some twine in the wagon that you can use for the lines." Matilda jumped up and hurried over to the wagon. "Here it is." When she turned around, North was standing right there.

"Thank ye," he said, his face coming closer. Then he kissed her, and she let him do it. "Matilda, ye have no idea what ye mean to me."

Her tongue shot out and she tasted his essence on her lips. "You mean a lot to me, too, North. I've really enjoyed being with you."

"I like being with ye and Robbie as well." He looked down at her goblet.

She picked it up and cradled it against her chest. "Please, don't tell me the whole reason that you've been so kind to me and my son is just to woo this away from me."

"Is that what ye think?" The hurt showed in his eyes. "I thought after the intimate time we've spent together, ye'd trust me by now."

"Should I?" She raised her chin boldly, her inner warrior traits rearing up within her. She couldn't help it. "I want to believe you, but something tells me that the true reason you've been nice to me and my son is only to get me to let down my guard so you can steal this cup away from me." She wanted him to know that she was on to his game and it wasn't going to work. "So, I ask you again. Should I really trust you?"

North looked deeply into her eyes without saying a word. She saw hope and sadness, and a little desperation within his silver orbs. Then, he took a step back and he shook his head. "Nay," he said in a soft voice. "I dinna suppose ye should trust me. Now, if ye'll excuse me, I have a promise to fulfill. And once the fishin' is over, we can go back to the castle at once."

He turned and walked down to the creek, leaving Matilda standing there with tears in her eyes. Why did she have to say that to him? She'd always been a defensive child, and also rebellious as she grew up. If only she'd stayed silent and not voiced her doubts about him, they'd still be having a special time together. Matilda cursed herself silently, and then she cursed North as well. Why did they have to be in this impossible situation? She knew now that there was no way things between them could ever end happily.

CHAPTER SIXTEEN

NORTH AND MATILDA barely spoke at all on the way back to the castle. North had thought things were going well between them, but now it was clear that Matilda still didn't trust him.

She shouldn't, he told himself. He had planned on having the cup in his possession by the time they returned to the castle. However, after seeing her distrust of him, he couldn't bring himself to steal it after all.

He truly did have feelings for Matilda, and he adored her little boy. Today had been fun, despite the trouble between them. He never thought he wanted to marry or that it was important. Hell, he thought his brother and friends were out of their minds when they did it. Now, he was starting to understand them a little better.

Having a family was important. He knew that, just by being an outcast from his clan. He'd seen how upset Matilda was today when she visited the site where she'd lost everyone she'd ever loved. Because of that, he saw her in a different light. She was hurting inside, it was obvious. He supposed that is why rumors had started about her being mad. It was the nightmares. That would drive anyone mad. When he and Nash had lost their parents, it was a hard blow as well. His parents, too, were murdered. He and Nash had found out the truth about that, while they were thatching roofs in the Highlands right before Nash married Kellina.

North and Matilda might be from different walks of life, and even different sides of the border, but they were still so much alike in so many ways. They'd both lost loved ones, and both he and she wanted things they could never have.

North knew what was missing in his life now. It was a wife and children to call his own. He had never felt so lonely or empty.

"I'd better get out here and walk to the castle by myself." He handed the reins to Matilda and jumped off the wagon while it was still going. "Are ye goin' to leave the wagon for the stable boy to collect?"

"Nay. I'm not going to sneak in or out of the castle anymore. If Marcus doesn't like it, I'll deal with him. I am going to ride through the gates with my head held high."

"All right then." He started walking and didn't look back.

"North, don't leave us," begged Robbie. He held up the one fish he'd caught today. "I want you to help me clean and cook my fish."

"I'm sorry, Robbie, I dinna think that would be a wise move," he called over his shoulder.

"Nay, it wouldn't," agreed Matilda, driving the wagon next to North as he walked. "Robbie, we'll take the fish to the kitchen and have the servants clean and cook it."

"But I want to do it myself, Mother. It's my fish."

"We need to get back to the castle before Lord Marcus sends a troop out looking for us." Without even a glance at him or a friendly thank you or goodbye, Matilda took off at a good clip for the castle, leaving North behind.

North's heart hurt as he saw little Robbie looking back at him over the side of the wagon. He seemed so sad. North wanted more than anything to teach him how to clean and cook a fish. The boy was young, but needed to learn how to take care of himself as well as his mother someday.

It was probably wise to keep his distance, he realized. Plus, he didn't want to upset Matilda since she'd already had such an emotional day, stopping by the ruins of the manor.

They both needed space. He needed time to think. The last thing he wanted was to anger Matilda because, if so, there was a good chance she would reveal his identity to Lord Marcus and the others. He couldn't have that.

North headed back to the castle on foot. He was still the assistant falconer, and if he was missing too long, questions would be asked, and suspicions raised.

As he headed over the drawbridge and into the courtyard, something caught his eye. It was the cart of a peddler. There were shoes hanging everywhere, so it had to be a cobbler or cordwainer, he realized.

"Where have you been?" came a low voice from behind him. He turned around to see Walter standing there with his arms crossed over his chest.

"What does it matter? I'm here now," said North. "Do ye need some help in the mews?" Since Walter knew North was a Scot, he no longer tried to hide it around him. He spoke in his normal way.

"I find it suspicious that you disappeared the same time as Lady Matilda and her son."

"Really? I didna ken she had left the castle."

"Like hell, you didn't," snapped the man. "Lord Marcus was furious when I told him that Lady Matilda and her son were seen leaving in the wagon and without an escort. I saw her go, you know."

"Ye told him? What business is it of yers?"

"What business do you have with the whore?" he asked in return.

North reached out and gripped the man by the front of his tunic. His jaw clenched and he felt the throbbing of a vein in his neck. "She is a lady, no' a whore. If ye ever call her that again, I swear, I'll kill ye."

Walter broke free of his grip and stumbled backward. "Ah, I see you've bedded her already."

"Stop it," spat North. "This is how rumors start. I willna allow it."

"You must know of her reputation," said the man. "I've heard that her late husband said she was barren and that she couldn't please him in bed."

"I said, stop it."

"It's said that she would bed everyone and anyone, trying to get pregnant. Even lowlifes like you. I wouldn't be surprised if that whelp of hers is a bastard."

North couldn't stand it anymore. He punched the man in the face, knocking him to the ground. Then he threw himself atop him, and the two of them rolled over and over, fighting and hitting each other.

"Stop this, anon!" Marcus walked up with several of his guards who pulled them apart. "What is the nature of this fight?"

North stood up, brushing off his clothes. He looked over to Walter who was grinning.

"Go ahead. Tell him," said Walter. "And then I'll tell him a few things as well."

North wanted more than anything to speak the truth. But if he said a word against Walter, then the fake falconer would reveal North's secrets as well. North had more than just himself to think about now. He might be able to take the punishment, but the last thing he wanted was for Matilda to be chastised or punished. The poor girl already had a horrid reputation that she did not deserve. Plus, he didn't want his brother and friends to suffer anymore because of him.

"There's no trouble," said North. "It was just a simple misunderstanding, my lord. It won't happen again."

"It better not," growled Marcus. "If you two can't get along, one of you will have to go."

"I really don't need an assistant, my lord." Walter stood up quickly. "And I'm sure a falconer is much more valuable to you than just an assistant."

"They'll both stay for now." Matilda walked up with Robbie

at her side. The dog followed. Robbie held up his fish.

"Look at the fish I caught today, Lord Marcus."

"You took the boy fishing by yourself, Matilda?" asked Marcus. "How could you? Do you know how dangerous that is?"

"We weren't by ourselves," said the boy. "We were well protected."

"What?" asked Marcus.

North held his breath, wishing the boy hadn't said that. He caught Robbie's eyes and slowly shook his head.

"What he means," said Matilda, "is that I had my sword. Plus, Gertie was with us."

"That dog is worthless," said Marcus. "All anyone has to do is throw it some food and it'll be their best friend forever. Matilda, I don't want you leaving the castle unescorted again."

She paused before she answered, glancing over at North. He was sure she was going to fight Lord Marcus' decision, but she didn't.

"Of course not, my lord," said Matilda, pulling Robbie over to her. "If you'll excuse me, I need to take Robbie to the kitchen so the cook can prepare his fish for him to eat."

She turned and left with the boy without saying another word.

"I can see now that I shouldn't have been gone so long today tending to things. What is that?" asked Marcus, pointing to the cart of shoes. "And why is it in the center of the courtyard?"

"A cobbler showed up here a little while ago," reported one of the guards. "He's been fixing everyone's shoes for the last few hours."

"Does anyone know him?" asked Marcus, sounding suspicious.

The guards looked at each other and shrugged. "He isn't our normal cobbler. The man said he was a traveler passing through," answered the guard.

"Excuse me," said a man, coming over to them. "Can I have my cart back now?"

"You're Edwin, our normal cobbler, are you not?" asked Marcus.

"Aye, my lord." The man lowered his head.

"Why is your cart here without you and what do you mean asking for it back?"

"A Scot paid me to borrow it and said he'd be right back. I was wondering if he was finished with it yet, since I have been waiting in the woods for a while now and he hasn't returned."

"Where is this man now?" asked Marcus, looking back and forth quickly.

"I'm not sure, my lord. He was here just a little while ago," answered a guard.

"I saw the fake cobbler head toward the back of the castle a few minutes ago," Walter told him.

"The back of the castle? Why on earth would he go there?" asked Marcus. Then a panicked look washed over his face and he drew his sword. "He's here to try to break those damned Scots out of the dungeon. Men, quickly, follow me."

"Bluidy hell," North mumbled under his breath, realizing now just who the cobbler was. It was Gavin, coming to try to free his friends.

North ran after the others, hoping to do something to keep Gavin from being captured as well. However, it was too late.

Marcus entered the dungeon first, with his guards right behind him. North heard fighting when he ran in, and stopped in his tracks seeing Gavin being held by both the guards. Marcus had his blade to Gavin's throat.

"Who are you and what are you doing here?" growled Marcus.

Gavin's eyes shot over to North for help, but North looked the other way. There was nothing he could do to help his friend that wouldn't get him thrown into the dungeon as well.

"I am Gavin MacKeefe and I am here to free my friends who have done nothin' wrong," yelled Gavin. Cam and Nash could be heard banging on the iron bars of their cell, calling out as well.

"You keep saying you're MacKeefes, but I have no proof," replied Marcus.

"Look at my plaid, unless ye're bluidy blind," spat Gavin. "I wear the MacKeefe colors."

"He could have taken them off a MacKeefe after he killed them," spoke up Walter, watching from the door.

God's eyes, North wanted to belt the man again. If he broke his damned jaw, mayhap he'd be able to keep the man quiet.

"Throw him in the cell with the others," ordered Marcus.

"Mayhap it's time to have a hanging," suggested Walter. "After all, these are the Scots who caused so much trouble at the dance."

"Mayhap it's time for you to shut your mouth," spat North.

"Both of you, out of here!" screamed Marcus.

North left right behind Walter, stopping when he saw Lady Amethyst and Matilda running up to the dungeon door.

"What is going on?" asked Amethyst.

"Another bloody Scot was caught, and I say it's time to kill them all." Walter had a mean streak in him and was starting to be a troublemaker.

"Walter, please go back to the mews anon," demanded Matilda, seeming very shaken.

Amethyst entered the dungeon while Walter left for the mews.

"Matilda," whispered North. "They are my friends. My family. Please, dinna let Marcus hurt them."

She raised her chin and looked directly into his eyes. "I think it is time for you to go back to the mews as well, since you are the assistant falconer. The lord of the castle will do what he pleases. So, if you have any qualms about it, you'll have to take it up with him."

"Matilda. Really?" North didn't understand why she was acting this way toward him. He felt so choked that he could barely speak. Her face remained stone-like, and all her loving and caring qualities seemed to have quickly disappeared. His dreams that involved Matilda seemed to be turning into a nightmare now.

North turned and headed back to the mews, realizing what a fool he'd been. He never should have gotten caught up with Matilda. His longing to possibly marry her and raise a family together was naught but a wild dream. He was a Scot and she was an English lady. They didn't belong together and never would.

He hurried back to the front gate instead of the mews, knowing he had to get back to his camp and collect the horses. After all, he was going to need them in order to help his brother and friends escape.

CHAPTER SEVENTEEN

"COUSIN, WHAT WILL you do with the Scots?" asked Matilda, watching the guards haul the one named Gavin to the cell with the others, throwing him inside. The iron gate closed with a loud clang behind him, sending shivers up her spine.

"Now that we've caught all three of them, there is nothing else to be done," said Marcus. "The prisoners will die by hanging in two days' time."

"What?" screamed Matilda, feeling her heart about beating out of her chest. "You can't do that. They don't deserve to die!"

"Matilda, you were almost abducted, and one of them tried to steal your goblet if I must remind you." Marcus shoved his sword back into the sheath. "I am an earl and a border lord. I deal with Scots quite frequently and, most of the time, they are trying to take off my head. I just can't take the chance that someone else will come trying to free them. Before I know it, I'll have an entire clan of Scots at my door. I need to nip this in the bud before things get out of hand."

"What about the messenger you sent to Glasgow?" asked Matilda. "Surely, you should wait for him to return. You don't want to kill our allies if they really are MacKeefes. If you do, we'll have a battle on our hands."

"I agree with Matilda," said Amethyst. "My brother, Onyx, would never forgive you if you killed off any MacKeefes. I just wish I knew where he was. He's traveling with his wife to see some of her relatives or I could have asked him by now if he knew these men."

"I am tired of waiting," growled Marcus. "I am going to take action, and don't try to talk me out of it." He turned to go, but Matilda grabbed Marcus' arm to stop him.

"Cousin, this is insane. You cannot kill innocent men."

"That's odd to hear you say that," said Marcus. "You hate Scots more than anyone after what they did to your family."

"Aye, but I . . . changed my mind. I'm sure they're not all bad," she told him, feeling horrible about the turn of events.

"Matilda," said Marcus, pulling her hand off his arm. "I can see now why my father sent you to live with me instead of staying with him. You are outspoken and need a man to keep you in your place."

"Marcus! Really," scolded Amethyst.

"I'm sorry, Amy," said Marcus, using his nickname for his wife. "But Matilda has always been uncontrollable."

"She's just a free spirit," said Amethyst, trying to help Matilda.

"She's only got one chance left to marry, and I am not going to let her blow it." Marcus scared Matilda when he said that.

"What?" gasped Matilda. "What do you mean, Marcus?"

"I mean that tomorrow morning, Lord William Gurney of Cornwall will arrive. He is the last suitor. I am going to secure a betrothal for you before he has the chance to even meet you."

"That's mad," she spat. "I should have some say so as to the man I marry."

"Nay, you shouldn't," he told her. "And I promise you, I am not going to let you have the chance to scare away another possible husband. You will marry this man, like it or not, and you will leave for Cornwall right after the wedding."

"Cornwall? That's so far south. I don't want to live there. My family is here," said Matilda, not wanting to go far from the Scottish border. If she did, she'd surely never see North again.

"I'm done talking. Now stay inside the castle walls, because if

I catch you leaving again without an escort, I'm going to chain you to your bed the way you've chained that goblet to your waist." With that, Marcus, stormed away, leaving Matilda feeling as if her life had just crumbled.

Crying, she ran to her tower room and threw herself onto the bed.

"Matilda?" There came a slight knock at the door and Amethyst entered, closing the door behind her. "Are you all right?" She came and sat down next to Matilda on the bed.

"I hate my cousin!" she spat, sitting up, wiping away her tears with her sleeve.

"There, now," said Amethyst, pulling a square of cloth from her pocket, and dabbing at Matilda's eyes. "Why is all this upsetting you so much?"

"Those men don't deserve to die," she said through ragged breaths. "It's all my fault."

"I agree they don't deserve to die and that my husband is acting harshly, but you can't blame yourself."

"I can, and I will. If anything happens to them, North will hate me forever."

"North?" Amethyst lowered her hand and looked at her quizzically. "Is there something you want to tell me?"

"Oh, Amethyst, I've gone and fallen in love with a Highlander." Matilda blurted it out, needing to tell someone before she burst.

"I don't understand. You love one of those Scots in the dungeon? How do you even know them?"

"Nay, not them," said Matilda, starting to have second thoughts about telling Amethyst after all. "Oh, never mind. You wouldn't understand."

"It's the falconer's assistant, isn't it?" guessed Amethyst. "He's the Highlander you're speaking of, right?"

"H-how did you know?"

Amethyst chuckled. "I am not blind. I see the way you two look at each other. Plus, I saw how hard he tried to keep you from marrying that last suitor. Not to mention, I'm used to hearing the Scots speak because of my brother. I noticed several times that Norton – or North, I guess, sounds a lot like Onyx."

"Oh, Amethyst, please don't tell Marcus. He won't understand."

"You've got to let him know, Matilda. If not, he's going to make you marry Lord William Gurney of Cornwall."

"I still have time," said Matilda, using the hand cloth to blow her nose. "The banns will need to be posted before the wedding. Isn't it usually three weeks' time?"

"It is. However, it can be as little as three days, which I highly expect Marcus to do."

"Then I still have three days. But in the meantime, those poor men are going to die in two. I have to do something to help them."

"Don't get involved, Matilda. This is a dangerous game you play."

"I have to get involved, don't you see? One of those men in the dungeon is North's twin brother. The other two are his good friends. Besides, they really are MacKeefes. They're not lying."

"Then why didn't their own chieftain acknowledge them?"

"He's ill. And delusional. If we can stall Marcus long enough to give the messenger enough time to get back from Glasgow, I'm sure everything will be cleared up."

"Matilda, it's a three-day journey to Glasgow and back, and the men in the dungeon are sentenced to die in two."

"Nay. I can't let them die. I won't."

"Why are they even here? I don't understand."

"They are here for this." Matilda held up the silver goblet. "North said this belongs to their other chieftain, Storm MacKeefe. It's North's fault it was stolen, and unless he brings it back, he'll remain an outcast of the clan forever."

"Is that so bad?"

"Yes, it is. The MacKeefes are North's family."

"Then why don't you just give him the goblet?"

"I – I don't know," she said, holding the cup to her chest.

"This is the last remembrance I have of my family. I was going to use it to attract a husband, but I don't want to do that anymore. I don't want to remarry. Ever."

"You mean, you don't want to marry anyone other than North," said Amethyst with a knowing smile.

"Oh, Amethyst, I thought he wanted me. We even made love, but now I'm not so sure. I don't think he wanted anything but this blasted cup all along." She removed the chain from around her waist and threw the cup down on the bed.

"What did you just say? You made love to him?"

Matilda sighed. "I know. You think the rumors of me being a loose woman are true, but I swear the only other man I've ever coupled with was Alaric."

Amethyst's frown turned into a grin. "How was it? Making love to a rugged Highlander?" she asked, and giggled, surprising Matilda that she wasn't being chastised instead.

"It was . . . wonderful." Matilda smiled now. "North is so gentle and kind and he brings out feelings in me that I've never felt with anyone before. Plus, Robbie and even Gertie like him. Oh, Amethyst, I think I am falling in love with him."

"Really?"

"Aye, I do believe so. But I also think he hates me now."

"Nay, I'm sure that is not true."

"Mayhap if I proved myself to him, then he'd believe that I am sorry about his friends and that I care for him as well."

"He's never going to forgive you if his brother and friends die. Matilda, we need to take matters into our own hands."

"What are you saying?"

"I'm saying that, at one time, I wanted to free prisoners in this same dungeon and had to stand up to Marcus about it. It's been many years, but I think it's time to do it again."

"Y-you'd help me free North's brother and friends?"

"Can you think of another way to save their lives, and to prove to North that you love him?"

"Only one other way," she said, staring down at the goblet, realizing just what it was that she needed to do.

═══◆·◦◇◦·◆═══

CHAPTER EIGHTEEN

"MATILDA," CALLED OUT Amethyst the next morning, as Matilda hurried down the stairs having overslept. She was supposed to meet with Amethyst in the kennels in secret earlier this morning. They were going to come up with a plan to help the prisoners. Now, Amethyst stood at the entrance of the great hall, looking upset.

"Amethyst? Why are you here instead of at the kennels?" she asked. "I am sorry I overslept, but I thought we were going to meet there."

"Plans have changed," said Amethyst softly, hurrying over the Matilda. "Lord Gurney is already here. Marcus must have sent word to him yesterday right after the incident in the dungeon. He probably travelled all night to get here."

"He's here? Now? Oh, no," said Matilda. "I don't have time for this."

"There you are, Cousin." Marcus walked out of the great hall with an overweight, balding man on his heels. Matilda's stomach lurched.

"Good morning," she said, trying to be polite.

"This is your betrothed, Lord William Gurney from Cornwall," Marcus continued.

"I haven't agreed to the betrothal, my lord," said Matilda sharply.

"It doesn't matter. I am your guardian. The contract is already drawn up and signed. The agreement is settled." Marcus wasn't one for dragging his feet. When he wanted something done, he did it right away. In this case, it was working against Matilda.

"It's signed already?" Matilda didn't like hearing that. Things were moving much too fast.

"And this is Father Bernard, who is going to marry you," said Marcus, introducing a priest who had followed them out of the great hall.

"Why is he here now?" asked Matilda. "We haven't even posted the wedding banns yet."

"No need for that. Father Bernard assured me that he'll handle any complaints. The marriage will take place now. Out in the courtyard."

"What?" Both Matilda and Amethyst said together.

"Marcus, this is all so sudden," said Amethyst. "Matilda has just met the man, and no preparations for the festivities have been made."

"That's right," said Matilda. "I'm sorry, I'm not ready. I don't even have a wedding gown. I'll have to order one to be made and that will take weeks."

"Weeks?" asked the man, coughing so hard Matilda thought he'd hack up a lung next. "I didn't travel here during the night just to be told I'll have to wait weeks to marry you. I thought this was a rushed deal."

"You won't have to wait," Marcus assured him. "The wedding will go on as planned. Matilda, you have plenty of nice gowns. Just wear one of those. Or better yet, just use what you have on."

Matilda looked over to Amethyst, begging her silently to help her out of this mess.

"Marcus, the feast will need to be planned, and the great hall decorated. There are many things to do for this wedding first," Amethyst told him.

"Nonsense." Marcus waved a hand through the air. "We'll

have the ceremony in the courtyard. It'll be fine."

"Nay, it isn't," spat Amethyst, trying her best to help stall the wedding. "Men have died in that courtyard. Blood has been spilled. Matilda deserves a proper place to be wed, with beautiful flowers all around her."

"Fine," said Marcus, blowing a puff of air from his mouth.

Matilda was just about to be able to breathe again, until she heard her cousin's next words.

"I don't normally allow anyone in there, but just this once, I'll grant permission for the wedding to be held in my secret rose garden."

"Nay," said Matilda. "That is your private place and it wouldn't be right."

No one was allowed into Marcus' garden except by invitation. His mother had loved roses, and the soft side of Marcus continued growing them long after his mother had died. He did it in her honor. That is where Marcus and Amethyst had been wed as well.

"I'll not hear another word about it. Now everyone, quickly, to the rose garden," said Marcus. "The wedding is about to begin."

Matilda pulled Amethyst over to the side and spoke softly. "Amethyst, I'm frightened. What are we going to do?"

"I'm sorry, Matilda, I don't know. My husband is stubborn and I can't always change his mind."

"Then I'll run away," she told her, feeling frantic.

"Nay, you can't do that. They've already drawn up and signed the papers. If you do that, it'll break the betrothal and it could mean war. Besides, you need to think of your son. If you won't do this for yourself, then do it for little Robbie. Isn't this what you wanted all along? To find a husband as well as a father for Robbie?"

"Oh, Amethyst, everything is happening too fast and my head is spinning right now. I haven't even had time to tell North that I'm sorry." Matilda looked down to her waist and unbuckled the clasp to the chain that held the silver goblet. "You've got to take this to the mews and give it to North." She pushed the cup and chain into Amethyst's hands.

"Matilda, what are you saying?" Amethyst looked down at Matilda's coveted possession and shook her head.

"I want him to have it. It'll mean he won't be an outcast anymore. If I can't marry him, then I want him to be able to be with the rest of his family. He deserves to be happy. I won't be able to live with myself if he remains an outcast. It's not fair to him. Amethyst, I have to help him."

"I'm sorry, but I can't take this to him." Amethyst spoke as they walked. Her eyes flicked over to Marcus and then back to her. "Don't you understand? This is part of the dowry. If I do that, Marcus will have my head. I'm sorry, Matilda." She shoved it back into Matilda's hands. "I want to help you, honest I do, but we are too late. Your best bet now would just be to marry Lord Gurney."

"I don't want him for my husband. He's disgusting," cried Matilda. "I love North. I want to marry him."

"I wish things could be different, but we have no power to change them."

"Ladies, hurry up!" Marcus called out from ahead of them. He was just about to enter the rose garden. "The priest has another wedding to officiate and needs to leave soon."

"Yes, Husband," said Amethyst, turning back and giving Matilda a big hug. "I'm sorry, Matilda. By marrying Lord Gurney, at least you'll have a father for Robbie. Mayhap in time, you could learn to love the man. It's a shame that things couldn't be different for you." She sadly turned and entered the rose garden.

"Never will I be happy with anyone other than North." Matilda was about to enter the rose garden when she saw Beatrice walking with her son. "Beatrice, come quickly," she said, glancing back at Marcus and then waving her over.

"My lady, what is it? Where are you going?" Beatrice hurried over to her with Robbie at her side.

"Mother, why is there a priest here and who is that bald man?" asked Robbie.

"Unfortunately, that is Lord Gurney, the man I'm being forced to marry," she answered.

"Oh!" gasped Beatrice, holding her hand to her mouth.

"Him? I don't want him for my father," whined Robbie. "I want North."

"Who's North?" asked Beatrice.

"Never mind," said Matilda, shoving the silver cup and chain into the nursemaid's hands. "Go to the mews at once. Make sure the assistant falconer, Norton, gets this. It is very important. Do you understand me?"

"Yes, my lady," said the woman, taking the cup. "But why, may I ask, are you giving it to him? Isn't this to be part of your dowry?"

"Please, I don't have time for questions. Just make sure he gets it."

"I want to see North," said the boy.

Matilda decided it would be best not to have Robbie there to witness this marriage. Her son was clearly upset. Matilda didn't want him to be scarred for life, watching his mother marry a man that neither of them even liked.

"Go with Beatrice then," she told her son. "And Beatrice, please tell North . . . tell Norton that he should leave the castle right away."

"Leave?" asked the nursemaid. "I don't understand."

"Tell him his services are no longer needed." It broke Matilda's heart to say that, but she had no choice. She knew North needed the silver goblet more than she did right now, and was willing to pay the price for giving it away. Hopefully, by the time Marcus and Lord Gurney discovered it was gone, North would be halfway back to Scotland. She decided that after the wedding, she would go to the dungeon herself and release North's brother and friends. She would not let them die! Matilda would do whatever it took to help North and his friends. Her only hope was that someday she would forget all about North MacKeefe. However, there were some things that would live on with a person forever, and she was afraid this was one of them.

"Aye, my lady," said Beatrice, turning to go.

"Wait," said Matilda, stopping her. "Also tell him . . . tell him I will always love him."

⇒⟫⟩⟨⟨⇐

NORTH KEPT HIS back to the wall and his eyes on the guards atop the battlements. He had his sword strapped on, as well as a dagger and an extra blade in his boot. He had to help his brother and friends escape before they were hanged in the courtyard on the morrow. If he had to kill off a few guards to aid him in the process, he no longer cared. He would free his brother and friends, or die trying.

North was just about to open the door to the dungeon when he saw the nursemaid, Beatrice, running to the mews. She held on to Robbie's hand. Gertie was with them also. In the light of the sun, he saw something in the woman's hand reflecting brightly. That's when he realized she had Matilda's chalice with her.

"Hmm," he said, wondering what she was doing. "It doesna matter," he told himself. He needed to stay focused. He needed to free the men from the dungeon. When he opened the door, the guard on watch duty looked up.

"What is it?" growled the guard.

North saw Nash, Gavin, and Cam jump up, looking out the cell door. They had such looks of hope on their faces. All he had to do was kill this one guard, steal the keys, and set them free. It shouldn't take more than a few minutes.

"What do you want, Norton?" asked the guard. "You shouldn't be in here."

North's hand wavered over his sword. Then his eyes roamed

back to the men in the cell. It would be so easy. He heard Gertie barking, and turned around and looked out the open door. It was odd that Beatrice and the boy were coming to the mews without Matilda. He wondered what they wanted. Then he started thinking about the cup. Why did Beatrice have it? Matilda coveted that thing with her life. She would never take it off, and she certainly wouldn't give it to a servant. Something was wrong here. Curiosity got the best of him and he stepped back out the door.

"Sorry to have disturbed you," he said to the guard. "I must have taken the wrong passage. It's easy to get confused in a castle this big."

His brothers and friends started shouting and banging on the door to the cell.

"Quiet down!" commanded the guard as North left the dungeon and closed the door behind him.

He hurried to the mews, and stepped inside. Beatrice was talking to Walter, holding out the cup.

"What's this?" asked North, ducking through the entranceway so as not to hit his head as he entered the mews.

"North!" cried Robbie, running over to him and wrapping his arms around North's leg.

"North?" asked the old woman. "I thought your name was Norton."

"Why are you here, Beatrice?" North asked. "And what are you doing with Matilda's silver goblet?"

The woman had been handing it to Walter, but she stopped and pulled it away. "I was told by Lady Matilda to bring this to you, immediately. When you weren't here, Walter said he'd give it to you."

"I'll bet he did," said North, taking the goblet attached to the chain from her. "Why would Matilda even part with this when it means so much to her?"

"And why would she give it to you?" asked Walter, sounding suspicious.

"My mother is being married to a bald, fat man," said Robbie.

"What did you say?" North looked down at the boy.

"That's right," said Beatrice. "She was entering the rose garden for the ceremony when she pulled me aside and said it was important that you got this cup."

"She did?" North swallowed deeply, looking down at the cup in his hands. He unclasped the chain and threw it to the ground. Then he stuck the goblet into a bag that he retrieved from a hook on the wall. "Why is she getting married now? And so fast?" he asked her. "Why did she ask you to give this to me, when it is obviously part of her dowry?"

"I don't know," answered the nursemaid. "I am just as confused as you. Lady Matilda seemed so upset. I've never seen her like that. She also told me to tell you that you should leave here at once."

"Leave?" he asked. "Whatever for?"

"Ah, it sounds like you're being dismissed," said Walter, enjoying this too much. "I guess Lord Marcus decided I am more important after all."

"I'm being dismissed?" North was confused. "Was there anything else she asked you to tell me?"

"I don't want him for a father," cried Robbie. "I want you, North." He once again gripped his little hands around North's leg.

"You did have something going on with the girl, I knew it!" said Walter.

"What does it matter?" North grunted. "Matilda is marrying someone else as we speak."

"I'm sure she doesn't want to marry this man," said Beatrice.

"How do you know?" asked North, still using his English accent.

"Because, if she did want to marry Lord Gurney, then why would she tell me to relay the message to you that she loves you?"

"She really said that?" asked North, feeling his heart bursting from his chest.

"She did," Beatrice assured him.

"I heard her say it, too," said Robbie.

"Thank you for telling me." North turned and ran out the door. He knew exactly what he needed to do next. No matter what the consequences were for him, he no longer cared.

CHAPTER NINETEEN

MATILDA'S KNEES KNOCKED together as she stepped up under the arch of roses, standing next to the repulsive man that she didn't love or even want. She knew of no way to stop this marriage from happening. Her cousin was an earl, and he'd already secured the betrothal with Lord Gurney. She was too late! If she left now, it would only cause trouble for Amethyst and everyone in the castle. She didn't want a war to break out between Lord Gurney and Marcus because of her. Besides, even if she ran away, she had nowhere to go.

She needed to think of Robbie, just like Amethyst had told her. Her heart ached for North, but it no longer mattered. As soon as she was forced to say her vows, she'd belong to another man. She would never see North again.

The priest started with the vows. She wasn't even listening, since her thoughts were far from here right now.

"I do," she heard Lord Gurney say.

Then she heard the priest asking her a question, and her cousin, Marcus, calling her name.

"Matilda? Say 'I do'," Marcus commanded.

"I – I . . ." She looked over at the man who was to be her husband, feeling as if she were going to retch. Do it for Robbie, she told herself. Do it for the alliance. "I . . ." She just couldn't say it.

"Matilda! Dinna marry him, please," she heard from behind

her. She spun around to see North running through the rose garden, heading toward them.

"North? Why are you here? I told you to leave."

"I ken," he said. "But I realize ye didna mean it."

"Assistant falconer, what are you doing?" growled Marcus. "This garden is private and off limits to you."

"I'm sorry, my lord, but I had to come. To stop the weddin'."

"Why are you talking like a Scot?" Marcus drew his sword. "You're working with those Highland prisoners in my dungeon, aren't you?"

"What is going on here?" asked Lord Gurney, wiping sweat from his brow. "I thought this was a wedding."

"You have imprisoned my brathair and friends, and they dinna deserve to die," spat North. "They did nothin' wrong. We are MacKeefes, and aligned with ye."

"Don't try to fool me," spat Marcus. "I don't believe that for a minute."

"It's true," said Amethyst.

"Amy? How would you know?" Marcus looked over at his wife.

"I only know because Matilda told me."

"Matilda is a foolish girl who believes anything. I know, since she is my cousin."

"I love North," said Matilda. "I am sorry, Lord Gurney, but I can't marry you."

"What is going on here?" shouted Lord Gurney. "I have a contract. You are supposed to become my wife."

"B-but I don't want to marry you."

"You have no choice, Matilda. We have formed an alliance," Marcus reminded her.

"Ye also have an alliance with the MacKeefes, yet ye seem willin' to break it," said North. "So, break this betrothal."

"Why would I do that?" asked Marcus, still holding his sword.

"Because I love the lass, and I want to marry her."

"You love her?" asked Marcus. "That's not even possible."

"It is true, we love each other," said Matilda.

Marcus seemed speechless, and shook his head. "I don't care. Marriage is for alliances, not love."

"But Marcus, that's not entirely true," said Amethyst. "After all, we love each other."

"We were forced to marry," Marcus reminded her.

"But we did fall in love," Amethyst rallied.

"As will Matilda and Lord Gurney over time," said Marcus.

"Let's get on with the wedding," complained Lord Gurney.

"I agree," said Marcus.

Just as the priest was preparing to continue, Matilda cried out. "I made love with North."

Everyone's mouths dropped open, and silence filled the air.

"Montclair, you didn't tell me you were trying to pawn off a whore on me. She might already be pregnant with that Highlander's baby." Lord Gurney looked disgusted by the thought.

"She's no' a whore!" shouted North, unsheathing his sword. "I'll fight to the death if I have to, but I willna let ye insult Matilda. She is such a wonderful lass."

"Nay, stop!" shouted Marcus. "Put down the sword, Norton . . . or North, or whoever the hell you are."

"I willna."

"You will, because I am breaking the betrothal and asking you, Lord Gurney, to leave in peace and forget all about this," said Marcus, causing Matilda to gasp.

"Gladly," the man grunted. "I should have listened to the rumors about this wench because they are obviously true. Hrmph! How could she sleep with a bloody Scot? She must be mad, like everyone is saying."

"You insult my cousin once more, and I'll personally run my blade through your heart," Marcus warned him. "Guards," he shouted, and four men came running. "Two of you please escort Lord Gurney and his traveling companions out of here. The other two stay."

"Aye, my lord," the guards answered.

Once Lord Gurney was gone, Matilda ran to North, and wrapped her arms around him. North lowered his blade.

"Lass, I truly do love ye and want to marry ye," North told her.

"Are you going to be my father?" shouted Robbie, running into the rose garden, followed by Beatrice and Walter.

"Only if yer mathair will have me," said North, giving Matilda a kiss in front of everyone.

"Marcus?" Matilda looked over to her cousin. "I would like to marry North. I love him."

"Well, if this is the way you two feel about each other, then I suggest you marry right here, right now. Before the priest leaves."

"Really?" asked Matilda excitedly. "You're going to allow it?"

"I don't see how I can refuse, since you've already announced to everyone that you two have been intimate," said Marcus. "No man will ever want you now, so I might as well stop trying to find one."

"Thank you, Marcus," Amethyst told her husband.

North stood next to Matilda. She smiled at him and took his hand.

"Ye're tremblin', lass," he told her.

"It's not because I'm scared. It's because I am so excited."

"Me, too."

"Lord Marcus, I need to leave," said the priest.

"Just make the wedding quick, then," Marcus told him. "Nothing fancy."

"Of course. Do you, Lady Matilda Lumley . . ."

"Montclair," she told the priest. "I have been using my maiden name since I've been a widow."

"Fine." The priest started again. "Do you, Lady Matilda Montclair take Norton –"

"North. North MacKeefe," Matilda corrected the man, interrupting once again.

"North MacKeefe," repeated the priest, sounding irritated

now. "To be your husband?"

"I do," she answered, feeling her head spinning again since this was all happening so fast that she wasn't even sure it wasn't just a dream. Was she really marrying again, and this time for love? It was almost too good to be true.

"And do you, North MacKeefe, take Lady Matilda Montclair to be your bride?" asked the priest.

"Aye, I do," North answered.

"Then I pronounce you man and wife. You may kiss the bride. I need to leave, Lord Montclair."

"Of course," Matilda heard her cousin tell the priest, and then he ordered one of his guards to see the man out.

"Matilda. We're married, lass." North kissed her passionately, and she melted in his arms. She never thought her dreams could come true, but they just did.

"You're my father now," said Robbie, jumping up and down. North scooped him up, and hugged Matilda.

"This is wonderful," said Matilda. "I am the happiest woman in the world." She couldn't stop staring at her new husband. If she hadn't been watching him, she might have noticed Marcus still gripping the hilt of his sword and his guard approaching North with his sword drawn.

"Matilda," cried out Amethyst.

Matilda saw what was happening, but she didn't understand it. "Marcus? What are you doing?" she asked.

"I'm sorry, Matilda, but he's a Scot and I still don't know if I can trust him," said Marcus. "Throw down your weapons, North."

"What?" asked North. "Is this some kind of trick?"

"Nay, no trick." Marcus moved closer with his sword drawn now. "Put down the boy and drop your weapons. Now. I'm sorry, but until I know who you really are, you're going to have to join your friends in the dungeon."

CHAPTER TWENTY

"WELL, BRATHAIR, NICE of ye to join us," said Nash with contempt in his voice as the guards tossed North into the dungeon cell and locked the door behind him.

"If you had any brains in your head, you would have let her marry the nobleman," said the guard. "Instead of trying to stop it, you should have hightailed it out of here while you still could."

"I never would have done that. Ever," spat North.

"Lord Marcus has had many Scots as prisoners," continued the guard. "I hope you don't really think he's going to let any of you go."

The guard left, closing the cell door and the outer door as well, leaving North and the other Scots alone in the near dark.

"It's rather chilly in here," remarked North, not daring to make eye contact with the others.

"Ye dinna say!" It was Nash speaking again. North finally looked up to see his brother shooting daggers from his eyes at him. He supposed he couldn't blame him.

"What the hell happened?" growled Gavin.

"Why didna ye release us earlier when ye had the chance?" asked Cam, sitting with his back against the wall.

"I'm sorry," said North. "I never meant for any of this to happen."

"I wish I'd never said I'd help ye now." Nash sat next to Cam and rubbed his sore ankle.

"If it wasna for ye, North, we would all be home right now in a warm bed with our wives," said Gavin.

"Aye. I ken." North felt really bad about all this, and didn't know how to make it right. "I had every intention of releasin' ye. But then, I got a little distracted."

"We noticed. With the lass," said Gavin.

"The Sassenach," spat Cam.

"The wench," added his brother, glaring at him from the dark. North didn't need to see the whites of his eyes to know it. He felt the tension in the cell between them and him, and he couldn't say he blamed them a bit.

"My wife," North said softly.

"What did ye say?" asked Nash.

"It sounded like he called the lass his wife," said Cam.

"I did," said North, releasing a deep breath and finally turning to face them. "I was just married to Lady Matilda."

"Ye liar!" Nash threw an empty metal plate at him that had held food. North jumped aside and the plate hit the bars of the cell, falling to the floor with a loud crash. "Do ye think tellin' us a fib like that is goin' to make us feel sorry for ye?"

"It willna," said Cam. "So ye might as well tell us the truth."

"Why are ye in here?" asked Gavin.

"I am tellin' ye the truth, I swear." North continued. "Matilda was bein' forced to marry some baldin', fat Sassenach that she didna want to marry."

"So ye intervened and got thrown in here," said Gavin. "Well, that is just great. We're really doomed now."

"I was thrown in here because Lord Marcus doesna trust us. He allowed me and Matilda to be married first, since she told everyone that we'd already slept together."

"Ye did?" asked Nash in surprise.

"He did," said Cam.

"Why didna I ken?" Nash wasn't happy to have been left out of the loop of information.

"I suppose we forgot to mention it," said Gavin.

"So what happens now?" asked Cam.

"I'm no' sure," said North. "They were goin' to hang the three of ye on the morrow."

"What?" all three of them said at once.

"Sorry," mumbled North.

"Oh, great! Well, now ye can join us," spat Gavin. "We'll all die together as one big happy family."

"God's eyes, North. Why didna ye try harder to get us out of here?" asked Nash. "I am yer own brathair, but yet ye left me in here the longest, to rot."

"I'm sorry, Nash. I am ashamed of myself." North looked down to the bag hanging at his side. "I was goin' to release all of ye, but I suppose I became too greedy."

"How so?" asked Gavin.

"I didna do it because I didna want trouble until I had this in my hand." He pulled the silver goblet out of his bag and held it up for the others to see.

"Ye finally have it?" Cam stood up and came over to inspect it. "So, ye managed to get it after all."

"Ironic that he has the means to free himself from bein' an outcast, but it willna matter since he'll be dead," said Gavin.

"He traded us for his doitit cup." Nash did not come over to join them.

"He was only tryin' to finish his punishment and no' be an outcast any longer," said Cam. "I can understand that."

"I understand, too, North, but couldna ye have done it a little sooner?" asked Gavin.

"I wish I had." North looked down at the cup, running his finger over the empty spot where the heart gemstone should be. His heart felt empty now, too. He pulled the stone out of his pocket and put it over the spot. "I was so close to findin' happiness for the first time in my life. I should have kent Lord Marcus wouldna really be supportin' me and Matilda as husband and wife. After all, he is a border lord, and I am a Scot."

"What are we goin' to do?" Nash finally got up and walked

over to join them.

"We need to escape," said Cam. "Unless we want to die on the morrow."

"I'm sure Matilda will try to convince Marcus no' to do anythin' until he has an answer to the missive that he sent to Callum," North told them.

"And what if she canna convince him?" asked Gavin.

"Or if Callum gets ornery and decides no' to agree that he kens us," added Cam.

"I wouldna put it past the old coot." Nash slammed his hand against the bars of the door.

"Ye're right," said North, putting the pink heart stone back in his pocket and the cup back into his bag. "We canna risk it. We're goin' to have to break out of here tonight, as soon as the guard nods off."

"Och, right, Brathair. And how the hell do ye suggest we do that?" asked Nash. "It's no' like we havena been tryin'."

"I've been kent to pick a lock now and then." North reached down and pulled a hidden dagger from his boot.

"How did that escape the guard's notice?" asked Gavin with a smile.

"There was so much commotion with the cryin' boy, the barkin' dog, and both Matilda and Amethyst yellin' at Marcus. I guess they were in too much of a hurry to imprison me to search me properly." North chuckled. "I gave up my weapons freely, and headed to the dungeon with my hands over my head. I did it so fast that they didna have time to check for hidden blades, or to even realize I had this on me." He patted the bag that held the cup.

"How did ye manage to finally get that away from Matilda?" asked Gavin.

"Aye, with it chained around her waist, it did seem impossible," said Cam.

"I didna take it from her," North told them. "She sent it to me with the nursemaid when she thought she was marryin' the

Sassenach."

"So, she gave it to ye freely?" Cam was confused.

"She really must be in love with ye, North, or she wouldna have done it," said Nash.

"Nay, she wouldna," North agreed. "She told me this was the last remembrance of her faither. He gave it to her when she was a child."

"How can that be?" asked Nash. "Storm had it. It was given to him by the king."

"I dinna ken," said North.

"I think she's lyin'," said Nash.

"Nay, I believe her, Brathair." North let out a deep sigh. "I am guessin' that mayhap this cup was really stolen from the English by the Scots years ago. Mayhap it was theirs all along. Then again, mayhap the English stole it from our king."

"Either way, what does it matter?" asked Gavin. "Now, ye will no longer be an outcast. Let's get the hell out of here, and go home to our wives."

"Aye," agreed Cam. "I canna wait any longer to be with Yvaine."

"I want to kiss Kellina," said Nash. "God's eyes, I hope she willna be too angry with me for leavin'."

"I miss Davita and her siblin's," said Gavin. "When I pretended to be a cobbler to get into the courtyard, it brought back too many memories of learnin' to make shoes from Davita. I really miss my wife."

"Well, it's almost time," said North, holding up his hidden dagger and looking at his reflection in it from the scant torchlight in the dungeon. "After tonight, we'll be back in Scotland. And ye three will be with yer wives."

There was silence when he didn't mention himself.

Finally, Nash spoke up. "Mayhap ye can bring Matilda with us."

"I wouldna do that unless her son and dog come, too," North told them. "But if I try to sneak all of them out of here, we will surely be caught."

"So, what are ye sayin'?" asked Cam. "Ye're willin' to leave them all behind?"

"She's yer wife now, Brathair," Nash reminded him.

"I dinna want to leave her behind, but I've already caused the lassie enough trouble. I'll get the three of ye home, and when the air clears, I'll come back and get her."

"Are ye sure?" asked Cam.

"We can help ye get the lass, the boy, and the dog out of here," offered Gavin.

"Nay." North wouldn't hear of it. "Ye've all done enough for me already, and I thank ye. This is my problem now. All I want is for all of ye to get back home to yer wives in Scotland where ye belong."

"Well, if ye're sure, then who are we to stop ye?" It was clear that Nash still hadn't forgiven North for his mistakes. "I see the guard and he's already noddin' off," said Nash. "Start workin' on the lock. We need to get movin' before Lord Marcus decides the only way we're leavin' here is without our heads."

CHAPTER TWENTY-ONE

ATILDA AWOKE THE next morning to hear shouting out in the courtyard. She had cried herself to sleep last night, longing to be with her new husband. She and Amethyst had tried to convince Marcus to let North and the other Scots go free. Sadly, he had refused. He had even forbidden either of them to visit the dungeon.

Marcus was upset about the broken betrothal with Lord Gurney. It hadn't ended well. Matilda could understand his concern that the man might come back with an army. Then again, Lord Gurney seemed like he didn't want her anyway once he'd found out she had coupled with North. Hopefully, he wouldn't pursue the matter further.

Matilda rolled over in bed, wishing there wasn't so much noise outside. She was lost in her thoughts of North, and wanted to close her eyes to be with him again. She snaked her hand under the pillow, her fingers touching something cold and hard. Sitting up in bed, she moved her pillow aside, and gasped when she saw her silver chalice. Next to it, was the small pink heart stone that she had lost on Grope Lane.

The warning bells rang out, signaling that something was wrong. Matilda's head snapped around and she looked at the open window. Right now, she half-expected to see North climbing into the room. Sadly, he wasn't there. There was no doubt in her mind why they were ringing the bells. It was because

North and his friends had escaped the dungeon during the night.

Part of her was relieved that they had gotten away. But another part of her was also angry. If North had sneaked into her room and left the chalice under her pillow, why hadn't he woken her up? He could have taken her with him or, at the very least, said goodbye.

What else made no sense to her was why North would leave without this cup. After all, if he returned to Scotland without it, he would still be an outcast. This goblet was even more important to North than it had been to her.

"Oh, North," she said, hurriedly getting out of bed, and pulling on her clothes. She needed to get down to the courtyard as quickly as possible.

She had just finished dressing when there came a slight knock on her door.

"North?" She spun around and ran to the door, pulling it open. "I knew you wouldn't leave without me."

She stopped dead in her tracks when she saw Walter, the falconer, standing there with an evil grin on his face.

"Walter," she said, taking a step back into the room. "What brings you here? Falconers are not allowed up by the personal chambers of the nobles."

"I came to see you, Lady Matilda." He stepped into the room, even though she tried to close the door. He pushed it open, spotting the chalice on the bed. "Well, if it isn't my lucky day after all. I knew if I waited long enough, I'd get what I wanted."

"W-what do you mean?" Whatever it was he wanted, she was not willing to give it to him.

He chuckled, making his way over to the bed. Then he snatched up the goblet, tossing it in the air and catching it again in one hand. "I have missed this for almost twenty years now. Ever since those bloody Scots betrayed me, leaving me for dead, and bringing back the goods to their damned king."

With his back to her, she noticed something that she hadn't before now. He had silver bands attached to the back of his boot heels. Her heart lodged in her throat. She hoped she was wrong, but she had a feeling she knew what he meant.

"I'm sure I don't know what you're talking about." She looked over her shoulder, slowly making her way toward her sword on the other side of the room.

"Don't even think about it." He reached out and yanked her back to him and threw her down on the bed.

"What do you want with me?" she cried. "Leave me alone! Guards! Help me."

"Shut your mouth before I rip out your tongue." He reached down with his gloved hand, holding it over her mouth. She tried to bite him and struggled with him, managing to rip off his falconer's glove. Her eyes focused on the long scar running down the top of his hand. Her heart jumped. This was no coincidence. She knew exactly who he was.

"You!" she spat, sitting up on the bed, scooching backward. "You're the man who killed my family."

"Actually, I only killed your parents. The Scots foolishly killed your brothers, but I suppose it was for the best. They would have only caused trouble."

"I r-remember you," she stuttered, so scared she could barely speak. "Y-you came after me in my hiding spot. I s-stabbed you on the hand with my eating knife."

He laughed. "So, you finally figured it out, you bitch!" He reached out and yanked her forward and then slapped her hard across the face. Pain shot through her, but she wouldn't give him the pleasure of hearing her scream or even cry.

"I don't understand," she said. "Why did you do such horrible things?"

"Your father and I were working together. That is, until he decided to betray me. So, I teamed up with some renegade Scots who promised me wealth and protection." He chuckled lowly, as if it amused him. "I should have known I couldn't trust a damned Scot. They abandoned me that day. Right after they robbed me, beat me, and left me for dead."

"I hate you," she cried, tears flowing down her cheeks. "Who are you, really? And why would my father have had anything to do with the likes of you?"

"I am Hubert of Canterbury."

"You were a guard," she said, remembering his name.

"That's right. I used to be, when I worked for your Uncle Gilbert. But he tired of me, and I was let go. I ended up getting a job as a guard, working for your father instead."

"Aye," she said, still trying to move away from him. "I remember you now. You used to bring me up to the battlements as a child and hold me up to look over the wall."

"I was tempted to throw you over many times, and now wish I had."

"You are an evil man. Get out of my chamber!" She bolted up off the bed, but with one blow of his arm, she fell back down again. Clenching her jaw, Matilda bit back the pain. "My father should have killed you instead of trusted you."

"Aye, I suppose he should have. However, he was just as greedy as me. He always wanted more than his brother, Gilbert, and I showed him how to do it. Our plan was that he'd attract the noblemen to his manor. When they weren't paying attention, I'd go through their things. We'd steal from the nobles, whatever we could, and divide the booty amongst us. We even stole things like this from the Scottish king himself." He chuckled and tossed the chalice up and down once more.

"Nay. That's a lie. That is my cup. My father gave it to me."

"Such a naïve child you still are. How do you think your father would come to have something as expensive as this in the first place?" He held up the goblet to admire it. "This is the goblet of a king, and the best thing he ever stole."

"Nay. That's not true," she cried. "My father was not a thief."

"He was, because I taught him to be," said Walter. "And if Robert Montclair hadn't taken too much for himself, he might still be alive today. I would have made him richer than his brother, and he would have someday had that castle he always wanted."

"My uncle," she whispered. "Is he in on this, too?" She asked about the man who had raised her – Marcus' father.

"Nay, he's just as clueless as you were. Or your mother and brothers."

"I don't understand," she said, needing to know more. "My father was not a bad man."

"Greed changes even the best of men," he told her. "Everyone wants more in life, and I just happened to be able to help him get it. Believe it or not, it's the truth."

"Why now? Why didn't you come for the chalice or me long ago?"

"I lived in France for years, trying to heal after the Scots attacked me. Besides, I had nowhere to go back to, since we burned your father's manor. I finally tired of France, and decided to return to England. Luck was on my side when I heard the rumors of the chalice being back here again. I knew I had to have it. That is what led me back to you."

"I knew there was something about you I didn't like."

He chuckled again. "Now that you have seen my face and know my story, I'm afraid it is time for you to go. I cannot have loose ends. Not at my age. I will remove the gemstones and sell them. Then this chalice will be melted down and bring me enough profit to live comfortably for the rest of my life."

"Why don't you just go back with those Scots you worked with?" she asked, hoping to keep him from killing her until she could devise a plan to escape. "No one would ever find you in Scotland."

"Those renegade Scots are long gone, Wench."

"Y – you killed them, too?"

"Nay. They were punished for what they did to me, by the hand of God. They all died aboard a ship they boarded that capsized in a storm. So, you see, I am on my own now."

"Matilda, did you hear that –" Amethyst stopped in the open doorway, her jaw dropping when she saw the falconer by her bedside.

"Amethyst, help me!" cried Matilda. "He is going to kill me."

Hubert yanked Matilda up off the bed, putting his arm around her, still holding the cup. He used his dagger in his other hand, and pressed it against her throat. "Say a word and she's dead," he ground out.

"Oh," Amethyst whimpered, slapping her hand over her mouth.

"That's the word," he said, pressing the blade closer.

CHAPTER TWENTY-TWO

NORTH RODE TOWARD the border with his brother and his friends, too sad to even talk. He had left the silver goblet under Matilda's pillow, and had been tempted to wake her and take her with him. But he didn't. He realized that, right now, that wasn't the smartest move. She was his wife, but taking her with him would have meant taking the boy and the hound, too. They would have slowed him down and he would have ended up being caught and thrown back in the dungeon. Even if they hadn't been caught, an action like that could have brought war between them.

"Dinna fret about it, Brathair," said Nash, slowing down his horse to talk with North. "Ye can always get yer marriage dissolved."

"I dinna want that, ye fool," he said through gritted teeth. "I love Matilda. She is my wife."

"If ye feel that way about it, mayhap ye can go back and get her someday," suggested Gavin.

"Aye," agreed Cam. "Since ye're no longer an outcast, I'm sure Storm will help to straighten things out. After all, the MacKeefes have an alliance with the Montclairs."

"That will never happen," said North.

"Why no'?" asked Nash. "Ye dinna think that Marcus will forgive us for escapin'?"

"Or forgive ye for marryin' his cousin, and then leavin' without her?" said Gavin.

"I did what I had to do," North told them. "It was for no' only Matilda's guid, but also her son's welfare. I couldna let anythin' happen to them. At least I ken she is safe at Montclair Castle. Besides, I dinna have the cup. I am never goin' home."

"What?" all three of the men asked at once. Cam and Gavin turned back and came to North's side.

"Please tell me I heard ye wrong," said Gavin. "I thought ye said ye didna have the cup."

"Ye had it in the dungeon," said Nash. "Ye showed it to us."

"What did ye do? Drop it?" asked Cam sarcastically. "Or mayhap stop at a tavern when we werena lookin' and use it to have a dram of whisky, and forgot it there?"

"Nay," explained North. "I kent how important the goblet was to Matilda. So I sneaked into her room last night and slipped it under her pillow."

"Ye did what?" Gavin's jaw twitched.

"We left our wives and traveled this far with ye to help ye, and ye still dinna have the means to end yer sentence," said Cam.

"No' to mention, ye left us to rot in the dungeon for naught." Nash glared at him, and it didn't feel good.

"Nash, stop it. Ye're goin' to have to get over it sooner or later," North told him.

"Do I now?" Nash didn't sound as if he agreed.

"Ye are a fool!" spat Cam.

"Nay, I'm a man in love," North answered. "If I didna love Matilda, I would have taken the cup and no' looked back."

"How is this any different?" asked Gavin. "Besides no' havin' the cup, ye left her and are no' lookin' back, unless I'm mistaken."

North hadn't been thinking clearly. Gavin's words made him feel unsettled.

"Ye're right," he said, stopping his horse and turning around. "I am a fool."

"Wait, Brathair. What are ye doin'?" asked Nash.

"I'm goin' back to live with my wife. I just hope Lord Marcus will let us stay at the castle, or we'll have to live in the woods."

"Ye canna be serious," North heard Cam say from behind him. "North, ye are a MacKeefe. Yer home is in Scotland."

"Dinna be daft," said Nash. "The MacKeefes are yer family."

"Unless ye've forgotten, I am still an outcast and will always be now," North said over his shoulder, still heading in the opposite direction. "I am no longer welcome in the MacKeefe Clan."

"North, wait," begged his brother, seeming to have a change of heart. "Think this over."

"I have," he answered. "I'll never take Matilda's only remembrance of her family from her, but I dinna want to lose her either. I'm goin' to ask if I can stay at Montclair Castle. It'll be my home from now on."

"Ye'd really leave us?" Cam called out.

"Go back to yer wives where ye belong, and dinna worry about me."

"Bid the devil, what is he doin'?" Gavin said to the others.

"I think he's gone mad," Cam answered.

"That's my brathair for ye," was the last thing North heard Nash say before North dug his heels into the sides of the horse and took off at a fast run, anxious to be back with Matilda once again.

MATILDA SCREAMED WHEN Hubert punched Amethyst in the face, splitting her lip and making it bleed. When Amethyst doubled over in pain, the evil man hit her over the head and threw her on the bed. She went limp, falling unconscious.

"Nay! Stop hurting her," Matilda cried out, once more lunging for her sword, but Hubert was too strong. He held her against him with his knife in his hand while he slipped the silver goblet into a bag tied to his waist.

"You're coming with me now," he growled. "You're my safe passage boarding a ship that is headed to France. I can sell the cup and live like a noble. I'll have a fresh start where no one knows who I am."

"I'll never go with you. I am married to North, and he is going to kill you." Matilda continued to struggle as he pulled her to the door.

"I think you're mistaken. I don't want you for my wife. You're too much trouble. I only want insurance to get out of the castle and onto the ship safely."

"My husband will hunt you down like a dog once he hears what you did."

"Do you really think I believe that? I watched last night as your husband and his friends left the castle without you," he told her, all but dragging her down the spiral staircase. "They are not even here. You should know now that you can never trust a Scot. Now, you'll help me, because if you don't, you'll never find out where I hid your son."

"Robbie?" she gasped. "What did you do to him?" Her heart beat furiously and anxiety made her entire body shake. Fearing for her life was one thing, but she never thought he'd stoop so low as to go after a child. Thoughts flooded her brain once again of the time when she was just a child and he had tried to kill her. Aye, he would do this. He wasn't lying. Robbie was in trouble.

"I haven't hurt him. Yet. But if you refuse to aid me, I'll never tell you where I hid him and he'll die. After all, he is bound and gagged so he'll be there for a long, long time."

"Nay!" she cried. "Please, let him go. I don't care what you do to me, but just don't hurt my son."

"I know you don't care about yourself, or you never would have slept with that bloody Scot. I see now that the rumors I've heard about you are true."

"You bastard! I swear I will have your head. You won't get away with killing my family, and I won't allow you to kill my son either."

"Well, now, I don't see how you're in any position to be telling me what I can or cannot do. Now, keep your mouth shut or your son will die. I'll have a blade at your back, so don't even think about running or calling out for help. You do, and I won't hesitate to kill you. We need to get to the stable without arousing suspicion. Thankfully, everyone is in such a frenzy about the escaped prisoners that I doubt they'll even notice us. I already have a horse saddled and waiting. All we need to do is keep invisible until we cross that moat."

Matilda's body trembled. She walked with Hubert out to the courtyard, feeling the tip of his blade pricking her back. She wished more than anything for her sword right now. All her years of training to fight, and when she needed to do it, she couldn't. Her mind went crazy worrying about Robbie. She had to do whatever was needed to assure his safety.

"Lady Matilda," cried Beatrice, running across the courtyard waving her arms wildly. "The prisoners have escaped and Robbie is missing. I just saw him an hour ago, but now he is gone."

Matilda stopped, her body stiffening.

"Keep walking," Hubert said in her ear. "Tell the old bat that your son is fine."

"Nay," she said stubbornly.

"Your choice. But your son's life depends on if I board that ship or not."

"Robbie is fine," she called out to Beatrice. "He's in my bedchamber taking a nap."

"Nay, you bitch," Hubert ground out in a low voice. "Why did you tell her that? Now, she'll find the earl's wife. Damn, I should have killed her when I had the chance."

It was the exact reason why Matilda told Beatrice her son was in her chamber. She figured, if Beatrice found Amethyst, she could help her, as well as tell Marcus. Her cousin would come looking for her, she was sure.

They entered the stable to find Theodore, one of Marcus' barbican guards mounting his horse. Hubert tried to move back in the shadows, but Theodore saw them.

"Matilda, I am sorry to tell you but the prisoners, including your husband, have escaped," the guard informed her. North and Theodore had been friendly to each other and this was probably one of the only guards who still liked North, even though he now knew he was a Scot.

Matilda looked back at Hubert and he shook his head, giving her a silent warning.

"Aye, I know," she said. "Where is Lord Marcus?" She felt Hubert squeezing her arm so tightly that she almost cried out.

"He took a dozen of his men and is out looking for the prisoners. I'm headed there now to help him." He started to ride forward, then stopped and turned his horse around. "Where are you two going?" he asked. "Lord Marcus requested that everyone stay inside the castle walls. Those Scots could be dangerous."

"Lady Matilda has required my help in finding her falcon that has broken its jess and is flying around loose," said Hubert.

"Oh. Good luck." The guard nodded. "Wait a minute. Lady Matilda doesn't have a falcon. She has a hawk."

Matilda's eyes shot over to Hubert. His blade poked her harder now, and she wasn't sure he wouldn't draw blood.

"Aye, that's true," said Matilda. "Hubert meant that both my hawk and a falcon escaped."

"Right," said Hubert with a chuckle. "I guess it is one big day for escapees."

"I guess so." The guard turned around and rode out of the stable. "Good luck."

"Good going," Hubert said, hauling her over to a saddled horse. "You purposely called me Hubert in front of him. Don't think I didn't notice. It's just a good thing that the idiot doesn't even know my name is supposedly Walter."

Matilda sat on the horse in front of Hubert as they left the stable and crossed the drawbridge. She tried to make eye contact with several of the guards and also some servants, planning on mouthing the word "help". Unfortunately, not a one of them would look at her. They probably thought she was naught but a trollop, taking off with the falconer after she'd married a Scot yesterday.

She cried out for North in her mind, wishing he had never left her. Matilda needed him now more than ever for her and her son. She had a feeling once Hubert boarded the boat, he wouldn't tell her where Robbie was. She also felt that she wasn't going to still be alive to look for him. She and her son would die just like the rest of her family at the hands of this horrible, wretched, wicked man.

CHAPTER TWENTY-THREE

NORTH RODE BACK to the castle as fast as he could go. He was anxious to hold Matilda in his arms once again and tell her he loved her. He knew that returning after they'd escaped wasn't going to bode well for him. He wouldn't be surprised if he ended up back in the dungeon again for a spell.

Lord Marcus might even hang him, but it no longer mattered. At least he would die being close to the woman he loved. He could only hope that the missive from Glasgow had arrived, and that Callum had confirmed that he knew them. If so, his troubles were over. On the other hand, if the old coot was feeling ornery, he might just have told the messenger to shove off, and not even given him a dram of his Mountain Magic before he left.

"Damn, why didna I just stay in the first place?" he spoke to himself. He heard a rider up ahead. Looking up, he noticed it was just one soldier. He could fight off one man easily, so he didn't hide. "Theodore?" he asked, noticing Lord Marcus' guard whom he had enjoyed drinking with on the battlements once or twice.

"North," said Theodore with a smile, stopping his horse. "I think I should warn you, Lord Marcus and a small troop of men are out looking for you and your friends."

"I ken," said North. "I expected as much."

"Why are you headed back toward the castle?" he asked. "I figured you'd be across the border by now. I know I would be, if I were you."

"I couldna leave. I already miss Matilda. I should have stayed there, but I had to help my friends. But now, I'm comin' back to Matilda – my wife. I want to tell her I love her."

"Well, you might have to tell her later. I just saw her leaving the castle with the falconer."

"With the falconer?" he asked in surprise.

"Aye. Sorry, North. I think she's already found someone new."

"I dinna believe it." This made North feel very uncomfortable. "She doesna even like the man. She would never get that close to him on purpose."

"Well, she said that she and Hubert were going out to look for her falcon, even though she has a hawk. They tried to cover up the mistake, but I didn't believe it. Something was odd about the whole thing."

"Hubert?" asked North, feeling confused. "Who is he?"

"He's the falconer," said the guard. "You should know him, since you were his assistant."

"God's eyes, nay!" spat North, suddenly remembering the scar he'd seen on the back of Walter's hand. Matilda's story came back to him of how she had stabbed her attacker when she was a child. He would bet anything that Walter – or Hubert was this same man.

"Theodore, I think Matilda is in trouble. That falconer is a fake and I am sure he means to hurt her."

"I'll go back and look for them," offered Theodore.

"Nay. I'll head back. Ye go and try to find Lord Marcus, and tell him the falconer has kidnapped his cousin."

THEY WEREN'T FAR from the castle when Matilda saw a rider up ahead, coming in their direction. As he got closer, she recognized the purple and green plaid of the MacKeefes.

"North," she gasped, surprised to see her husband headed back toward the castle. Especially since he'd already left with his friends.

"Damn it," spat Hubert, directing the horse off into the woods. He rode faster and faster. When Matilda turned her head and looked back, she realized North was gaining on them. He was an experienced rider.

"Stop!" North called out, but Hubert didn't even slow down. When North got closer, he cut them off, forcing their horse to stop. "Unhand my wife," he yelled, pulling his sword from his sheath.

"Don't come any closer or she dies," shouted Hubert.

"North, he's got a blade to my back, and he's taken Robbie," Matilda called out. "Don't kill him. If you do, we'll never find out where he's hidden my son."

"God's eyes, can this get any worse?" spat North. "What do ye want? Money? Gold? Whatever it is, I can give it to ye. Just dinna hurt Matilda or her son."

"What I want is to see every Scot's head on a pike."

"Talk that way again, and I'll have yer head on a pike," warned North, his face growing red with anger.

"Escort me to the ship that is leaving for France," said the man. "Get me there safely, and then I'll tell you where I hid the boy."

"I dinna believe ye."

"You don't have a choice. It's either that or I'll kill the girl right now and let the boy die all alone in the dark."

"North, please," cried Matilda. "I can't let anything happen to Robbie. He is all I have."

"Nay, that's no' true, lass. Ye have me, too. I made a mistake by leavin'. I came back because I want to be with ye and Robbie forever."

"Why did you return the cup, North?" asked Matilda. "That was your only means of redeeming yourself. Without it, you will be an outcast forever."

"I'd rather be an outcast than live without ye, my love."

"I've had enough of this," said Matilda. Her head shot backward with a jerk, and she hit Hubert hard.

"Ow!" he cried out.

Then she elbowed him in the gut, grabbing his hand that held the dagger. The horse reared up, neighing, and in her struggles, her hand got cut. They both fell to the ground, and she felt as if the air had been knocked from her lungs.

"Matilda!" yelled North, jumping from his horse. Hubert scrambled over the ground, unsheathing his sword and bringing it down toward Matilda. Matilda closed her eyes, realizing she was about to die.

NORTH'S SWORD HIT Hubert's, knocking it out of the man's hand. Then North kicked him and dropped his sword, punching Hubert in the face over and over again. If they had known where he'd hidden Robbie, the man would be dead right now. He heard Matilda crying softly from behind him.

"Bid the devil, I wish I could kill ye, because it would make me more than happy," spat North. When the man laid there still, and with his eyes closed, North turned and fell to his knees by Matilda. She was bruised and bleeding and had a big bump on the back of her head.

"North, you saved me."

"What were you thinkin', lass? Ye didna need to get hurt. I had him."

The pounding of thundering hoofbeats shook the earth, telling North that someone was either coming to his aid, or coming to collect him to throw him back into the dungeon. Either way, he didn't care. At least he was with Matilda once again. He helped her sit up, and held her closely in his arms.

"Are ye all right?" he asked.

"I am, now that you're here."

"I wanted to kill that bastard. I still do."

"I'll never give a bloody Scot the privilege of killing me," came Hubert's voice from the ground as he pushed up to a sitting position. "I'll make sure it never happens."

"North!" Matilda's eyes opened wide.

North released Matilda, pulling his spare dagger from his boot, and jumping to his feet. Hubert raised his blade above his head, but instead of attacking North, he plunged his dagger into his own heart. His eyes bulged out and he dropped the blade as he coughed up blood. Then he fell back down on the ground.

"Nay!" Matilda crawled over the rocky ground to get to him, shaking him, and yelling at Hubert now. "Don't die, you bastard. Tell me where you hid my son. Tell me. For God's sake, I need to know!"

Blood dripped from Hubert's mouth, and he looked right at her. "Since I couldn't kill you . . . I'll have my revenge . . . on your son, instead." Hubert died with his eyes wide open.

"Nay! Nay, wake up." Matilda shook the man violently. "Tell me where you hid Robbie. Tell me. I need to know."

"Matilda, stop it. It's over." North removed her hands from the man's body, pulling her back into his arms. "He's dead, lass."

"He can't be." Her tears flowed like a river now. Her body shook, and she looked like she was going to faint.

"North, we're here!" North's brother, Nash, rode up with Cam and Gavin right behind him.

Gavin jumped off his horse with his blade pointed at Hubert's chest.

"Dinna bother. He's dead," announced North. "He tried to kidnap Matilda, and then he killed himself." North stood up, still comforting Matilda in his arms.

"What's that?" Cam dismounted, and reached into the man's pouch and pulled out the silver goblet.

"It looks like it's North's ticket home," said Gavin, bending down and closing Hubert's eyes. "I canna believe this. What is goin' on here?"

"Help me get the bastard atop a horse and I'll tell you everythin' on the way back to the castle." North realized he was asking a lot, thinking they would go back to the place from where they'd just escaped. "Forget it. I'll go by myself. Ye three head home to yer wives where ye belong. They'll be waitin' for ye."

"Nay. I'm no' goin' anywhere without ye, Brathair," said Nash from atop his horse. "We are in this together until the end."

"Even if it means gettin' thrown back into the dungeon at Montclair Castle?" asked North.

"I suppose I could use a little rest before we ride home," said Gavin, flashing him a smile.

"And I never got to finish carvin' my name in the back wall of the cell," said Cam with a grin.

"I'll never understand ye three." North took the goblet from Cam and handed it to Matilda.

"What's there to understand?" asked Nash. "We're family."

"Enough said." North smiled, feeling lucky to have two families now who would stand by him through thick or thin. "Let's get back to the castle."

"Nay, North," said Matilda, still looking very upset. "Hubert died before he could tell us where he hid Robbie. We have to look for my son."

"Damn, that's right," said North, running a frustrated hand through his hair.

"The boy's missin'?" asked Cam, concern sounding in his voice.

North headed to his horse. "I'm goin' out to look for him. The rest of ye take my wife and the dead body back to the castle."

"I'm goin' with ye," said Gavin, mounting his horse as well.

"North, wait," said Matilda. "Hubert said he saw you ride out, and Beatrice said she'd only been looking for Robbie for the last hour. That means Hubert never left. I think he hid Robbie somewhere inside the castle walls."

"The mews?" asked Nash.

"Or mayhap the dungeon," said Cam.

"We'll check all those places and more," announced North. "Matilda, I swear to ye, we'll find Robbie and he'll be just fine. I promise ye that from the bottom of my heart."

Chapter Twenty-Four

MATILDA SEARCHED THROUGH the hay in the mews, calling out for her son. Marcus and his men hadn't returned yet, but Amethyst had been there to greet them, and told the rest of the guards what had happened. She warned them not to put the MacKeefes back into the prison cells. Everyone around the castle helped with the search, and Gertie barked like crazy, knowing something was wrong.

"God's eyes, where is he?" asked North, starting to feel as if they were never going to find the boy.

"We've been searchin' for an hour now," said Gavin. "No one has found even a clue."

"Mayhap we should take a break," suggested Cam.

"Nay! I willna stop until I find the boy," said North.

"Then I suggest we go outside the castle gates to look," said Nash, coming down from the battlements. His ankle was doing much better, and he barely limped at all now. "I looked over the battlements, and there are a lot of places he could have hidden Robbie."

Gertie barked again, pulling on North's plaid, trying to get him to play.

"Stop it, Gertie. No' now," scolded North.

"What are we goin' to do?" asked Cam. "The longer it takes, the slimmer the chances are that we're goin' to find him alive."

"Shhhh," said North, seeing Matilda approaching. By the

frown on her face, he could tell she'd had no luck in finding the boy either.

"Did someone check the dungeon?" asked Matilda.

"Aye," said Cam. "Three times. The lad isna there."

Gertie barked some more, running in a circle now, making so much of a ruckus that North could barely think. "Quiet down, Gertie. And leave me alone. I dinna have time to play."

"That hound is givin' me a headache," complained Nash.

All of a sudden, North had an idea. "Gertie, come here." He got down on his knees and held out his arms.

"North, please," said Matilda. "There is no time to play with the dog now. We need to find my son."

"That's right, and I know someone who can help us find him."

"The dog?" Cam made a face.

North scratched behind the dog's ears and even let the damned thing slobber on him. "I just realized that all those times I played hide and seek with Robbie and Gertie, it is now goin' to come in handy."

"What do you mean?" asked Matilda.

"Gertie, find Robbie," North coaxed the dog. "Go on. Sniff him out. Find Robbie, Gert."

The dog barked and barked, and finally started sniffing the ground, walking in circles. Then she ran off toward the back of the castle.

"This way, everyone," called out North, running the fastest, stopping when he followed the dog into the secret rose garden. The dog ran in a circle around a shed, and then continued to bark at a pile of split logs stacked up next to it.

"Check inside the shed," North commanded.

"We already did," said Gavin. "He's not in there."

"The lad has got to be here somewhere. Gertie keeps barkin'."

"North, I think I know where he is." Matilda gripped North's arm. "My cousin has a secret oubliette under the wood pile. It's where he keeps his private stash of Mountain Magic. It's where I got the Mountain Magic that I brought to our outing. Hubert said Robbie would die in the dark. It's darker than anything in that hole."

"That's got to be it," said North, rushing forward, throwing the stacked wood everywhere. He got to the bottom of the pile where the dog was barking, seeing a metal handle on a round, wooden lid.

"That's it. Open it!" cried Matilda. "Oh, North, I am so scared."

"Stand back, everyone," North commanded, ripping open the door, looking down into a hole that was about waist-high. Sure enough, Robbie was in there. "He's here!" North pulled the boy out, ripping off his gag and untying his hands. Robbie started crying.

North hugged him protectively to his chest.

"Robbie, thank God you are alright." Matilda rushed forward to hug her son. North pulled them both in, not wanting to let either of them go. The dog continued to bark, and came over and slobbered on North once again, and he didn't even give a damn. The dog got in on the hug as well.

All that mattered to North was that the people he loved were safe. He felt it in his heart that he had found love in his life and never wanted to lose it. He would always have the MacKeefes, but now he had a new family. His family. A family he would always protect, and never let go.

MATILDA HUGGED AND kissed Robbie, feeling so relieved that they had found him and that he wasn't harmed.

"Thank you, North," she said. "I am so glad you decided to return." She looked over to Amethyst, seeing her bruises and swollen lip. "Oh, Amethyst, I am so sorry." She jumped up and gingerly reached out to touch Amethyst's face. "I will get my healing herbs and take care of this for you right away."

"You're hurt, too," said Amethyst, touching Matilda's cut on her hand.

"I'm fine."

"What happened to that awful man?" asked Amethyst.

"His dead body is in the courtyard," said North. "He willna bother anyone ever again."

"Amethyst! Are you all right?" Marcus ran into the secret garden, followed by Beatrice. "I just heard what happened." He pulled his wife into his arms and hugged her.

"Oh, Robbie, you're alive," cried Beatrice, running over to hug the boy.

"Lord Marcus," said North, standing up to confront the man. "I apologize for causin' ye any trouble, but I couldna let my brathair and my friends die, so we had to escape."

"Well, North," said Marcus, using North's real name. "It seems you had no reason to leave, and that I have been overly cautious. I'm sorry."

"What do ye mean?" asked Nash.

"While I was out searching for all of you, I met my messenger on the road, coming back from Glasgow." He released Amethyst and pulled a parchment out from under his doublet.

"I hope Callum isna pretendin' no' to ken us," said Cam.

"Aye," agreed Gavin. "I really dinna want to go back in that cell again."

"And neither will you have to," said Marcus with a smile. "Callum sent word that he indeed knows North, Nash, Cam and Gavin MacKeefe. He also said that he was the one who sent you here, to look for and retrieve Storm MacKeefe's silver goblet."

"Finally," said North with a deep sigh. "So, are my brathair and friends free to go then?"

"Of course, said Marcus. "And you are, too, North."

"Nay, I'm no'." North shook his head.

"Why not?" asked Matilda. "I gave you the silver cup. Use it to get welcomed back into your clan." She pulled the silver chalice out from the bag slung over her shoulder and handed it to him.

North's gaze devoured the cup, and she saw a glimpse of hope, and lots of want in his eyes. He reached out for it, but before he touched it, he pulled his hand back and shook his head.

"Nay, I canna. I gave the cup back to ye," said North, pulling Matilda into his arms and looking longingly into her eyes. "I could never take away the last remembrance of yer faither. It's yers, lass, and will always be."

Matilda glanced over to see everyone staring at her. She wanted to tell North what she'd learned about her father from Hubert, that he was a swindler and a thief. If Hubert wasn't lying, then her father was not the man she thought him to be. She was planning on telling Marcus, and also her Uncle Gilbert. But then she realized if she told the truth, everyone's image of her father would be sullied. She didn't want her family to suffer if rumors got out that Robert Montclair had a dark side to him. With Hubert dead now, her father's secret died along with him. She wanted to keep it that way. That was not how she wanted her father to be remembered at all.

"I no longer need this," she said, handing it to North once more. "I think it would be better off in the hands of your chieftain, Storm MacKeefe."

"But, I thought it meant somethin' to ye, lass," said North, hesitantly taking it from her.

"The only thing that means anything to me is what I remember about my father . . . about my family. No one and nothing can change what I know. And that is all I need. My memories will keep my family alive. No cup can do that, nor do I want it to. Please, give it to your chieftain, and send it back where it belongs."

She decided she would tell North all about her father someday, but this was not the time to do it. Today was a happy day, since no one but a dark-souled man had died. Robbie was alive and North was with her. She was North's wife now, and that made her happy. She couldn't ask for anything else, and neither did she want to. As long as she was with those she loved, her life's purpose was fulfilled. No more would vengeance darken her heart. Instead, it would be lit up by love.

"I suppose you'll be leaving for the Highlands right away then?" asked Marcus.

"Oh, nay. Please, stay. All of you," said Amethyst. "We never had the chance to celebrate Matilda and North's wedding."

"I agree," said Marcus. "As soon as we get things cleaned up, I'll have the cooks put together a grand feast. The musicians will play music, and we'll all dance."

"Will we all drink Mountain Magic?" asked Matilda, motioning to the hole in the ground with Marcus' secret stash.

"I've been discovered, it seems," Marcus said with a low chuckle. "Well, I can't think of anyone better to share the brew with other than the Highlanders. After all, it was one of theirs who made it."

"Where will you two live, now that you're married?" asked Amethyst.

"I would never dream of pullin' Matilda away from her home," said North. "I am more than ready to stay here with ye and Robbie, Matilda. That is, if Lord Marcus will allow it."

"And Gertie, too?" asked Robbie.

"Gertie, too," laughed North, patting the dog on the head.

"North, I don't want you to have to leave your brother or your clan," said Matilda.

"Well, what should we do?" asked North.

"Mother, I want to live in the Highlands," said Robbie, jumping up and down.

"I guess you have your answer." Matilda giggled, pulling her son to her in a big hug.

"Really, lass?" asked North. "Ye would come with me to live in the Highlands?"

"Aye, if it would make you happy," she answered.

"Would it!" North picked up Matilda, making her squeal and spinning her around.

"I want to do that," said Robbie, pulling on North's sleeve.

"Ye're next," he told the boy, spinning him around as well.

"I dinna want to ruin this happy moment," said Nash. "But when do we eat? I am famished."

"Me, too," said Cam. "We didna have anythin' but bread and water in the dungeon."

"I will more than make up for that tonight," announced Marcus. "We'll have stuffed swan, roasted pig, and even cockaleekie soup and skirlie."

"We will?" asked North in surprise. "How do ye even ken about those Scottish dishes?"

"Don't forget, my wife's brother, Onyx, is a MacKeefe as well," said Marcus.

"I still dinna understand that," Nash spoke up. "Onyx is a MacKeefe, but yet Amethyst isna?"

"Well, aye and nay," answered Amethyst, gingerly touching her hurt lip. "It's a long story. Let's just say that when my brother comes to visit, we eat a lot of Scottish foods to make him feel at home."

"But he lives in England with his wife most of the time," said Gavin. "So is he English or Scottish?"

"I'd say he's both," said Amethyst. "However, if you want to know his story, you'll have to ask him. After all, he gets a little crazy if someone tells it wrong."

"A little?" asked Nash. "The man is mad."

Amethyst smiled, her eyes twinkling. "Well, I suppose that is why everyone calls him a Madman MacKeefe."

CHAPTER TWENTY-FIVE

THE DAY WENT by quickly, and before North knew it, everyone was gathering in the great hall for the wedding feast. He had bathed and donned his plaid, and even washed his hair. He wanted to look and smell good for his new wife.

North stood at the foot of the dais, anxiously waiting to escort Matilda up to the raised table that was reserved for the nobles.

"Wow," he heard Nash exclaim, and looked to the door where Amethyst and Matilda had just entered. Robbie walked at Matilda's side. They were all cleaned up, and dressed in fresh clothes. North's biggest surprise was that Matilda was wearing a skirt made from the MacKeefe plaid.

"Losh me, ye look guid in the MacKeefe colors," said North, walking up and offering her his arm. "Where did ye get that?"

"My brother leaves some of his plaids here so he can change before he goes up to the Highlands," Amethyst explained. "I thought it was time for Matilda to wear one since she is a MacKeefe now as well."

"I want to be a MacKeefe. Can I have a plaid, too?" asked little Robbie.

"Robbie, come sit with me," said Beatrice, hurrying over to get the boy.

"Ye'll get a plaid as well, dinna worry, Robbie," North called out as they headed over to the trestle table to eat.

"May I escort ye up to the dais? Matilda MacKeefe . . . my wife." It felt damned good to say that, although North never thought he'd be getting married, like his brother and friends.

"I'd be honored, Husband."

MATILDA FELT LIKE she was in a dream. Sitting next to her husband, they feasted on some of her favorite foods such as roasted game hens with savory herbs, sweetmeats, and hand pies made from apples with cinnamon and nutmeg. She also tried haggis for the very first time, as well as some of North's favorite Scottish dishes that she was surprised didn't taste bad at all.

"I like this hand pie," said North, near the end of the meal. "I've smelled the spice in it somewhere before but I canna remember where. What is it called?"

"It is cinnamon mixed with mace," she explained. "It is probably the mace you are talking about."

"Mmmm, I like it."

"Just don't like it too much," she told him. "Mace can be dangerous if it is taken in large doses. A lot of herbs and spices can, but most people don't know it."

"Really?" he asked. "How dangerous? Will it make me . . . randy?" he whispered in her ear.

"Nay, not that," she giggled. "But it could cause side effects and even hallucinations."

She saw North stop chewing and his eyes opened wide.

"What's the matter?" she asked him. "Is something wrong with the pie?"

"Nay. I just remembered where I smelled this spice before. It was when our chieftain, Ian MacKeefe, dropped a pouch right before we left. I picked it up and handed it to him, and it was filled with this spice."

"Are you sure?" asked Matilda. "That is a lot of mace. Too much. Is he ingesting it?"

"I believe so," said North. "He was hiding it, like he didn't want anyone to know. He called it somethin' like the dust of the fairies. I just thought he was goin' mad."

"Didn't you say he has been ill lately? Falling over and acting as if he is losing his mind?"

"Aye," said North. "No healer can figure out why."

"My guess is that it's the mace. Or too much of it, anyway."

"Can it be remedied? Can he return to normal if he stops takin' it?" asked North.

"I believe so, but it might take a while. I have some herbal potions that can help cleanse him. I'll bring them with me, and attend to him myself to help cure him."

"Ye do that, and ye'll be the most liked lady at the castle," he told her.

After the meal, they danced, and everyone joined in to help North and Matilda celebrate their marriage.

"The boy's tired, my lady," said Beatrice, walking over with Robbie in her arms. "He's had a big day." Robbie had his head down on Beatrice's shoulder and his eyes were half closed.

"Time for bed, Robbie," said Matilda, giving him a kiss and running a loving hand over his head.

"Can we go to Scotland tomorrow?" asked the little boy.

"Of course, we can," said North.

"And Gertie, too?"

"Yes, Gertie, too," said Matilda, smiling. "We would never leave her behind. She's family."

"What about Beatrice?" asked the little boy. "Can Beatrice come with us? She is family, too."

"Well, I don't know," said Matilda, looking up at North.

"Oh, you don't want me, my lady," scoffed Beatrice. "I am old and I'm sure you'll have lots of help at your new home."

"Nonsense," said North. "Beatrice, ye are welcome to live with us, and I would be honored if you joined us."

"Oh, please do," said Matilda. "I would like that, and it would mean so much to Robbie."

"Are you sure?" asked Beatrice.

"Quite sure," said North.

"Oh, I don't know what to say. This is such a wonderful offer. I've always wanted to see Scotland before I die."

"Beatrice, say yes." Amethyst overheard and came rushing over.

"I don't want to leave you, Lady Amethyst." Beatrice seemed to be having a struggle with her decision.

"My children are old enough not to need a nursemaid anymore," Amethyst told her. "Besides, you can come back and visit whenever you want. I think you should go with them."

"What will Lord Marcus say?" asked the old woman, seeming flustered.

A male voice answered. "Marcus will say, if you don't go, I'll send you there myself." Marcus walked up with a tankard of Mountain Magic in his hand, looking very relaxed. They were all happy, having had the potent brew. It was needed after a day like today.

"Then I say yes," answered Beatrice with a large smile. "Oh, the boy's fallen asleep. I'd better get him to bed and start my packing."

"Isna there someone else that should be gettin' to bed as well?" asked Nash, watching them, along with Gavin and Cam as they drank more than their share of the Mountain Magic.

"I think, my brathair's right, Wife," said North, sweeping Matilda off her feet.

"North, put me down. Everyone's watching." Matilda giggled, feeling a little tipsy.

"No' until I get ye to the bedchamber." North took the stairs at a near run. Matilda held on for dear life since he was taking her to her tower room, and the winding staircase was steep.

When he got to the top of the stairs, he kicked the door open with his foot, heading right over to the bed, putting her down, and kissing her passionately.

"Close the door, North," she told him. "I'll light a candle."

"Nay, no candles. I want to look at the stars," he said, closing the door and hurrying back to the bed.

"You do?" she asked. "I thought you wanted something else."

"I do want that, too. But the window is open and the sky is beautiful tonight. I want to make love to my new wife with the stars and moon watchin' over us for guid luck in our future."

"Is that a Scottish superstition?" she asked, while pulling off her clothes.

"Nay." He yanked his tunic over his head and threw it across the room. "I just made it up."

"I see." She finished undressing, settling herself beneath the covers. "I never knew you were such a romantic, North."

"Dinna ye ever wonder why my parents named me North?"

"I suppose I do. It isn't that common of a name."

"It's because when I was born, the North Star was shinin' down brightly on my wee body." He stripped naked, snuggling under the covers with her.

"Really? That is interesting. Since Nash is your twin, why didn't they name him after a star or the moon, or even a direction?"

"Nay, he was named after my mathair's favorite ash tree, but dinna tell him I told ye. He doesna feel as important as me when it comes to our names."

"Well, North Star, come on over here and make me feel important." Matilda held her arms open, and North pressed his body up against hers, kissing her everywhere, making her giggle.

It didn't take long before they were both aroused. His hands slid down her body, causing a tingling sensation to run across her skin. He was so gentle and caring. She never thought a Highlander would be that way.

When he entered her, he moved slowly, gliding in and out, letting her set the rhythm. She saw stars when he brought her to climax, but they were the ones in her mind. And when they were both sated, they lay in each other's arms, staring out the window at the moon and stars, enjoying the beautiful, magical night.

"Oh, North, look!" Matilda pointed out the window. "I just saw a shooting star."

"Make a wish," he told her. "Quickly."

"I don't need to," she said, looking over to him, kissing him, feeling very important. "My wish has already come true. I am your wife. I have a husband that I am in love with, and a wonderful father for Robbie."

"I love ye, too, lass. But is that all ye want? Are ye sure?" North reached over and kissed her on the nose.

"I'm sure. Is there anything you wish for, North?"

"Like what?" he asked.

"Like . . . more children?" Matilda felt sensitive about this subject, but wanted to bring it up. "I mean, I am older than most women when they marry. And it took me a while to conceive Robbie, so I can't promise you that I'll ever be pregnant or have children again."

"If we do, I would love it," said North. "However, I dinna ever want ye to feel old or lesser of a woman if ye never have more children. It's no' up to us. It's up to God."

"But I want to give you children, North. Lots of them," she said, starting to feel emotional.

"We have Robbie," he told her. "And Gert. Although, I canna say I want a daughter as big as her that slobbers."

That made her giggle. "You always know how to make me laugh," she told him.

"I will accept what life gives us, and no' be longin' for more, ever again, lass."

"What do you mean?"

"I mean that I have always wanted things I couldna have in life. Some people even called me greedy, and I ken now that I was."

"Nay, don't say that. You're not greedy, North."

"I dinna want to be. Never again. But of course, how could a man want more when he already has everythin' he could possibly want?"

When he kissed her this time, she knew that he meant it. Matilda had longed for a man to love, her entire life. Now, she had one that she loved and who loved her in return.

"I agree," she told him, snuggling up against him, staring out at the night sky. "I have everything I have ever wanted, with you. I am looking forward to a new life. With my new family in Scotland, as the wife of North MacKeefe."

❖∘◇∘❖

CHAPTER TWENTY-SIX

Hermitage Castle, Scotland

IT HAD BEEN three days now since North had returned to Scotland with Matilda and Robbie – his new family. When they found out that Callum and Storm were in Glasgow, North and his friends decided to surprise them by just showing up at the Horn and Hoof Tavern – where this all began.

Lady Clarista and Lady Wren were with them, as well as their ailing Chieftain, Ian MacKeefe. North drove the wagon with all of them, plus Robbie and Gertie in the back. Matilda rode up front with him. Nash, Cam, and Gavin, escorted them atop horses of their own.

"So, I'm finally going to see the famous Horn and Hoof Tavern," said Matilda, all smiles since they'd crossed the border. "I've heard so much about it that I can't wait."

"Mother, I spilled cider on my plaid," said Robbie, standing up in the back of the cart, holding on to the side. Robbie had been so excited to be dressed like a MacKeefe now that he even wanted to sleep in his plaid.

"Sit down, Robbie. We'll take care of that when we reach the tavern," said Matilda, over her shoulder.

"Robbie, come sit by me," said Lady Wren, holding out her arms.

Clarista kept administering to Ian, herbal potions concocted by Matilda. Plus, they found and took away the bag of mace from him that seemed to be causing all his problems. Somewhere, he heard mace would make him younger, and he'd secretly been ingesting more than was safe. With Matilda's ministrations, Ian's memory already seemed better. Matilda said he would make a full recovery, but it was going to take some time.

Everyone was happy about that. Now, Ian wouldn't have to step down as chieftain after all.

"We've arrived at the Horn and Hoof," Gavin called out over his shoulder as they approached the tavern. There were a lot of horses tied up in front, and it looked to be even busier than usual.

The door to the tavern slammed open, and Davita, Kellina, Yvaine, and Cam's young daughter, Avianca, rushed out to greet the men.

"Kellina. Ye're here?" Nash was the first to dismount, rushing to his new wife, pulling her into his embrace.

"Aye," she said with a smile. "Lady Wren sent a messenger pigeon from Hermitage Castle to the Highlands, tellin' us ye were comin' here, so we left right away."

"Sorry to ruin the surprise," said Wren, as North helped her out of the back of the cart. "I just thought it would be nice if the girls were here when we arrived. I knew how much they missed their husbands."

"Ye dinna hear us complainin'." Gavin jumped off his horse, holding out his arms for Davita.

"Ye have no idea how much I've missed ye, Wife." Cam dismounted and ran to Yvaine, hugging and kissing her. Next, he picked up little Avianca, hugging her as well.

"We thought ye were never comin' home, Da," said Avianca, already accepting him and Yvaine as her parents after being orphaned recently.

"Who's that?" asked little Robbie from the back of the wagon.

"That is Avianca," North explained. "Mayhap ye two will want to play together with Gertie." The dog barked and bolted out of the wagon. North grabbed Robbie as he was about to jump, and put him on the ground. Robbie ran after Gertie, and over to meet Avianca.

After helping Ian and Clarista from the wagon, North put his arm around Matilda. "Are ye ready to meet Callum?" he asked. "The man can be quite ornery sometimes, but dinna let that scare ye."

"I'm ready to experience everything," she said, giving him a kiss.

When they all entered the tavern, Storm hurried over with two tankards in his hands. "Welcome back," he said. "North, I think ye might need a little Mountain Magic by now."

"Thank ye," said North, reaching out for the tankard. Nash snatched it away before he could take it.

"If ye kent what we've been through, ye'd understand why I need this more than my brathair right now." Nash took a gulp, looking over to North. "Och, what the hell." He handed it to North. "After all, we're brathairs, so I dinna mind sharin'."

North had just taken a drink when he heard the clanging of a bell. He looked up to see Callum hitting a stick against a bell that was mounted on the end of the drink board.

"What's that?" asked North, having never seen this before.

"It's new. It was all my grandda's idea," Storm told him in a low voice. "He said it's to maintain order in his tavern. Whenever he rings it, everyone needs to be quiet and listen to him."

"Who's talkin'?" snapped Callum, stretching his neck to see over the crowd.

"Sorry, Grandda," Storm called out. "I was just explainin' yer new rule to North."

"North? Is that thief here? He's no' allowed in here anymore until he's finished his sentence."

"He has," said Storm, looking over to North. "I think ye'd better go up there."

"Aye," said North, draining the tankard and handing the empty vessel back to Nash.

"Wait, I'm coming, too." Matilda held on to his arm, and they made their way to the drink board with Storm right behind them. Ian was already sitting there having an ale.

"Well?" sniffed Callum, looking over to Matilda. "Who the hell is she?"

MATILDA WASN'T SURE what to expect when she met Old Callum MacKeefe, but the little, old, wiry man almost made her laugh aloud. He had long white hair and looked skinny and frail. He wasn't really any taller than her, yet everyone seemed to fear him.

"This is –" North started, but Matilda took his arm and whispered to him.

"I'll handle this," she said, stepping forward and curtsying to the old man. "I am Lady Matilda Montclair from Northumberland," she told him. "It's a pleasure to meet you."

"Lady Matilda MacKeefe," North corrected her, stepping forward as well. "Callum, meet my new wife."

"Hrmph," Callum grunted, looking her up and down. "Well, she seems to have manners. No one else ever curtsies to me. I like that."

Matilda released the breath she'd been holding. Part of her had been amused by the old man but, deep inside, she was just as frightened of him as everyone else.

"Did ye find the cup, North?" asked Callum. "Because if no', ye might as well just turn right around and head back out that door."

"He has it," said Matilda, looking over to North. She pulled it out of her bag and handed it to him. "Go ahead, dear. Give Storm back his goblet."

"Are ye sure about this, Matilda?" North asked in a low voice. "It's been a part of yer life for so long."

"I'm sure," she told him. "It's been with the MacKeefe Clan even longer. Go ahead."

North took the goblet, and handed it to Storm.

"Aye, it's guid to have this back." Storm immediately picked up a bottle from the drink board and poured some Mountain Magic into his cup. Then he raised the goblet to his mouth, taking a drink and letting out a satisfied sigh. "Everythin' tastes better out of this goblet." He put it down on the drink board when he was finished.

"There is somethin' else," said North, taking the pink rose quartz heart from his pocket. "This was once embedded in the goblet. However, with yer permission, Storm, I'd like to let Matilda keep it. Ye see, it once belonged to her."

"What in the name of the clootie does that mean?" snapped Callum.

"Nay, North, it's all right," Matilda told him, but she could see how much North wanted her to keep it.

"I'd like to have this made into a necklace for ye, Matilda," explained North. "After all, it was never in the goblet since Storm had it."

"I dinna mind," said Storm. "After all, it is a little too girlie of a thing for me to have on my goblet. Grandda, is it all right with ye?"

"Why should I care about that? Do what ye want," answered Callum.

North gave the pink heart to Matilda, and she closed her fingers around it. "I thank you, North. I will wear it in remembrance of the family I loved and lost."

"Enough with this doitit clishmaclaver," said Callum with a snort. "North MacKeefe, ye are no longer an outcast of the clan."

Everyone cheered and cups were raised in the air in celebration.

"Congratulations, Brathair. Ye deserve it," said Nash.

"We all do," said Cam. "This has been a long, hard road for all four of us."

"I agree." Gavin pushed his way through the crowd to join his friends.

The conversations became louder and, once again, the sound of the irritating clanging bell was heard. Several shhhhhs were heard, and finally everyone quieted down once again.

"My son would like to say a word or two," announced Callum.

Ian stood up, holding on to the drink board to keep him stable. "I wanted to apologize to the clan for my unacceptable behavior lately."

"Ye were ill, ye couldna help it," someone in the crowd called out.

"Nay, I was foolish," stated Ian. "I wanted to be young again, and almost killed myself tryin' to do it. But now, I realize that I am happy bein' who I am, no matter how old I am." He put his arm around his wife.

"We dinna think of ye as auld, Da," said Storm.

"That's right," added Nash. "Besides, Callum is always goin' to be aulder than all of us."

Callum's head snapped up and he wrinkled his nose. "Who said that?" He looked from one person to the next.

"Watch it, Nash," North whispered. "We dinna want to end up in the dungeon again."

"I think it is time I remind everyone what is expected of ye once ye step foot in my tavern." Callum hobbled over to the swinging kitchen door and closed it, revealing a parchment tacked to the back. Everyone moaned. "Haud yer wheeshts," he said. "Damn it, where is my pointer?"

"Here it is," said Cam, handing it to him.

Callum pulled down a rolled-up piece of parchment tacked to the back of the door, displaying the rules of his establishment.

"What's that?" whispered Matilda.

"It's what got me and my friends into trouble in the first place," North answered.

"Now, everyone, pay close attention," said Callum. "Violatin' any of these rules will result in a punishment, or possibly bein' an outcast, as North and the others can attest to."

Groans went up from the crowd.

"Rule number one, and the most important of all the rules."

Callum slapped his pointer stick against the parchment. "Never . . . I repeat, never waste my Mountain Magic."

"I agree," called out Gavin. "Someone pass me a bottle of the brew. I dinna want it bein' wasted." Everyone laughed.

"Hush," snapped Callum, slapping the parchment again. "Rule number two is no feet on the tables." Several men near the back of the tavern could be heard scraping their boots on the tables as they lowered their feet to the floor and adjusted themselves on their chairs.

"What's number three?" someone called out.

"Number three is . . ." Callum looked over to Cam. "Mayhap ye'd like to read this one, Cam, since ye're the biggest offender of this rule."

"I'd be happy to," said Cam stepping forward. "Number three is no touchin', pinchin' or kissin' the wenches unless they are whores. Callum, I must point out that I am a married man now, so I would never even think of breakin' this rule again."

"Ye do and ye'll have to answer to me," said Yvaine playfully, making everyone laugh. "And I assure ye, Callum's punishments will seem mild to mine."

"Good one, Yvaine." Cam stepped back and put his arms around his wife. "Although, I ken ye are jestin'. Are ye no'?"

"Break the rule and we'll all find out," yelled out Nash.

"Nash MacKeefe, ye need to read the next rule so ye willna forget it," ground out Callum.

"Me?" Nash's smile disappeared and he swallowed hard.

"Go on, Brathair." North pushed Nash forward and he stumbled, catching himself on the drink board.

"North, are ye daft?" Nash growled, holding his tankard with two hands. "Ye almost made me spill my Mountain Magic."

"Read it!" Callum slammed his wooden pointer against the chart on the back of the swinging door.

"Rule number four." Nash cleared his throat and then continued. "Never damage anythin' inside the tavern."

"That goes for burnin' down the place, too," Callum told

him. "Rule number five. North?" said Callum, almost making North choke since he was drinking at the time.

"Go on, dear. It's your turn." Matilda giggled and pushed North forward, gently.

"I'm goin', I'm goin'." North got to the front. "Rule number five." He turned and read out the rule with his back facing the crowd. His voice was muffled and it was hard to hear him.

"We canna hear ye back here," someone shouted from the far side of the room.

"Louder," yelled someone else.

"Turn around, North." Gavin reached out and turned North around to face the others. "Now, what does it say?"

"It says, no one touches Storm MacKeefe's silver chalice. And believe me, I never will again." North hurried back to Matilda.

Callum continued. "Number six is no spittin'." He glared at Gavin when he said it. "Number seven is no vomitin', urinatin' or defacatin' inside the tavern walls. That goes for all of yer doitit pets as well. Gavin, read the next one since ye are a big offender of it."

"Me?" Gavin's open palm thumped against his chest.

"Go on, dear," said Davita.

"Fine," Gavin mumbled, not even having to look at the list to know what it said. "Rule number eight is no fightin'." He said it into his tankard as he kept his eyes downward and took another drink of Callum's famous potent brew.

"Oh, Gavin, it looks like you get to read the next rule as well," said Davita, stretching her neck to see it.

"Davita," he said, glancing over to Callum who was looking back at him with a raised brow. "Och, all right." Gavin walked up, looking closely at the parchment. "Rule number nine is . . ."

"Turn around," everyone in the tavern called out to him, together.

He turned around to face the crowd and continued. "It says never step on, or soil Callum's Cordovan leather boots."

"That's right. I love my boots," said Callum, sticking out his foot to admire it just as Gavin started to walk back to his wife. Gavin jerked backward, so as not to step on Callum's foot, causing him to fall to the floor since he couldn't keep his balance.

"My tankard was empty," Gavin called out, holding the cup above his head. "I didna spill a drop, I swear. And, neither did I step on his boot."

Someone started clapping in the crowd, and they all joined in.

"I'll read the last rule," said Storm, stepping up to the front. "It says anythin' Callum says, goes. Well, that's it."

"Wait!" Callum called out, taking a quill and a bottle of ink from behind the drink board and walking over to the list. "Number eleven is goin' to be that everyone hauds their wheeshts when they hear my bell."

More groans went up as he started to ink the rule onto the list. The sound of a little girl squealing came from the kitchen, followed by a little boy laughing, and also the sound of a barking dog.

"I think that's Avianca," said Cam.

"It also sounds like Robbie," said North.

"And Gertie," added Gavin.

"We'd better see what's goin' on," Nash suggested.

The four men hurried toward the kitchen. But before they got there, the door swung open from the other side and the dog ran out, followed by the two children. The men all jumped backwards, but the door knocked into Callum. The old man lost his balance and dropped the bottle of ink atop his boot. "Damn it," he swore, looking down, knocking into a bottle of Mountain Magic under the drink board. The bottle went crashing to the ground, making a mess and spilling Mountain Magic everywhere. "God's eyes, nay," shouted Callum, spit drooling down his chin as he tried to steady himself against the drink board, accidentally hitting Storm's silver chalice, knocking it to the ground. When he tried to catch it, his feeble old body stumbled, and he reached out to steady himself, grabbing on to Matilda instead.

Everyone started talking, and commotion broke out. Gertie

ran over and jumped on Callum. The hound slobbered all over him, and then peed on the floor.

The sound of the bell ringing brought the chaotic room to silence once again. It was Ian ringing the bell this time, getting everyone's attention.

"It seems to me, that my faither has just broken some of his own rules," said Ian with a grin.

"That's right, ye did, Grandda." Storm went up and looked at the back of the list. "It looks like ye broke rules number one, three, four, five, six, seven, and nine." His finger thumped against each one of them as he listed them off.

"Storm, haud yer wheesht or I'll belt ye one," yelled Callum.

"Ye do that, and ye'll be breakin' rule number eight," Gavin called out. "I ken that rule well."

"It was an accident. Besides, I didna break rule number three," said Callum, in his own defense.

"I'm sorry, Callum," Matilda spoke up. "But they're right. You did touch me trying not to fall."

"And she's no' a whore," North added his comment to the conversation.

"Well, the damned dog urinated on the floor, no' me," said Callum.

"I hardly think we can punish a dog," said Storm.

"Gertie is my dog, Callum," Matilda told him. "Therefore, you can punish me instead."

"What? Matilda, nay," North said, but Matilda winked at him and curtsied to Callum.

"Och, hell, why did ye have to curtsy?" grunted Callum. "I willna punish the lass. We'll just forget all about it."

"Well, we certainly canna forget about all the rest of yer own rules that ye broke," said Ian. "After all, ye wouldna let Gavin, Cam, Nash and North get away with it, so neither should ye. Storm, we need to hold council and decide how Callum will be punished."

"Mayhap Gavin, Cam, Nash, and North can help us decide

Callum's sentence," said Ian.

"Stop!" yelled Callum, hobbling back up to the list of rules. "I've decided to do away with all these doitit rules." Callum ripped the parchment off the back of the door and threw it to the ground and stomped on it. "It's too hard to keep up."

"Grandda, ye're really gettin' rid of yer list of tavern rules?" asked Storm with a chuckle.

"Just so he will no' be punished for breakin' them," said Nash, stepping behind Gavin after he said it. Callum looked up and glared at Gavin.

"What did ye say?" Callum asked him.

"I think it's a guid idea to forget the rules and just go back to bein' a happy clan," Ian interrupted.

"I agree," said Storm. "Let us all lift up a cup of Mountain Magic to welcome Gavin, Cam, Nash, and North MacKeefe back into our happy family."

Cheers went up from everyone, and Callum grabbed a bottle and started pouring drinks. "Everyone drinks for free today," he called out.

"Grandda, the MacKeefes always drink for free," Storm reminded him.

"Well, everyone here that isna a MacKeefe gets a free drink as well."

Little Robbie and Avianca stood on their toes, grabbing the long rope attached to the bell, and started ringing it. They laughed as they did so.

"Who's ringin' my bell?" Callum spun around and saw the children. "Oh, hell, go ahead and play with it. Have fun ye little troublemakers, I dinna care."

Storm picked up his silver goblet, taking a drink as he walked over to North and Matilda. "So, how does it feel no' to be an outcast anymore?" asked Storm.

"Words canna express how happy I am to be back with my clan – my family." North put his arm around Matilda and pulled her closer. "Both of my families, that is."

"How about ye, Matilda?" asked Storm. "I heard yer family once owned this cup." He held up the goblet. "I hope ye willna miss it too much."

"Laird MacKeefe, I assure you that I will never miss that silver cup again," said Matilda, looking up at North. "After all, I have everything I could have ever dreamed of now that I married the man I love."

"But this cup is silver and once belonged to our king. Its worth is beyond compare," Storm told her.

"It's worth might be beyond compare, but I assure you it can't even come close to the wealth I have in my life," Matilda answered, putting her arm around North and pulling in Robbie with the other. "You see, Laird MacKeefe, I am in love with a Highlander who means the world to me. North MacKeefe is not only the ideal husband, and a wonderful father, but he is also as good as gold. So, with Highland gold in my life, I no longer have any need for *Highland Silver*."

I hope you enjoyed North and Matilda's story and will take a moment to leave a review for me. North, as well as Matilda, had hard lives, but learned that happiness doesn't come from materialistic objects, but rather from the love we feel for one another. The love they found together was worth more than silver or gold.

Matilda was a secondary character in my book, *Amethyst* – Book 4 of my **Daughters of the Dagger Series**. If you'd like to read about not only her, but how Amethyst and Marcus got together as well, please be sure to read this story. Don't miss the **Daughters of the Dagger Prequel** as well.

Storm, Ian, Renard, and Callum MacKeefe can first be found in my **Legacy of the Blade Series**, as well as in many series afterwards, such as my **Madman MacKeefe Series**, and **Seasons of Fortitude**, among others. Storm's younger son, Hawke's story takes place years later in **Highland Storm** – Book 1 of my **Highland Chronicles Series**.

Onyx MacKeefe, that madman, can be found in **Onyx** – Book 1 of my **Madman MacKeefe Series**.

If you want to read more about the pirates, Coop, Goldtooth, and Stitch that were on Grope Lane, they are all secondary characters in **Tristan, Mardon**, and **Aaron,** of my **Pirate Lords Series** trilogy.

Please be sure to visit my website at www.elizabethrose novels.com to find out more about my books. I write not only

Highland, but English medieval, contemporary, paranormal, fantasy, and western romance, too!
Elizabeth Rose

ABOUT THE AUTHOR

Elizabeth Rose is an Amazon All-Star, and bestselling, award-winning, author of nearly 100 books and counting! Her first book was published back in 2000, but she has been writing stories ever since high school.

She is the author of contemporary, western, paranormal, and her favorite – medieval romance. You'll find sexy, alpha heroes and strong, independent heroines in her books. Sometimes her heroines can even swing a sword. She loves adding humor to her work, because everyone needs to laugh more in life. Her **Bad Boys of Sweetwater: Tarnished Saints Series,** was inspired by people, places, and things in her own life. The location is the lake and small town of Michigan where she grew up visiting her grandparents.

Living in the suburbs of Chicago with her husband, she has two grown sons and one granddog – so far. A lover of nature, Elizabeth can be found in the summer swinging in her "writing hammock" in her secret garden, creating her next novel. Her secret garden is what inspired her series, **Secrets of the Heart**, which of course centers around a secret garden too!

Elizabeth's current and upcoming books will be published by *Dragonblade Publishing* and independently too under *RoseScribe Media Inc.*

<u>**Social Media:**</u>
Elizabeth's Website: elizabethrosenovels.com
Newsletter Sign Up: bit.ly/3aK66i2
Eizabeth's Private Readers' Facebook Group:
facebook.com/groups/1069264379873015
Facebook: facebook.com/ElizabethRoseNovels
Goodreads: goodreads.com/author/show/89482.Elizabeth_Rose
Bookbub: bookbub.com/authors/elizabeth-rose